WILD WEST CHRISTMAS

D0003405

KATHLEEN Y'BARBO

Lena Nelson Dooley

Darlene Franklin

Vickie McDonough

BARBOUR
PUBLISHING

© 2009 *Charlsey's Accountant* by Lena Nelson Dooley
© 2009 *Lucy Ames, Sharpshooter* by Darlene Franklin
© 2009 *A Breed Apart* by Vickie McDonough
© 2009 *Plain Trouble* by Kathleen Y'Barbo

ISBN 978-1-60260-566-4

All scripture quotations are taken from the King James Version of the Bible.

Cover model photography: Jim Celuch, Celuch Creative Imaging
Interior Illustrations: Mari Small, www.thesmallagencynj.com

This book is a work of fiction. Names, characters, places, and incidents are either products of the author's imagination or used fictitiously. Any similarity to actual people, organizations, and/or events is purely coincidental.

Published by Barbour Publishing, Inc., P.O. Box 719, Uhrichsville, OH 44683, www.barbourbooks.com

Our mission is to publish and distribute inspirational products offering exceptional value and biblical encouragement to the masses.

ecpa Member of the
Evangelical Christian
Publishers Association

Printed in the United States of America

Charlsey's Accountant by Lena Nelson Dooley
Charlsey Ames is the son her father would never have—riding, roping, working the ranch with the best of them. Horace Miller III, an accountant from back East, is intrigued by the feminine Charlsey until he learns she dresses like a man out on the range. Can these two stop judging each other long enough to recognize the future God has planned for them?

Lucy Ames, Sharpshooter by Darlene Franklin
Lucy Ames's dreams come true when her sharpshooting makes her the star act of Major Paulson's Wild West Show. Gordon Paulson is traveling with his parents for one last season before accepting a teaching position at West Texas Christian College. As Lucy's and Gordon's love for each other grows, will God weave their gifts and dreams into a single calling?

A Breed Apart by Vickie McDonough
The only thing Sarah Ames is good at is training horses. When her pa hires a stranger, Carson Romero, to take over her job, Sarah is hurt and angry. She suspects the handsome half-breed is a rustler and keeps her eye on him, but the man seems above reproach. When cattle go missing, Sarah no longer wants to believe Carson is the thief. Could Carson have stolen her heart as well as the cattle?

Plain Trouble by Kathleen Y'Barbo
Bess Ames believes the Lord created her to take care of her pa while the other sisters were meant to be married off. Now that the last girl's gone, wouldn't you know that the one man who ever made Bess's heart flutter, Texas Ranger Joe Mueller, is back in town? Can the plain daughter learn to believe she's no longer Bessie Mae, plain as day?

CHARLSEY'S ACCOUNTANT

by Lena Nelson Dooley

This book is dedicated to the other authors who worked on this novella collection with me—Kathleen Y'Barbo, Vickie McDonough, and Darlene Franklin. One of the best things I've gained from this writing life is special friends such as the three of you. Thanks for the fun ride through Texas.

Thank you, Rebecca Germany, for allowing us the opportunity to bring Horsefly, Texas, to life.

And this past year, God has brought several new people into the critique group that meets in my home. Each of you joins the other members in improving my writing. Betty Wood, Kellie Gilbert, Julie Marx, Mary Williams, Marilyn Eudaly, Michelle Stimpson, and Carol Wilks. Happy to have you aboard.

No book is written without the love and support of my husband, James. We've walked a long road together, and it gets better every year. I thank God for bringing you into my life just at the right time.

Chapter 1

Texas Hill Country, Spring 1890

Harold Miller III twisted on the train's bench, trying to find a more comfortable position. Every time he moved, all the thin padding under the leather upholstery shifted away from him. After spending the night in the Pullman, he wished for his plush feather bed back home. If his father hadn't insisted he come out West, he'd be rested, not aching and weary. Just the thought brought a strong twinge in his stiff neck. And he'd be working with the numbers he loved, instead of heading toward some godforsaken place in Texas. Why would anyone name a town Horsefly? He hoped it wasn't an indication of what he'd find when he arrived.

The monotony of rail travel compelled him to purchase a dime novel before he boarded. In any other circumstance, he never would have considered reading one.

He preferred the classics to this drivel. After pulling the paperback book from his pocket, he studied the cover. A pen and ink sketch of a cowboy in full regalia—hat, boots with spurs, long-sleeved shirt, bandanna around his neck, and chaps over his trousers—was crowned with the title *Black Bart's Nemesis.* He opened it to the middle where he'd left off reading the exciting but preposterous tale.

> *James Johnson vaulted into the saddle from across his horse's rump and took off flying over the vast prairie after Black Bart. This time the dastardly outlaw would not get away.*
>
> *Leaning close to Champion's neck, he urged the strong stallion faster and faster, hoping Bart wouldn't start shooting at him. He didn't want to have to kill the man. He just wanted him brought to justice. Thudding hooves stirred up smothering clouds of dust, and the outlaw and his horse left a wake of waves in the tall, dry prairie grass, much like the waves on the ocean.*

Harold doubted the writer of this book had ever seen an ocean, especially if he compared it to dry prairie grass. And dust couldn't be compared to the salty tang in the cooling air currents blowing across open water. He remembered sitting on the dock at his family's cottage on Cape Cod, tasting the familiar fragrance, with the waves lapping under his feet.

James pulled his bright red bandanna over his nose to keep from breathing too much dirt into his lungs. Hot wind fanned by the mad dash across unfamiliar terrain jerked his hat from his head. If he hadn't had the cord knotted under his chin, he'd have lost his prized Stetson. Instead it bounced against his back, keeping time with the hoofbeats.

He was fast approaching his prey when suddenly Champion pitched forward and fell to the right. James had to leap sideways from his saddle to keep the gigantic horse from crushing him. Momentary fear robbed him of breath. Quickly he jumped to his feet, sucking deeply of the hot, dry air that brought a slow-burning sensation to his lungs. He pulled off his hat and surveyed the damage while he beat his headgear against his leather chaps, trying to get some of the accumulated tan dust off.

He walked wide around the troubled horse, trying to find what had tripped his usually sure-footed mount. Of course, the prairie dog town had been hidden by tall grass, and Champion stepped into one of the holes. "Oh, d—."

Harold refused to voice the curse word even in his thoughts.

"I hope you didn't break your leg."
The horse rolled back and forth, his hooves flailing,

before finally making it up on all four hooves.

James stared ahead, watching the figure of Black Bart and his mount recede until he was just a bouncing dot on the horizon. "Foiled again! But tomorrow is another day."

"Don't believe everything ya read in them dime novels." Harold stared up into the face of the friendly conductor. "I'm sure that's true. I only brought it to help pass the time."

"Ya did say you're gettin' off in Horsefly, didn't ya?"

Feeling uncomfortable holding a conversation with the man who towered over him, Harold rose to his feet. "Yes."

"We'll be pullin' inta the station in about five minutes."

"Thank you." Harold tipped his hat before turning and shoving the book into his black leather Gladstone traveling bag.

The conductor ambled farther down the car.

"Sir," Harold called after him.

Without breaking stride, the man wheeled around and returned in a trice.

"Will I be able to hire a buggy in Horsefly, or will I need to ride a horse?" He hoped the conductor couldn't tell how much he dreaded the last alternative.

"Hey, Charlie!" one of the cowhands shouted, catching Charlsey's attention. "Bring on the next 'un."

Charlsey Ames settled her sombrero more firmly on her head and opened the chute. A half-grown calf stumbled toward her. She bulldogged the Hereford and slid it closer to the huge fire, trying to keep the smoke out of her eyes. Today was unusually hot for spring. It felt more like summer. Too bad they needed such a strong fire for the branding irons.

When the reddened metal touched the calf, the acrid stench of burning hide filled her nostrils, a truly unpleasant odor, mixed with excrement and other things that accompanied it. Branding wasn't one of her favorite chores, but she could rope the calf and tie its legs together faster than any of the other hands. That way the calves didn't suffer as much trauma because their branding was over quickly.

While she was bulldogging the next calf, her father rode up and dismounted. Funny how she could be intent on what she was doing, but also aware of all her surroundings. Pa said that made her the best hand on the ranch, though her sisters might disagree. And the cowboys respected her.

She released the calf and stood, winding her lariat into a manageable circle then swiping her sleeve across her sweaty brow.

"Charlie!" Once again the cowboy shouted for a calf.

Pa held up his hand. "Not right now. I need to talk to Charlie a minute. Why don't the rest of you take a short break?"

The cowboys rushed toward the chuck wagon for coffee, and Charlsey approached her father. "What's going on?"

"I forgot to tell you I received a telegram yesterday from Harold Miller in Boston." He took off his hat, wiped his forehead with his bandanna, then stuffed the soiled cloth into his back pocket. "He bought a packing plant in Chicago, and he's sending his son to buy some of our beef."

Charlsey broke up a dirt clod with the toe of her boot. "Have you met his son?"

"Nope, and I haven't seen Harold in over thirty years. Not since we worked the King ranch together. He lives somewhere back East." He put his dusty Stetson back on his head. "I was actually surprised he wants to buy cattle from us. I didn't know he'd kept up with me all these years."

Charlsey stared across the fence line toward the undisturbed pasture, brilliant with bluebonnets, Indian paintbrush, and buttercups. She loved the colors of spring and the fresh fragrance of wildflowers. "When do you expect the younger Mr. Miller?"

"Today or tomorrow. If I knew for sure which day, I'd send a wagon for him, but I can't have one of my hands sitting at the station most of two days." Pa reached for his horse's reins. "I've alerted your sisters. We might have company for a few days. You'll want to dress for dinner. . . and all that stuff."

His offhand wave told her what she needed to know about his expectations. She didn't mind entertaining guests, but it would be a bother in the middle of branding.

Harold exited the rail car onto the wooden platform. He surveyed the thriving western town surrounding the depot. Trees shaded many of the streets. Not the majestic white pines, hickory, hemlock, ash, and maple trees he was familiar with near his home in Massachusetts. The buildings were not the same either. Although a few were built of wood, most had rock walls. Others were part rock, part wood. *Interesting.* Not at all like in the dime novel he'd been reading.

He welcomed the coolness when he entered the depot. Stone walls evidently helped combat the higher temperature. But even inside, he was glad he'd chosen to wear his lighter-weight suit, a blend of wool and silk. After glancing at the people around him, he knew the four-button cutaway and his flat-crowned derby would stand out in this town. Not one man wore a suit. Their headgear didn't resemble his either.

He hoped to conclude business in a timely manner and be on his way back to civilization. He'd have to purchase something to wear if he stayed more than a day or two. They all looked cooler in their colored cotton shirts and denim trousers.

When the stationmaster finished talking to the family clustered near the counter, Harold approached him.

"Where can I hire a buggy?"

The man glanced up from the paper he was writing on and peered at him over the top of his spectacles. "Depends on where you're going."

Harold cleared his parched throat. "I need to get to the Ames ranch."

"Too bad you didn't get here half an hour ago." The man spoke with a lazy drawl. "One of their hands picked up a shipment. Could've hitched a ride with him."

"That would have been nice." Did everything in this town move as slowly as this conversation? Harold just wanted the information so he could find somewhere to get a drink.

"You'll have to cross the tracks." The man laid down the pencil and pointed. "Go about four blocks south. Livery's on the other side of the street. Can't miss it." He picked up the pencil again then looked back at Harold. "Before you go, you're welcome to head out back and get a drink from our well. I know how hot and thirsty you get traveling on the train."

The man must have been a mind reader. After thanking him, Harold hefted his bag and headed to the water. He cranked the wooden bucket down. It took awhile before he heard a splash. *A deep well.* When he finished cranking the filled container up out of the opening, he set it on the waist-high rock wall surrounding the well, spilling some of the water on the leg of his trousers in the process. With this heat, it should dry quickly, and the cold water felt good against his leg. He just hoped the fabric wouldn't wrinkle much more than it already had.

A long-handled metal dipper hung on a nearby nail. Rather primitive, but Harold was thirsty enough to drink out of almost anything. He dipped it in the liquid and welcomed the soothing coolness as it slid down his parched throat.

Three full dippers later, he trudged down the dusty street. Thankfully, several patches of shade kept the sun off most of the time. He passed cross streets with houses nestled among trees. Flowers grew in many of the yards.

With a name like Horsefly, he hadn't known what to expect. The town was much more pleasant than he'd thought it would be.

Soon Harold was ensconced in a black surrey with bright red fringe skirting the top. Reviewing the liveryman's detailed instructions, he settled back and enjoyed the ride. The horses handled easily, affording him the chance to study the landscape. He headed back north, and after passing the depot, he encountered a hotel. He considered checking in now but decided against it. He'd wait until he got back from the ranch.

Down the road a bit, a saloon stood on the other side of the street. Just before he reached the building, the swinging doors flew open, banging against the wall, and two men tumbled through. They rolled off the boardwalk, landing in the dust punching and kicking each other. Gawkers filled the open doorway, and their raucous taunts held many words Harold preferred not to hear. Maybe Horsefly was more like the dime novel than he had first thought.

Leaving the town behind, he turned onto the road the livery owner indicated he should take. It led over a couple of hills. Scattered trees and bushes rested beside large rock outcroppings, and grass seemed abundant. This area wasn't dry and dusty like in *Black Bart's Nemesis.* He shouldn't have even started reading that junk.

After the first couple of miles, he topped a higher hill, and a large valley spread before him. Glints of sunlight caught his eye from a river that meandered through the scene below. Trees grew along the banks of the river, and a meadow in the distance had a distinct blue cast to it. He knew they had bluegrass in Kentucky, but he'd never heard of any in Texas.

Finally, he topped another smaller hill and gazed across a field of blue flowers unlike any he'd ever seen. Other colors—red, pink, and yellow—dotted the azure blanket covering the ground. He just might like being in Texas—so different from what he'd heard and read in that stupid novel.

He knew the moment he reached the Ames ranch. Above the gate, ironwork proclaimed ROCKING A, and at each end of the sign were capital *A*s on rockers. Probably the brand. Strong fences stretched as far as he could see. He followed the drive around another hill. It led to the two-story ranch house built out of the same sandy-colored stone he'd seen on some of the buildings in Horsefly.

Harold tied the reins of the buggy to the hitching rail by the fence around the yard and walked up on the porch. Before his fist had time to tap the door, it opened.

"You must be Mr. Miller." A tiny young woman with flashing brown eyes and dark hair smiled up at him.

He quickly removed his hat and held it in front of him. "At your service, ma'am."

"Pa said to send you out to the pasture." She continued to give him instructions, her hands doing as much talking as her mouth.

Harold followed the twin dirt tracks past various out-buildings before he topped another hill. On the other side, he found the Texas from his dime novel. Tall prairie grass covered the ground and rippling waves rolled in the occasional breeze, but it wasn't the dry brown as described by the author of *Black Bart's Nemesis*. Instead, the tall, skinny stalks were light green, not the rich green of grass back home.

A short distance away in a clearing without any vegetation, a raging bonfire stoked the heat in the already hot air. He thought about removing his suit coat, but he wanted to make a good impression. His linen shirt had to be a mass of wrinkles after the day he'd had, and they could already see all the wrinkles on the dried leg of his trousers.

As he approached the group of busy cowboys, a horrendous odor overcame him, making him want to retch.

Whatever could that smell be? Surrounded by smoke, dust, and bawling cattle, he needed a breath of fresh air. Grabbing his handkerchief from his pocket, he covered his nose and mouth.

"Charlie." A raucous call rang out. "Bring on the next 'un."

A slim cowboy, in a hat larger than anyone else was wearing, pulled a lever to open a gate. A young cow stumbled out of the chute. That same cowboy jumped from his horse, roped it, tied all four legs together, then dragged the animal closer to the fire. Another man lifted what had to be a branding iron. Harold had never seen a real one before. When the hot iron touched the calf, he understood where the putrid burning odor came from as he heard the sizzling sound and watched steam escape from under the metal utensil. And the ground was littered with filth.

Fascinated, he held the handkerchief closer to his nose as he watched the cowboy quickly untie the calf and release it. Then the one called Charlie turned toward Harold. Eyes the clear blue of the Texas sky above them stared hard, and a look of disgust covered Charlie's lightly tanned face. Or was it disdain? *What was that all about?*

Chapter 2

Under any other circumstances, Harold would have accepted the invitation to stay at the ranch until he and Mr. Ames concluded their business. But not today.

On the way back to town, he mulled over his options. He didn't fit here in Texas, and he hated the feeling. He'd always been secure and strong. He felt neither right now.

Since he had stepped from the train onto the platform in Horsefly, no one looked at him with respect as they did in Boston. That had to change. What was the phrase that caught his eye while he was reading *Voyages of Radisson*? "When in Rome, do as the Romans do."

He glanced around, glad no one shared the road with him. They'd surely think him daft to be talking to himself.

While he drove through town, he glanced at Kofka's Mercantile across from the saloon. Merchandise spilled onto the boardwalk out front, and enough dust and grime covered the windows that he couldn't see inside. He assumed many of the coarse men who frequented the bar across the street shopped in the mercantile. He could get outfitted there, but he wondered if there was a more appropriate place. He had noticed a store more to his liking on the way out of town, but his mind had been on other things. Just past the hotel, Eberhardt Emporium came into view, looking very much like a store back home. This one probably served more discerning customers. He wanted to blend in, but not at the expense of his superior standards.

After returning the vehicle to the livery, Harold headed up Main Street through the residential section and past the railroad station to the emporium. A bell above the door signaled his entrance. Although a couple of the customers glanced his way, they quickly returned to their own business. He headed toward the men's section, keeping his eyes out for any other men. He wanted to get a feel for what they wore.

He picked up a white shirt with a tiny black woven stripe. The cotton fabric had a good feel to it. He didn't want anything that would be too stiff.

The bell rang again.

"How are things at the bank today?" The friendly storekeeper greeted the newcomer.

Harold glanced over his shoulder and quickly perused the banker. The man wore a long-sleeved white shirt with a vest buttoned over it. His neckwear differed greatly from the cravat Harold had on. However, the man still looked businesslike, and he had to be cooler than Harold had been since he rode into the Texas heat.

As he moved through the men's section, he found black trousers made from a heavy cotton twill; but they weren't as stiff as the denim trousers he'd started to buy. Soon his arms held several items to purchase.

Charlsey let her chestnut mare, Dancer, jog toward the house while she enjoyed every nuance of nature's display. Nothing was quite as breathtaking as a Texas sunset.

The blazing sun turned into a glowing red ball bathing trees and fields in a golden haze. As the sphere started sliding below the horizon, wide fingers of bright orange, yellow, and pink shot in an arc across the sky then melted into the twilight colors of plum, pale lavender, and rose. Molten gold rimmed the few clouds scattered around. They soon absorbed the mingled hues around them until the sky dropped its indigo shade pierced by twinkling stars.

Charlsey handed Dancer off to Bart, the youngest stable hand, and headed up to the house. She usually unsaddled her own horse, curried her, and fed her before going in for supper. But Bart would have to take care of her this time. With Mr. Tenderfoot from Boston coming, she had to hurry to be ready for their fashionably late dinner.

As usual, Sarah was working with a horse in the corral. All that girl ever thought about was horses.

"Sarah"—Charlsey stopped for a moment—"you'd better hurry up or you'll be late for dinner."

Sarah gave a quick wave, and Charlsey continued toward the house.

She took two steps at a time to reach her upstairs bedroom and flung open the door. "Oh, good."

Someone had brought in the large copper bathtub, and a little steam rose from the water. After flinging her sweaty work clothes and unmentionables into a heap, she slid beneath the surface and let the warm water soothe her aching muscles.

How she wished she could just relax this evening, instead of treating Boston like a special guest. At least he had declined Pa's invitation to stay at the ranch. He said he was staying at the hotel in town. She guessed spending an evening with the man wouldn't be too bad, since he wouldn't be underfoot all the time. She couldn't get his grimace when he arrived at the branding out of her mind. Imagine covering his nose with his handkerchief. *What a prissy tenderfoot!* Where did he think all those roasts and steaks he ate came from? They didn't magically appear on his table. A lot of messy things happened along the way. Maybe he needed an education in the facts of real life. Too bad tonight wasn't the time to do it. Maybe he'd be gone by morning, and she could get him out of her hair. . . out of her mind.

The hour had come to face his fear. Harold straightened his new white Stetson, curling the brim to match those worn by the other men. He squared his shoulders inside the western dress shirt and vest, straightened the lengths of his string tie, and pointed his booted feet toward the livery. So what if he hadn't ridden a horse since he was ten—when the wretched mare bucked him off and ran away, dragging him behind. He was now a man, and he would ride a steed to the Ames ranch this evening.

"When in Rome, do as the Romans do." The whispered words once again bolstered his courage.

The walk to the livery invigorated him. "Hey, Sam, where are you?"

The livery owner stepped from the tack room. He chewed on a piece of straw while he gave Harold an up-and-down stare. "So, Mr. Miller, back already?" He scratched his neck where the top of his red union suit peeked out. "Want me ta hitch up the surrey again?"

Harold wondered how the man could stand the added warmth from his winter underwear in this Texas heat. "Do you have a strong horse with a good disposition?"

Sam pulled the piece of hay from the side of his mouth. "You gonna ride somewhere tonight?" Skepticism tainted his tone.

In for a dime, in for a dollar. Harold wished these pithy sayings would stop popping into his mind. "I'll be dining at the Ames ranch. I thought I'd ride a horse this time."

The tall, thin man studied him for a moment before he turned toward the stalls. "Gotta gentle palomino mare. Sunshine. She'd be easy ta handle. Been out that way several times."

Harold hurried to keep up with Sam's long strides, hoping the horse's disposition matched her name. "She sounds like exactly what I'm wanting."

After they finished their business and Sam saddled Sunshine, Harold swung up into the saddle. . .*on the first try*. Wearing the right clothing made him feel like he belonged in the western saddle, which was very different from the English saddle he'd used as a boy.

"How long will the livery be open, Sam?"

"I close up before I go home to supper, but there are a few stalls out behind the hotel. You can keep Sunshine there until tomorrow."

Harold turned the mare around, and she danced a few steps in the dirt. She had a little spirit, too. He'd have to show her he knew what he was doing.

He headed north through town. The noise level at the saloon had reached a high pitch. Music, laughter, and loud voices blended into an unpleasant cacophony, complete with expletives Harold had never uttered, even when he was a boy trying to sound tough.

As he turned onto the road leading to the ranch, he felt as though he were on a different planet thanks to the bright moon steeping the landscape in a silver glow. As Sam said she would, Sunshine followed his lead, and soon they settled into an easy gallop.

After she finished her bath, Charlsey took awhile getting ready. The only time she usually dressed up was for church on Sunday or for a social. She had piled her abundant, fine hair into a poufy, upswept style with a cluster of curls nestled on her crown, but some of the strands kept slipping out of the confining pins. Tired of fussing with the ornery tresses, she left a few wispy curls along her cheeks and around the back of her neck. She stared into the cheval glass, actually pleased with the effect.

Now what should she wear? She pulled a dark skirt and white dimity blouse from her wardrobe then dropped them on her bed. She didn't want to look too stodgy. She wanted something to add color. After picking out several other garments and rejecting them, she finally chose a rose-colored dress sprigged with tiny white flowers. The bodice fit nicely and dipped to a deep point at the front of her waist. The round neckline dipped, too, but not far enough to be immodest. White lace outlined the waist, neckline, and cuffs of the long puffed sleeves.

Charlsey twisted and turned trying to get all the buttons fastened up the back. Her sisters were all down in the kitchen. She'd just have to go down there and have one of them close the gap she couldn't reach. Leaning close to the looking glass, she pinched her cheeks. Then she pressed her lips together until they glowed a soft red. Good. Nothing about her looked like a cowhand tonight.

Just as she reached the bottom of the staircase, a strong knock rattled the door. She took a deep breath and opened it, careful to keep her back turned away.

Standing in the light spilling from the opening

was a complete stranger who stole her ability to speak. Breathless, she continued to stare, forgetting everything else.

He had removed his hat and held it in his hand. His smile fashioned a deep crease in one cheek. The bold spark in his eyes deepened their color to match the Hershey bars Charlsey loved. One errant curl sprang from his restrained dark hair and hovered above one eyebrow. If a more handsome man existed in Horsefly, she'd never seen him.

A chuckle started deep in his chest and rumbled out in a melodious laugh. "May I come in?"

Charlsey nodded, pulled the door open wider, and stepped out of his way. What was she thinking, keeping him standing there so long? And what did he think about her staring at him? "May I take your hat?" Her words came out breathy. *What is wrong with me?*

He handed the headgear to her. For a moment, she held it while he glanced around the foyer, and she studied him. Dressed in some of the finest clothes available in town, he must have shopped at Eberhardt Emporium to get that quality. The neckline of his black leather vest dipped low, and the bow of the black string tie couldn't disguise the strength in his chest and shoulders. She had a hard time breathing because his presence overpowered the room. Where had this man come from?

Finally, Charlsey found her voice. "I'll tell Pa you're here. You can wait in the parlor."

She led him to the doorway, whirled around, then fled.

After the awkward welcome by the woman he now knew as Charlsey, the youngest of the Ames daughters, Harold enjoyed the warm reception by the other three sisters. He wondered how a man could have such a successful ranch with four daughters and not even one son.

The meal the women served proved as delicious as any he'd ever eaten: tender steak that almost melted in his mouth, vegetables that wouldn't be available in Boston for weeks, featherlight rolls slathered with butter. All of this topped off with the best peach cobbler his tongue had ever tasted—the kind that had a way of melting in the mouth all the way to a man's heart. These women would make some men very happy husbands.

The members of the Ames family were congenial dinner companions. . .all except Charlsey. The beauty with unbelievable blond hair and eyes the color of the Texas sky hardly talked during the meal. Every time he looked at her, a blush stained her cheeks, and she lowered her gaze and concentrated on the food. Occasionally, he caught her father or one of her sisters staring at her with a questioning expression. Evidently, this wasn't her usual demeanor. Maybe she was embarrassed because she'd turned her back on him with some of her buttons undone. He swallowed a chuckle, not wanting to make her feel any worse.

After they finished, Mr. Ames stood. "Charlsey, bring

the coffee into the parlor, and we'll all enjoy a visit with Mr. Miller."

For some reason, this brought a deeper flush to her face. Every time he glanced at her eyes, they reminded him of someone. Harold hoped she would relax in the parlor so he could get to know her better.

Chapter 3

Harold leaned into the comfortable wingback. The bloodred velvet chair hugged him, reminding him of home. Even though the walls of the ranch house were built of rock inside and out, the parlor welcomed him almost as much as the one back in Boston.

"So how many head of cattle are you looking to buy?" Mr. Ames sat across from him, one foot propped on the other knee.

Bess Ames cleared her throat. "Pa, you can talk business in the daytime. Tonight is a social occasion."

Chagrin dimmed the older man's eyes, and he gave a sheepish smile. "You're right." He nodded toward Harold. "Forgive me. Since my wife's been gone, Bess often has to keep me in line. I find it hard to take time away from the ranch work."

Sarah rushed through the doorway. "I'm so sorry I

can't stay and visit with you, Harold, but Larry just came to the back door. My favorite mare is foaling. I've got to go help."

Before he could answer her, she disappeared. He raised an eyebrow at Mr. Ames. "Does she always move that fast?"

"Not always, but that girl can be a real whirlwind." He rose and shook his head, chuckling. "I'm afraid I'm going to bow out, too. It's the mare's first foal. There could be trouble."

Right after he exited, Charlsey entered carrying a tray with a silver coffeepot and china cups and saucers.

Harold shot to his feet and relieved her of her burden. "Where do you want me to set this?"

She stared at him as if he had grown a third eye. Maybe the men around Horsefly weren't chivalrous. Or maybe the answer to his question was obvious.

"Over there will be fine." She waved toward the low table in front of the tapestry-upholstered couch. "I'll serve you."

He set down the heavy tray, and Charlsey perched on the front of the couch cushion, her back as straight as if a rod ran down her spine. *Mother would applaud her carriage and comportment if she were here.*

"Do you take cream or sugar in your coffee, Mr. Miller?" Charlsey glanced up at him without raising her head. "Or both?"

His gaze fastened on the long lashes framing her wide

blue eyes. Fascinated, he couldn't tear his attention away. She looked as if she were waiting for something.

Oh yes, she asked me a question. He cleared his throat. "No. Black is just fine."

When Harold reached for the coffee, his fingers brushed hers. A jolt ran up his arm, startling him. The cup rattled until he steadied the saucer with both hands.

Charlsey sipped her coffee, not taking her eyes from him. Hers didn't rattle. Maybe she didn't feel what he had.

"This is really good, Charlsey." Lucy's voice intruded upon his thoughts.

He'd almost forgotten she and Bess were in the room.

"Yes. . .good." He drank too fast. The hot liquid made his eyes water and burned all the way down his throat. He set the coffee on the side of the table nearest him.

Wondering why all three women stared at him, he shifted in the chair. "So, Charlsey, did you attend a finishing school back East?"

Her mouth opened, but she quickly pressed her lips back together.

"Our mother taught us all we know about being ladies." Bess answered for her sister. "She felt it was an important part of a young woman's education."

Once more, Harold had blundered, but he hadn't meant to insinuate that the West was backward. Maybe he should just go back to town.

Bess rose. "Charlsey, I'm going to check on those in the barn, see if they need coffee to carry them through the night." She turned toward Harold, and he rose, too. "Good night, Mr. Miller. We enjoyed having you here."

He reached to tip his hat, but his hand encountered only air. So he raked his fingers through his hair instead. "The pleasure is all mine."

When Lucy followed Bess, Charlsey couldn't believe they had all deserted her, leaving her alone with the stranger she wasn't even sure she liked. But when his fingers had brushed across hers, a tingle started churning in her stomach, and her coffee hadn't settled it down yet.

"How long do you think you'll be with us, Mr. Miller?" She forced a bright smile.

He studied her for an uncomfortably long time before answering. "I asked all of you at dinner to please call me Harold."

Rich masculine tones swirled around her, wrapping her in a blanket of unease. "Harold." She gave him a small nod, feeling entirely out of her element. None of the men from around these parts had ever unsettled her.

"And may I call you Charlsey?" His easy smile filled her with warmth.

She set her coffee back on the tray. She didn't need the heat. Glancing around, she couldn't see anything to fan herself with. "Yes. . .Harold."

Charlsey squirmed. Why did this man make her feel so uncomfortable? She glanced across the room, her gaze lighting on a new book.

"Harold, do you like to read?" Literature should be a safe topic. Next to working cattle, reading was her favorite pastime.

"Oh yes. I've spent many hours in our library." His eyes twinkled. She'd struck gold with reading.

"We don't have a library, but as you can see"—she waved toward a long bookcase—"we have a large assortment of books. And each bedroom has a similar collection." Charlsey gasped. Why had she mentioned the bedrooms? She felt her cheeks flush. Would he think her too bold?

He leaned forward. "So, Charlsey, what's your favorite book?"

She had to think a minute to decide which of the many she should pick. "I like biographies. We have a collection of them about American statesmen. I've read most of them. I also like *Imitation of Christ* by Thomas à Kempis."

"I've read that one, too. It gave me many days of thought-provoking insight." He leaned back, a pleasant expression on his face. No denying how handsome the man was.

"I know what you mean." Charlsey was anxious to further explore their common interest. "What's your favorite book?"

She held her breath awaiting his answer. His choice of reading matter should tell her a lot about the man. None of the cowboys had even a passing interest in books, so she hadn't had many discussions like this. Her pulse quickened, and she leaned forward.

"I've enjoyed biographies of American pioneers and statesmen—Washington, Franklin, Daniel Boone, David Crockett, even Kit Carson."

Quite a wide variety.

"Recently I picked up a copy of *Buffalo Bill: From Prairie to Palace*. I had started reading it, but alas, I didn't include it when I packed for the trip." He gave a rueful smile. Her heart flip-flopped in her chest. "I'll have to wait until I get home to finish it."

Charlsey laughed. "I hate to start a book and not be able to finish it right away, don't you?" Releasing a deep breath, she relaxed, surprised she was enjoying this city slicker.

He gazed straight into her eyes. "Don't you read anything just for fun? Everything you talked about was deep reading."

"I have enjoyed reading novels by Mrs. Mary J. Holmes, especially *Homestead on the Hillside* and *Lena Rivers*." She clasped her hands in her lap. "I'm sure you haven't read anything by her."

He threw back his head, and a hearty laugh rang out. "No, I haven't. But novels are fun to read. I think I've read all of Hawthorne's." He paused and studied her. "I have a confession to make."

Whatever could it be? His look of chagrin made her think it might be unsavory. Maybe she shouldn't feel so comfortable with him.

"I actually brought a dime novel on the train ride."

She giggled, the depth of him as surprising as the next chapter of a new book. "What is the title?"

"*Black Bart's Nemesis.*" He emphasized the words as if he were reading one of the dime novels right now.

"You do know that most of the dime novels are exaggerations of life in the West."

He grinned and nodded. "Of course I do, but the rootin', tootin', shoot-'em-up story helped pass the time on the trip." He paused for several seconds. "Why in the world would anyone name a town Horsefly?"

"There've been lots of stories, but no one knows for sure." Charlsey smoothed a large wrinkle in her skirt. She'd heard the question often enough from visitors to their town. "The one I like best is about a German immigrant who said he'd never seen such large horseflies, so they called the settlement Horsefly, which has now grown into our lovely town."

They explored music, politics, even Texas cattle ranches before he finally rose from his chair.

"I hate to bring an end to our evening, but I must get back to town." Harold clasped her fingers and raised her hand to his surprisingly soft lips.

Charlsey hadn't ever had a man kiss her hand. *Or anything else for that matter.* She felt a hot shiver creep up her back. A second glance made her decide she liked a man with good manners.

After he released her hand, she followed him to the

door. He settled the Stetson on his curls, still in disarray from his swipe through them. She wondered what he would have thought if she had straightened them for him.

Whew. When he was gone, she'd have to loosen her stays.

He opened the door and his boot heels clicked along the wooden porch. He glanced back at her before starting down the steps.

"Mr. . .Harold. . ."

Turning on the third and last step, he removed his hat and smiled at her. "Yes, Charlsey?"

They stood eye-to-eye. "Will you. . .be joining us. . . for dinner tomorrow?" *I can't even speak normally.*

"I'd be delighted to." His eyes twinkled. "Thank you for the invitation. Good night, Charlsey." He thrust his hat back on his head and whistled as he walked away, going around the house toward the barn. The way Harold's voice caressed her name gave it a femininity she'd always felt it lacked.

When Charlsey went into the kitchen, Bess had completely cleaned it up. *Good.* She wouldn't have to do it. She hurried upstairs to get ready for bed. When a knock sounded on her door, she was almost finished braiding her hair. It had to be Bess. She was the only one who knocked so softly.

"Come in, Bess." Charlsey continued staring at her reflection in the cheval glass. *How does Harold see me?*

Probably not the way she saw herself. Too short, hair too light, eyes too big for her face.

Dressed in her nightgown and robe, Bess dropped onto the foot of the bed. "Do you want to tell me what the problem was tonight?"

Charlsey tied a rag around the end of her long braid. "You mean besides making a fool of myself when I answered the door?"

"How did you do that?" Wrinkles of puzzlement divided Bess's brows.

A flush once again crept up Charlsey's cheeks. She knew how red they must look. "I didn't recognize Harold, and he flustered me so much, I turned my back on him. He had to have seen the gap in the back of my dress."

"Oh dear, maybe he wasn't looking."

Charlsey wished she could believe that, but she could still feel his eyes staring at her back, branding her.

"He didn't say anything about it."

Charlsey gave a very unladylike snort. "He's too much of a gentleman to do that." She wrinkled her nose. "But he wasn't that nice when he came out to the branding. Tonight he was like a different person. Which one is the real man?"

Bess stood and put her arms around her. "Charlsey, I've never seen you like this. You've never let any man affect you this much."

Charlsey hugged her back. "I know. What do I do about it?"

Bess chuckled. "Just give the man a chance, and talk to the Lord about it."

Charlsey had already been talking to Him about that most of the day.

⁓⁓⁓

Even though she had worked hard, Charlsey didn't sleep very well. When she arose just before dawn, her legs and arms recoiled from having to move. But those calves wouldn't brand themselves. She stretched to get the kinks out of her neck and shoulders. Before donning her denim trousers and long-sleeved plaid shirt, she braided her hair in one long braid, pinning it into a coil on the top of her head so it would fit in the crown of the sombrero.

After a quick breakfast, she rode Dancer to the branding corral. Without saying a word, she headed for the chute. When she finished bulldogging the first calf, she moved to the next one, establishing a rhythm that worked for over an hour.

"Hey, Charlie. Bring on the next 'un."

She was already tired of hearing that shout, but she pulled the lever, holding her reins in one hand and her lariat at the ready.

When she released the calf after it was branded, Pa's voice rose above the clamor. "Charlie, come with us."

Sitting on the large palomino next to her father, Harold stared straight into her eyes, but not an ounce of recognition flickered in his. *What is the matter with him? Where is the man who kissed my hand?*

She gave her dad a wave and headed toward Dancer, mounting her in one smooth motion.

"You men carry on." Several of the cowboys gave an offhand wave in answer to Pa's command.

She rode Dancer up to the side of Pa opposite Harold. That way, she could see him when she glanced at Pa. Even though he was dressed in a long-sleeved plaid shirt and denim trousers, Harold had gone back to being Boston, instead of the friendly man from last night. She rode along silently, listening to the two men discuss business and wondering if she'd done something wrong—something that displeased him.

"So do you only run Hereford cattle?" Even his accent was more precise this morning. "I had heard there were longhorn cattle in Texas."

"Oh, we have longhorns, too." Her father's deep voice felt comforting in her confusion. "Several cattlemen brought in Herefords, because they produce a higher quality of beef. More tender. But it wouldn't be a Texas ranch without longhorns. Let's show him, Charlie." He wheeled his horse and headed toward the far pasture. "I like to keep them separated. Keep both strains pure." He had to holler to be heard above the hoofbeats and the wind whistling in their ears.

They loped over one hill and down across a valley. Boston kept up pretty well, but he didn't ride as smoothly as she or Pa. Maybe he was too focused on keeping his seat to give her any attention.

Wait a minute. I don't want his attention. Or did she? Conflicted, she rode silently, enjoying the feel of her powerful mare as Dancer's gait ate up the ground, allowing Charlsey to wrestle with her thoughts.

As they topped the second hill, the herd came into view. Pa reined in his horse. She stopped beside him.

Boston followed suit. "Wow. Look at the length of those horns. I wonder how they keep from hurting each other."

What a strange thing to say. Charlie stared at him, and he turned to look at her. His gaze roamed over her face and settled once again on her eyes. But he looked confused. What was the matter with him?

If she had her way, she'd just turn around and ride back to the branding. But her father led them away from the longhorns and toward where the rest of the Herefords were pastured.

They continued all the way around the large valley, waving at the hands who were riding herd.

"So, Harold, I'll ask you what Bess wouldn't let me ask last night." Pa took off his hat and wiped his brow with his bandanna. "How many head are you wanting to buy?"

Harold planned to stop at Eberhardt Emporium on his final trip into town from the Ames ranch. These last five days were some of the most interesting he'd had in a long time. Being on Sunshine and observing the cowboys cut his cattle from the herd made him feel as if he were part of the West. . .almost.

The evenings spent with the Ames family proved lively. Sarah insisted he go to the barn and inspect the new foal. Lucy demonstrated her sharpshooting abilities. And Bess stayed near the house and made sure delicious meals were on the table every evening. Supper, as these Texans called it.

Harold wondered what Charlsey did during the daytime. She never talked about it. But he enjoyed discussing so many topics with her in the evenings. She awakened his mind in a way no other woman had. If he were truthful, she awakened more than his mind; but he was destined to go back to Boston eventually, and Charlsey was a true Texan. He wished his time in Horsefly wasn't coming to an end, but he needed to accompany the cattle to Chicago. He'd watch the men load them into cattle cars on the train later today, then head for his place in the passenger car. And he had to keep a good account of the money he'd used.

He rode Sunshine to the livery.

"Sam, thanks for letting me get to know Sunshine." Harold unfastened the cinch.

"This the last day you'll need her?" Sam went about the business of removing the bridle.

"Unfortunately. We've become good friends." Harold reached for a brush to curry the mare.

"I'll take care of that, Miller. You go on along."

"Thanks, Sam."

Harold strolled north on Main Street, soaking up the feel of this Hill Country town. The quieter pace was deceptive. The mostly rock structures, the scrubby mesquite trees, the smell of dust baking in the Texas sun. A lot of business took place here. He'd have a lot to tell his parents when he arrived home.

He stopped in the Emporium to purchase a hand-painted china plate for his mother. The scene reminded him of the first time he saw a field of bluebonnets. He also needed to buy a bag to carry all his western clothes. When he found the store was out of leather Gladstone bags, he bought an extra-heavy canvas one instead.

Harold took one last long gaze up Main Street toward the bank and hotel before he stepped up into the passenger car. He settled in his seat, but before the train pulled out of the station, a man ran out of the bank waving a gun and holding a bulging canvas bag. Dressed all in black and riding a black horse, he thundered out of town. Lagging far behind, but gaining on him, a cowboy, dressed like the one on the cover of the dime novel Harold read on his way to Texas, leaned close to the neck of his powerful mount.

Mesmerized, Harold stared at the first man. He looked exactly the way Harold had imagined Black Bart.

Immediately after Harold realized that, the outlaw cut out across the open prairie, heading straight for a rocky outcropping with trees clustered about. The second man turned, too, hard on his heels.

Harold leaned close to the window and stared after them until they entered a clump of trees. Maybe dime novels weren't all exaggerations.

As the train gained speed, Harold relaxed against the hard seat and relived each moment of the time he'd spent with the Ames family, Charlsey foremost in his thoughts. *Will I ever see your beautiful blue eyes again?*

Chapter 4

After Harold left town, Charlsey tried to forget the man, but he had invaded her heart and mind and settled in to stay. His behavior during their evenings was so different from the way he acted during the day. Maybe he had a problem with a woman wearing trousers and doing what many people considered man's work.

Charlsey had ordered a recently released book, *Strange Case of Dr. Jekyll and Mr. Hyde*, written by the Scottish author Robert Louis Stevenson. She had only read part of the story, but it reminded her of Harold.

In the evening, he was the perfect gentleman. *A very handsome gentleman*. They shared many interests. When they discussed books, she should have asked him if he had read Mr. Stevenson's. What would Harold think about the story of the man with the personality split along the lines of good and evil?

Harold's two personalities weren't good and evil, but he definitely exhibited two different ones. In the daytime, he was all business, concentrating on her father and not even speaking to her, even though Pa had her ride with them every day. But the evenings were an entirely different thing—talking and laughing, enjoying each other. She'd never had a special relationship with any man the way she did with Harold's evening personality. That was the one she missed, the one tangled in her thoughts all day and in her dreams at night.

She couldn't spend her time thinking about the wonderful part of Harold without also taking into account his business personality. Daytime Harold, or Boston as she often thought of him, had been colder, calculating, and still something of a dandy even in the cowboy clothes. How could she miss the company of such a man?

A month. Harold had been gone from Boston a very long month. Now he was aboard a train nearing his hometown. When his father asked him, he hadn't wanted to go to the wilds of Texas. He hadn't even wanted to leave the accounting office. *But I'm glad I did.*

He still liked balancing numbers. That skill had come in handy as he did business with Mr. Ames, with the railroad to transport the cattle, with the packing plant at the stockyards in Chicago, even for obtaining his tickets on the passenger cars.

In addition, his horizons had broadened. Exploring

the vast country opened vistas of knowledge he never would've obtained any other way. The variety of scenery he'd ridden through amazed and delighted him. The large fields of colorful wildflowers. Valleys dotted with long-horn or Hereford cattle. The meandering river lined with mesquite and weeping willow trees. Picturesque Horsefly. *Texas isn't the only place I went.* But it was the one that stuck in his heart.

Look at his personal accomplishments. He could ride a horse as well as the next person. Well, maybe not the cowhands. Enough to know he enjoyed partnering with the animal stretching and bunching powerful muscles beneath him. He'd ridden herd with the Rocking A cow-boys, helping them control the cattle he purchased.

Then there was Charlsey, the most fascinating woman he'd ever met. At that thought, his heart hitched, and he breathed out a deep sigh. He had to reason a way to go back to Texas.

The train pulled into the station. His parents waited on the platform. They must have missed him. Suddenly he realized how anxious he was to see them. Before the passenger car came to a complete stop, he stood on the steps, ready to alight.

"Harold!" His mother's velvety voice rose above the cacophony, and she rushed into his arms. "I missed you."

He kissed her cheek. "I missed you, too." He savored the familiar lilac scent that always surrounded her.

Father gave him a long, piercing look. "Did everything

go all right?" At Harold's nod, he picked up Harold's leather Gladstone. "Let's go home. The carriage is waiting, and Cook fixed all your favorites."

Harold waved toward the baggage car. "I have a couple more things. I'll pick them up and meet you out front."

Charlsey knew what would take her mind off the brown eyes alive with interest that haunted her days. She threw herself into ranch work, starting before dawn and not returning to the house until well past twilight. No matter how tired she was, that one-dimpled smile intruded into her dreams.

She let Dancer have her head as they started toward the barn. The mare stretched her legs in ever-lengthening strides on her way to food and rest. Charlsey wished she had somewhere to go and be totally alone for the evening, but who could be by herself with a houseful of sisters?

Tonight she turned her mare over to Bart and headed to the house, fatigue dragging every step. She didn't see any of the other girls on the way to her room. A tub of hot water awaited her. She'd have to thank someone. *Probably Bess.* She'd slipped deep into the water when her door opened a crack.

"Charlsey"—Sarah's head peeked around the corner— "can I come in?"

"Sure." She hoped her tone didn't sound as hesitant as she felt.

Sarah stood tall and slim, with dark hair and eyes. *Just*

like Bess and Lucy. All her sisters took after Pa, but not Charlsey. She had to be like their mother. Not that she could remember her. Her earliest memories were of riding the range nestled in front of Pa, his strong arm keeping her safe.

"I wanted to talk to you." Sarah gathered up the dirty clothes Charlsey had left scattered around the room as she removed them. After piling them beside the door, she plopped down on the rug and sat cross-legged beside the bathtub.

"Okay." Charlsey picked up the bar of Cashmere Bouquet soap and sniffed the soft floral fragrance before using it to lather her washcloth. "What do you want to talk about?"

"You." Sarah just sat there staring at her.

Charlsey dropped the soap in the soap dish sitting on the floor and scrubbed her arms. "What about me?"

"You"—Sarah cleared her throat—"haven't been yourself since Harold came."

Not Sarah, too. "In what way?" Charlsey lifted one leg out of the warm water and scrubbed it.

"That first night he was here, you were so quiet at supper. You always keep conversation lively at the table."

"I talked to him afterward, didn't I?"

Sarah pleated the hem of her skirt with her fingers. "I don't know. I went to the barn."

Charlsey continued bathing as they talked. "That's right. Everyone left me alone with him. I had to talk to him. No one else would."

Her sister wouldn't let the subject go. "You spent every evening with him. What did you talk about?"

Why do you want to know? "I enjoyed being around him while he ate supper with us. We talked about everything from books to politics."

"And that's all?" A frown marred Sarah's face. "Didn't you connect in any other way?"

Where is all this coming from? "Actually, when we were together out on the ranch in the daytime, I didn't like him very much."

"Why?"

"He was so different. Didn't even acknowledge me. Now can you hand me that towel?"

Sarah obediently unfolded the cream-colored Turkish towel and held it up so Charlsey could step out and wrap it around herself. "You've been different since he left. More distant. And you're working yourself to death."

Might as well tell her what she wants to hear. "I'm trying to get that man out of my mind."

Sarah walked to the door and turned back. "Must not be working." Then she slid into the hallway, closing the door behind her.

"No, it's not." Sarah's words mocked her.

As Father said, Cook had outdone herself preparing all of Harold's favorites. After eating heartily, he pushed himself back from the table.

"Amanda"—Father clasped Mother's hand in his—"I want to ask our son about the business side of his trip if you don't mind. He's regaled us with plenty of other information during dinner."

Mother frowned for a moment then smiled. "All right, but I may claim him for myself tomorrow."

Harold rose from the table and followed his father to the study. *I have to keep my mind on business instead of Charlsey.*

While Father filled his pipe with his favorite tobacco, Harold arranged his thoughts in an orderly manner and waited for Father to join him. Soon aromatic smoke wreathed the room as Father sat across from him in his favorite leather chair.

Father plied him with questions that drew an enormous amount of information from him. Finally, Father leaned back and blew a smoke ring toward the ceiling. "How is my old friend Frank Ames?"

"He's done really well for himself. He's one of the leading ranchers in the area."

"I heard he married. Tell me about his wife." Father set the pipe in a glass ashtray on the table beside his chair and leaned his forearms on his thighs. "Is theirs a happy marriage like your mother's and mine is?"

I didn't expect that question. "The only thing I know about his marriage is that they had four daughters, and Mrs. Ames died soon after Charlsey was born."

"I'm sorry to hear that. Must've been hard for him,

raising daughters alone on a ranch."

Harold nodded. "I'm sure it was. But they're fine young ladies."

Father quirked his brow. "Are they, now?"

Harold wanted to distract him from that train of thought. "How well did you know Frank Ames?"

"When I went out West as a young man, we both worked on the King ranch in South Texas. A finer man, I've never known. That's why I wanted to buy our cattle from him. Why do you ask?"

Harold scratched the day-old whiskers on his cheek. *How should I word this?* "Do you think he would ever have a liaison with another woman?"

"I don't think so. Frank's the man who introduced me to Christ. Surely he wouldn't leave his Christian convictions behind. What makes you think he did?"

Harold didn't want to malign the man, but that young cowboy looked enough like Charlsey to be her brother. "A young man works for him, who looks enough like one of his daughters to be his son. He didn't eat with the family, or even come to the ranch house while I was there. I only saw him out on the range."

"That sounds strange. Maybe he's a cousin or something." Father picked up his pipe again, puffing thoughtfully.

"Looking like he did, he'd have to be a first cousin." Hopefully that was true. Harold didn't want to believe Frank Ames would flaunt a love child. But then, maybe that was why Charlie never came to the house.

Chapter 5

Harold stretched one hand across his forehead and rubbed his temples with his thumb and fingers while he tried to focus his eyes. The long lines of numbers all melted together, and his thoughts took him back to Texas. A little break might do him good. He leaned back, folded his arms over his chest, and let the memories flow.

Charlsey Ames floated down the staircase, a smile illuminating her features. Lively sparks in her beautiful eyes dared him to come closer. She extended a hand toward him, and he pressed his lips to her fingers. Her lyrical voice welcomed him into the parlor.

His chair almost tipped over, and he sat up straight. *Stop thinking about her.*

Once more, he tried to make sense of the numbers dancing across the page. Why wouldn't they line up?

Since he arrived home, he hadn't spent a single day

outdoors. Instead, he'd been trying to catch up with how the business had progressed while he was gone. He hunched his shoulders and stared at the columns of numbers. A fly started buzzing around his head. So hard to keep the pesky things outside. At least it wasn't as big as the horseflies in Texas. *Horsefly.*

He imagined himself stepping from the bright Texas sunlight into the cool dimness of the livery stable. Sam had Sunshine saddled for him. Like a regular cowboy, Harold swung up onto the horse's back, settling into the comfortable western saddle. After riding north on Main Street, he and his favorite mount took the road that led out of town, then over a hill toward the ranch. Sunshine soon achieved an easy lope. The wind against Harold's face cooled him and invigorated his mind. His excitement built as the ranch came into sight. He left the horse in the barn and trotted up to the ranch house, anticipating his imminent meeting with the woman of his dreams. His knock brought Charlsey to the door. Texas-sky-blue eyes stared at him, surrounded by a cloud of white-blond hair swept up from around her face, except for a few wispy curls that caressed her cheeks and neck. Her smile arrowed straight to his heart.

Daydreaming was getting him nowhere. Every thought brought him back to the same thing. . .the woman who'd stirred his heart like no other. Pining away over her wouldn't balance the accounts.

Concentrate!

Harold wondered why his father sent word for him to come up to the top floor of their building. As the electric elevator made its slow ascent to the fourth floor, a feeling of accomplishment swept over him. At least he'd finally balanced the books. Even if it had taken him more than a week. Something that had never happened before.

When the car stopped, he opened the gate and followed the hall to his father's office. At his knock, the door opened wide, and Franklin, his father's secretary, welcomed him in before leaving, shutting the door behind him.

"You wanted to see me, Father?" He dropped into the leather chair in front of the desk.

His father tented his fingers and studied him for several long moments.

Harold revisited the day's events. Surely he hadn't done anything wrong. Had he? Not that he could remember. At least, not since he arrived home from his business trip.

"Son, are you happy?" The question broadsided him.

Am I happy? He didn't know how to answer. He'd come back to the accounting he hadn't wanted to leave in the first place. And after a long line of checks and balances, he enjoyed conquering the numbers; but that wasn't as satisfying as it had been before he'd gone to Texas.

Thoughts of Texas always led to Charlsey. *What is happiness anyway?* Talk of happiness drew him to the woman who filled his daydreams.

Father stood and came around the desk to sit on the corner nearest him. "From your hesitation, I take it that you're not sure."

Nothing like getting right to the point. "I'm not really unhappy." He shifted in the chair.

Father crossed his arms. "I know you didn't want to leave your office and go on the trip to Texas and Chicago, but I thought it would be good for you. Broaden your horizons."

"It did that, all right."

Harold wondered where his father was going with this conversation. He didn't waste business time on idle chatter.

"I get the feeling you wouldn't mind going back to Texas." Father stared at him under his beetle brows.

His heart lightened, and he smiled. "You're right." He didn't want to give away the real reason.

His father gazed across the room at the painting of cowboys and Indians by Frederic Remington that he'd recently acquired. Harold wondered if his father was remembering his trip to Texas as a young man.

"Going to Texas and working on a ranch changed me. It gave me a whole new perspective on life." His father rubbed one hand across his chin and cheek. "What would you think about us buying a ranch in Texas?"

Harold's breath caught. *Where did that idea come from?*

"I heard about one for sale north of Fort Worth, and

I'd like to invest in it."

That was quite a ways from Horsefly, but a lot closer than Boston. "Where do I come in?"

Father stood and stuffed his hands into the pockets of his suit trousers. "I thought I might send you back to the Ames ranch to learn all about ranching. If we purchase the new property, you could take over the management."

"Do you mean—?"

"I haven't thought it all out yet, but once you got the ranch organized, you wouldn't have to spend all your time in Texas. You'd want to keep a watchful eye on all our holdings. Everything will belong to you someday."

"That's a lot to think about." *What an understatement.*

"You don't have to decide right now. Think it over. But I'll want you sitting in on all the meetings about the possible purchase of the ranch."

"I'd like that." Maybe seeing Charlsey again wasn't just a dream.

It's not working. No matter how hard Charlsey toiled or how exhausted she was when she went to bed, Harold Miller III would not leave her alone. . .day or night. While she was out on the range, he galloped through her thoughts. In the few days he'd been here, he'd developed into quite a horseman. Of course, he may have ridden before he came.

But if he could already ride, why did he come out in a surrey when he first arrived? Wouldn't it have been easier to ride a horse? When she and Pa took him around the ranch the next day, he'd seemed a little uneasy in the saddle. By the time they drove his cattle into town and loaded them on the train, he rode like a seasoned cowboy.

Nights were even worse. Harold waltzed through her dreams. Sometimes she'd dream that he'd hold her close. While she stared up into his warm chocolate eyes, his face would slowly descend toward hers until it was a breath away. Then she would awaken with a start.

How would it feel for his lips to touch mine? No one had ever kissed her lips.

She would never know. She'd probably not see the man again, except in her dreams. How could she be so drawn to such a man? She'd just have to force him from her mind.

With the sun descending close to the horizon, Charlsey headed Dancer toward the house. She usually enjoyed the multicolor display, but today a gray mood doused the rainbow. Would this madness never end?

After taking care of Dancer, Charlsey went to her room to wash up. With all that riding today, she needed to change clothes, too. She cleansed her hands and face and loosened her braid from the pins, letting it fall over one shoulder.

She slipped into a housedress and stared at the mirror above the bowl and pitcher on her washstand. Although her skin held a healthy glow, dark smudges under her eyes revealed her lack of sound sleep. *Lord, I need Your help. I must get over this fascination with Harold.*

Everyone had arrived at the kitchen table before her, and they looked up expectantly when she walked through the doorway.

"Guess what, Charlsey." In place of Sarah's usually solemn demeanor, a huge grin split her face.

Charlsey slid into her chair and placed her napkin in her lap. "I'm sure I don't know."

"Mr. Miller wrote a letter. It's addressed to our family, so we wanted to wait till we were all together to read it."

Charlsey turned from Sarah toward her father, but he nodded to her oldest sister. "I asked Bess to read it to us."

Clenching her hands in her lap, Charlsey closed her eyes for a moment. She didn't care what the man had to say. If only she could get up and walk away from the table. But if she tried, she'd have to answer too many questions.

Bess carefully opened the envelope. She pulled out two pages of expensive-looking paper and unfolded them.

Charlsey could tell from where she sat that the handwriting was precise. Not at all like Pa's chicken scratch. Sometimes his notes took her awhile to decipher.

"Dear Ames family, time has really flown by since I left you."

Maybe for you it has. Charlsey almost snorted at his words.

"Thank you for your warm hospitality while I was in

Texas. All of you are often in my thoughts and prayers."

All of us? If he'd had traveling companions, maybe she could be thinking about more than just the one man. A warm flush crept up her neck and settled in her cheeks. She ducked her head, hoping no one would notice.

"It has taken several days to tell my parents about all of my adventures in Horsefly. We've laughed together about many of the things that happened."

Now we're funny. Nothing in her thoughts and dreams had been funny. Memories of the evenings blessed her heart, and the snubs on the range made her angry. She took a deep breath and slowly let it out.

"Father asked many questions about you, Mr. Ames. He counts your time together on the King ranch as some of his fondest memories. I was able to assure him that you've done quite well for yourself, and he was pleased."

The words about ranch work brought back the pain of the way the man shunned her during the day. Why had her resolve melted in the evenings when his smile stole her heart? *Stole my heart?* That couldn't be.

"Bess, I miss the wonderful meals you prepared for us. And the lively conversations around the dining room table." Bess smiled before continuing. "Sarah, I'm wondering how your new foal is doing. Have you thought of a name yet?"

Smiles must be contagious. Sarah caught one when Bess read her name. Charlsey didn't find anything to smile about.

"Lucy, I'm sure you're still practicing sharpshooting. I'd love to watch you again. Maybe we could have a shooting contest someday."

Charlsey watched a silly grin adorn Lucy's face, too. *Wonder if he'll say anything about me.*

"And I couldn't write a letter without mentioning just how much I enjoyed the evenings I spent with Charlsey. Of necessity, they came to an end far too early."

All eyes turned toward her, and the warmth spread over her from head to toe. *Must be the hotter weather this year.* Too bad she didn't have a fan with her, but she didn't want to call attention by using her hand or napkin to try to cool herself. She was glad when their eyes returned to the letter and Bess.

When Bess finished reading, she served supper. Charlsey had been hungry when she started to the house this evening, but each bite she took seemed to grow in her mouth instead of diminishing before she choked it down with a drink of water. She scattered her vegetables around her plate with her fork while her sisters chattered about their recent guest and ate every bite on their plates.

How could a man living over a thousand miles away keep turning her world upside down?

Charlsey let Dancer lope across the valley to the river. She didn't care what her mount did. All she could think about was that maddening man. She'd had a hard enough time trying to push him out of her thoughts. Then yesterday they'd received that letter, and now it was an impossibility.

His melodious baritone voice swept through her dreams the few times she'd slept last night. And his face... today she couldn't get his chiseled good looks out of her mind. Pa had given her a welcome day off from work, but she'd dressed in her men's clothes and gone riding, hoping to shake the visions of him from her head.

Dancer picked her way through the thicket and stopped on the riverbank. Charlsey slid from her back and dropped the reins, letting the ends touch the ground. She patted her horse's neck and walked out on a large rock jutting over the stream. As a young girl, she'd spent many a day lying in the sun in this very spot, hidden from prying eyes by the trees and underbrush. She studied the eddying currents for a few minutes before settling onto the rock to sit with her legs over the side, high above the rushing water below.

Summer heat made her want to shed her outer clothing and take a swim, but this time of year the river still flowed too fast for that. In August, the level would be low enough and a welcome respite from the oppressive heat.

She wished she had brought her fishing pole. Several good-sized catfish lived in this section of the river. A mess of fish would have made a delicious supper and maybe, just maybe, gotten her thoughts on other things.

Wonder if Harold likes catfish. What difference would that make? The sooner she forgot him, the better.

The sound of approaching hoofbeats snapped her out of her reverie. Whoever it was should pass right by without seeing her.

"Charlsey!" Lucy's voice sounded close. She burst through the trees on her horse. "I thought I'd find you here. Pa sent me to fetch you."

Charlsey stood and reached for Dancer's reins. "What does he want?"

"Come to the house." Lucy rested her hands on the saddle horn. "He just got back from town. Mr. Miller is in Horsefly, and he'll be here for supper."

He can't be. Charlsey's mouth opened and closed, reminding her of the big catfish in the river. "But we just received his letter yesterday. He didn't say anything about coming back."

"I know. Isn't it exciting?" Lucy, grinning as big as Texas, wheeled her horse and headed back toward the house.

That's not what I'd call it. What was the man doing coming back? Why did her heart jump into her throat? Her pulse pounded. Excitement rushed through her like the Guadalupe River below, churning and disrupting her almost settled thoughts about the man. Charlsey swung up into the saddle and turned Dancer toward home.

Chapter 6

Charlsey turned, looking in the mirror. This time when she saw Harold, there would be no repeat of their first meeting. Her cheeks turned pink thinking about it.

Taking another glance, she was glad she had purchased this gorgeous dress in the Eberhardt Emporium, even if it had been after Harold left for Boston. Now she'd have a chance to wear it and hopefully show herself to the best advantage. She loved the pastel flowers sprigged across the dusky blue background that emphasized the color of her eyes. She hoped he would notice.

The fitted bodice sported a line of white buttons up the front. She could reach every one of them. No gap, and she made sure each button was completely through the buttonhole with no chance of slipping out.

As she brushed out her hair and worked it into a passable upswept style, she wondered why Harold had returned so soon. Only one day after his letter, which contained not one word about him coming to Texas. She hoped seeing him again would help her push him out of her thoughts, especially when he returned to Boston, which he undoubtedly would do.

While she descended the stairs, a sharp rap sounded on the front door. She'd wanted one of her sisters to answer the door when he arrived, instead of her. *No such luck.*

Charlsey grasped the knob and pulled. As she glanced up, her gaze collided with Harold's and held far too long for her comfort. *Or maybe not.* Feasting on those chocolate eyes brought back all the good memories. Easy conversations that connected them intellectually. . .and on other levels. When his eyes danced with interest about a subject, they enticed her into the heart of the discussion. Such a kinship. . .a connection, she'd felt with him. But there was something else there, too. Something she couldn't quite name. Maybe that was the reason she couldn't rid her thoughts of him.

After the first shock of seeing him, she stepped back. "Harold, please come in." She bit the excitement out of her voice, she hoped.

Her words broke their gaze. He glanced beyond her shoulder. She turned, surprised to see Pa coming down the hallway. Why hadn't she heard his boots pounding a cadence on the wooden floor? Their guest captured her attention to the point that everything else around her disappeared.

Pa's face shone with genuine affection as he clapped Harold on the shoulder. "Glad you could join us for supper. I believe Bess has everything ready."

The two men headed into the dining room, leaving her holding the door. Almost the way Harold treated her out on the range, as if she were invisible. That put a damper on any warm feeling she had toward him, except her fingers itched to push back the errant curl that fell across his wide forehead.

She huffed out a breath, shut the door a little too loudly, and followed them to the table, quickly slipping into her usual place.

Harold eased himself into the chair across from Charlsey. He studied her face. With her downcast eyes, he felt sure she avoided looking at him. She hadn't done that when she opened the door. Their gazes locked and held in a strong, almost breathless way. Something he'd never experienced with any of the women Mother paraded through his life, hoping for a daughter-in-law. None of them ever touched that deep place inside him where he and Charlsey shared similar views on God, family, and the future. Not that they'd ever really discussed a future together, but the desire for one had tugged him back to Texas as much as his father's plan to purchase a ranch.

They bowed their heads before Mr. Ames pronounced the blessing on their food and their lives. But when Mr. Ames finished, Charlsey still didn't look at him. He hadn't meant to walk past her, but her father had interrupted them. Bemused, Harold followed along. Now he wished he'd said something to her before he left her holding the door. His mother had taught him better manners, even though Charlsey couldn't tell this evening.

Finally, her beautiful blue, piercing gaze speared him. "Mr. Miller, why have you returned to Texas?"

The icy tone of her voice didn't bode well for him. She'd called him Harold when she opened the door. *What happened to that?*

"Didn't your father tell you?" He glanced toward the head of the table.

"I wanted to wait until you were here, so you could tell the girls." Mr. Ames took a bite of his delicious-smelling steak.

Harold glanced around, and all four sisters trained their attention on him, stifling him. He looked straight at Charlsey. "My father plans to purchase a ranch north of Fort Worth. He wants your father to teach me how to run it."

After the initial surprise, her features hardened for an instant before she adopted a bland expression that completely hid her feelings. "How long do you plan on staying here?" The quiver on her last word cut straight through him.

"That will depend on your father. When he thinks I've learned enough to be able to take over the ranch, I'll leave." Stated baldly like that, the plan sounded cold. . . unfeeling.

He was anything but unfeeling toward Charlsey. Maybe they'd be able to spend part of the evening in discussion as they did when he had been here before. That was what he missed most about Texas.

Unfortunately, when Harold finally took his leave, it was from the whole family, not just Charlsey. The evening had been enjoyable, but not one member of the Ames clan left the parlor until he departed. At least Bess hadn't stopped them from discussing business, and he and Mr. Ames had worked out all the details with the four sisters looking on and even making suggestions.

Tonight didn't go as I'd hoped. He slammed his hat on his head and started toward the barn.

Charlsey hung back while Lucy, Bess, and Sarah headed to the kitchen to clean. "Pa, can I talk to you a minute?"

He looked up from reading the *Horsefly Herald Gazette*, which he'd picked up as soon as Harold left. "This is the first chance I've had to look at the news. Is it important?"

She dropped onto the edge of the sofa. "It is to me."

Pa folded the paper and laid it on the table. "Okay, sugar, what do you want to talk about?"

She gripped her hands until they hurt. "I'd really like to head out to the north line shack tomorrow. Some of the fence needs mending. I could stay there a few days and take care of it."

Puzzlement quirked his brow. "Why'd you want to do

that? I can send a couple of the hands out to take care of the fence. They would get it done quicker with two of them working together." He paused and studied her. "What brought this on anyway?"

Heat crept up her neck into her cheeks. She wanted to cover them with her hands.

Pa had already seen the blush, because his eyes narrowed. "Something about Harold bothering you, gal?"

This was worse than she had anticipated. "I'd just rather not work with him is all." She didn't want Pa to guess the depth of her feelings for one of the man's personalities.

"I can take care of that without you banishing yourself to the line shack." He picked up the paper. "You wouldn't even have a way to bathe out there. . .or anything else you need."

The snap he gave the paper before he opened it signaled an end to the conversation.

She flounced out into the hallway and up the stairs to her bedroom. How in the world would Pa help her stay away from Harold? . . . *And why would he want to?*

Harold rode his newly purchased horse, Sunshine, to the Ames ranch. In his saddlebags, he had enough western clothes for a week. He hadn't checked out of the hotel room because he planned to return to town to have his laundry done. And he needed a place to go if he wanted to have time to himself.

He hoped to catch sight of Charlsey as he rode toward the ranch office in the north end of the barn, but she was nowhere to be seen. After dismounting, he knocked on the frame of the open doorway.

Mr. Ames swiveled in his chair and rose. "You got here plenty early, Miller." He grasped Harold's outstretched hand. "Do you want to stay at the house or in the bunkhouse? Either's fine with me."

Harold shoved his hands into the front pockets of his denim trousers. "If I'm going to understand about a cowboy's life on a ranch, I'd better live in the bunkhouse."

The ranch owner shook his head. "Not much space for each man. Just a bunk and a place for a trunk if you have one. You're not used to living like that."

"If you and my father could do it when you were young men, then so can I." He rocked up on his toes and down again.

"Well, I respect you for it. You'll learn faster that way." Mr. Ames sat back down. "Do you want the boys to know why you're here?"

He thought about the idea for a minute. "Not right away. If we don't tell them, maybe they'll accept me sooner."

"Probably right about that." Mr. Ames got up and studied a chart on the wall.

Wanting to see what it was, Harold joined him.

With long, thin fingers, the rancher traced a line of boxes, most with names on them. "These represent the bunks. See, they're stacked two high." He looked back over his shoulder. "When your dad and I worked the King ranch, the bunks were stacked three high. I sure didn't want the top bunk."

When the man started toward the door, Harold followed him. They went to the bunkhouse that was nestled on a rocky knoll surrounded by live oak trees. Not far away, a small cottage sat facing the ranch house.

"Who lives there?" Harold waved toward the tiny house.

"The foreman and his wife. Actually, sometimes Martha helps the girls with the housework if they're too busy to do it."

Made sense to Harold. But if the girls needed help sometimes, what kept Charlsey busy during the day? Maybe she volunteered in town with the children or at the church. *A worthy endeavor, for sure.*

For a week, Charlsey managed to stay away from Harold in the daytime. Sometimes she caught a glimpse of him across the way, but she'd been busy and so had he. Their evenings were a different story. Even though she'd hoped for a return of their happy times before he went back to Boston, they hadn't had a single evening alone. Pa and one or more of her sisters joined them in the parlor every evening.

Last night, Harold kept everyone laughing with his tales of reading *Black Bart's Nemesis* and expecting Texas to be like the dime novel. A smile tugged at her lips at the memory. He told about watching a similar event play out in Horsefly before the train left the station taking his cattle to Chicago.

She stuck in a final hairpin and tipped the cheval glass so she could check her hem. *Just right.* As much as she loved her family, maybe tonight she and Harold could spend a little time alone. She needed to catch a glimpse of the side of the man she'd come to, dare she say, love when he was here before.

After the lively dinner conversation, Sarah and Pa headed out to the barn to check on a sick horse. Lucy offered to help Bess clean up the dishes.

Finally, Harold held out his arm to escort Charlsey to the parlor. She slipped her hand through, noticing how muscular he was. Her fingers tingled from the rock-hard feel of his forearm under her hand.

She settled on one end of the sofa, hoping Harold would share it with her. Instead, he eased into a wingback chair and propped one booted foot on the opposite knee.

Wonder what direction our conversation will take tonight.

He cleared his throat. "Charlsey, I'm glad we're alone this evening. I've been wanting to ask you something."

Must be important since he seems so nervous, tapping his fingers on his leg. . .limb. . .or whatever is the proper thing to call it while he jiggles it up and down. "What do you want to know?"

He dropped his foot back on the floor and rose in one fluid motion like the caged tiger she'd seen when the circus came to town, pacing across the rug toward the fireplace. He rested his hands on the carved walnut mantel.

Will the man ever say what he wants?

After turning back toward her, he shoved his hands into the back pockets of his clean denim trousers and rocked up on his toes, then back down. She'd never noticed him doing that before. Maybe she should prod him to get to the question.

She started to open her mouth but shut it again when he finally spoke. "I'm wondering about the young cowhand who works for your father."

Young? All the cowboys were almost as old as Pa.

"I saw him more when I was here before, but he doesn't live in the bunkhouse." He raked his fingers through his hair, making more than one errant curl dangle above his eyes. "I see him occasionally, but not up close." Once again he cleared his throat. "Is he maybe a cousin or something? He favors you more than your sisters."

Charlsey froze. Her heart stopped, then beat a staccato in her throat. He could only be talking about her. *Does he really not know?*

Harold turned his back toward her. "I even asked my father if your pa could have been involved with another woman."

She shot to her feet. "How dare you think such a thing!" She didn't care that she was shrieking. "You are so dense."

He whipped around, pain streaming from his eyes. "I'm sorry." He took a step toward her.

She backed up a step.

"I heard the other cowhands call him Charlie at the branding that day I arrived."

Trembling from head to toe, she tried to control her anger. "That was me!" She thrust her thumb toward her chest. "I'm Charlie."

His mouth dropped open as if he couldn't comprehend what she was saying. "You? . . . But he wore trousers."

"Of course I wear trousers when I'm working the ranch. Did you think I did it in a skirt?"

"I didn't know what you did all day." Shoving his fingers back through his hair, he stared at her. "Decent women don't wear trousers."

"You don't think I'm decent?" She spat out the bitter words, her fists clenched against her hips. "I thought we were becoming good friends, maybe more, but I can see now that we have nothing in common." She stomped out of the parlor and up the stairs, never looking back.

The nerve of that man!

Chapter 7

Instead of heading to the bunkhouse, Harold veered to a rocky outcropping bathed in silvery moonlight. He wasn't ready to face any of the other cowboys. How had he not known? When "Charlie" rode with her father and him the first time he came to Texas, she didn't join their discussions, so he didn't hear her voice. But those eyes. . .he'd always felt drawn to those eyes. Now he knew why.

If he'd had a lick of sense, he'd have remembered that Charlsey looked like their mother and the other girls took after their father. If Mr. Ames had been with another woman, the child wouldn't have looked like Charlsey. How had he even considered the idea about such a godly man?

What was he going to do? He'd been entertaining the idea that Charlsey might be the woman God intended for him. But that would never happen. Her scandalous behavior was completely unacceptable. What would his mother think if she ever found out the whole truth about Charlsey? If only he could talk to his father.

As he started toward the bunkhouse, he noticed Sarah leaving the barn and heading to the house. He made his way to the barn through the shadows cast by the mesquite trees and live oaks, careful not to stumble over a rock or step into a hole. By the time he reached the moonlight again, Mr. Ames was shutting the door.

"I'd like a word with you, sir." Harold stopped a few feet from the older man.

Mr. Ames studied his face a moment. "Sure. Would you like to come back up to the house?"

Harold thrust his hands into his pockets. After making his decision, he wanted to get it over with as soon as possible. "No. I just wanted to say that I need to go home right now."

With narrowed eyes, Mr. Ames gave him a puzzled look. "Something happen I need to know about?"

"No, sir." Harold concentrated on the toe of his boot drawing circles in the dust.

"You comin' back?"

How should he answer? He glanced up. "I'm not sure."

⁓

Charlsey muffled her sobs with her pillow. She wasn't even sure whether she cried because she was hurt or angry. She just needed to release a passel of pent-up emotions.

"Charlsey?" A knock followed Bess's tentative call.

She didn't answer. She didn't want to see anyone right now, especially not Bess.

The doorknob turned, but she had locked the door when she came in. She knew one or more of her sisters would try to talk to her. *But not right now.*

"Charlsey, open the door."

The doorknob jiggled, reminding her of Harold's jiggling leg, and she didn't want to think about that man.

"I know you're in there." Bess's tone had turned plaintive. "Let me in."

"What's going on?" Lucy didn't try to keep her voice down the way Bess had.

"I don't know. You heard the yelling as much as I did. That's all I know." Bess's answer was as loud as Lucy's question.

"Charlsey!" When Lucy rattled the knob, the whole door shook.

"Go away." Charlsey tried to keep her voice from trembling. "I. Am. Not. Opening. The. Door."

For a while they tried to wheedle her into complying but finally gave up.

She didn't know if she could ever tell anyone why she felt so foolish—allowing herself to fall for a man who didn't respect her. In her mind, both of the personalities of Mr. Harold Miller III coalesced into one man, a man she couldn't abide. Not now. . .not ever.

During the long train ride to Boston, Harold replayed his

time in Horsefly. Before tonight, he'd considered it some of the happiest times of his life. He had really taken to ranching. With his accounting background, he'd caught on quickly to the office work. He hadn't realized how much bookwork ranching entailed. Keeping track of all the cattle, the breeding, the branding, the sales. And the Ames ranch was very successful.

The time he'd spent out on the range with the cowboys had been enlightening, too. He'd learned to work with the other cowboys like a team, rounding up cattle, moving them to other pastures. He'd even helped fix fences. The other cowboys rode into town in the evenings, so they didn't realize he was spending time at the main house with the family. They accepted him as one of them by the second day. He hated to see that come to an end.

What could he do now? Charlsey wouldn't ever want to see him again. And even if she did, could he really introduce her to his mother? She would not fit into his world, and she surely didn't want him in hers.

If Father still wanted to buy the ranch, he'd run it for him. Even though it had only been a week this time, he felt he had a grasp on ranching.

When the train pulled into the station, his father waited for him, worry puckering his brow. "What brought you home so soon? The telegram didn't give any details, except when the train would arrive."

"Can we wait until we're back in the office to discuss it?" He didn't want to get into a serious discussion in such a public place.

"Your mother expects us home. She's had Cook preparing a veritable banquet." Father picked up his Gladstone bag while Harold went for the trunk. "That woman spoils you."

Harold smiled at his father's quip. "She just knows I like to eat."

All the time they traveled the busy streets of Boston and throughout the meal, Harold kept a facade of normalcy. He didn't want to upset Mother, and he didn't want to talk to his father until they were alone. He had really messed up this time. Why hadn't Father left him to his accounting? He'd never have been in a fix like this.

When he followed his father into the study, he finally relaxed. As usual, Father sank into his favorite leather chair and started filling his pipe. Not until the aromatic smoke wreathed the room did Father ask his first question.

"Are you ready to tell me what's bothering you?"

Was he ready? He wasn't sure, but no way around it now.

"Have you already purchased the ranch in Texas?" If Father hadn't, then there might not be a problem. . . . Except that Father would make him face what happened anyway.

With a nod, Father asked, "Why is that important?"

"It's probably not." He stared at the Remington painting, wishing he were still out on the range. "I may have made a terrible mistake."

Father laid his pipe in an ashtray and leaned forward, his expression intent. "What kind of mistake?"

"Remember when I mentioned that young cowboy at the Ames ranch? Well, I was wrong. Mr. Ames didn't do anything wrong. Charlie is Charlsey." He rubbed the stubble on his chin.

"And you thought she was a man?" A hint of glee colored Father's words.

"Well, she wore men's clothes. A big hat, a big shirt, and loose...trousers." With the last word heat suffused his cheeks.

A loud guffaw bounced around the room. "Oh...this is...priceless." His father interspersed the words with more laughter.

Harold didn't see anything funny about it. He frowned. That set Father off again. This conversation was going downhill fast.

"Is that why you hurried home?" Father's tone grew serious.

Harold inhaled a deep breath and let it out slowly. "I wanted to talk to you."

With a nod, Father smiled. "I'm glad you did. So tell me all about it." He picked up his pipe and took a long draw, leaning back in the chair.

Might as well get it over with. In a monotone, he recounted his final confrontation with Charlsey.

After pondering his words, Father finally spoke. "You really did say she isn't decent?"

"I didn't mean it that way, but she wouldn't be acceptable in Mother's circle of friends."

Laying the pipe back in the ashtray, Father leaned forward with his forearms on his thighs. "The Bible talks about people looking at outward appearances but God looking at the heart. When you were home last time, you shared things with me that led me to believe you had a heart connection with the girl."

"I thought we did." He envisioned the times they'd spent together. "I was beginning to believe she was the woman God intended for me, but that can't be."

With a chuckle, Father stared at him. "The Bible also says that His ways are higher than our ways, and His thoughts than our thoughts." He got up and strode to the massive fireplace, stopping to stare into the mirror above the mantel. "I never told you about almost missing out on the woman God planned for me. I had too much pride."

"Pride about what?" This sounded interesting and took the attention off his own mistakes.

"Actually, the sinful kind that causes a man to be puffed up and not listen to the Lord." He turned and stared at Harold. "I was a poor cowboy, recently returned from the Wild West. Your mother, the daughter of a banker here in Boston. I misjudged her. Thought she'd consider herself above me. So I kept myself from being hurt by holding myself aloof."

Aloof? From what he'd seen of his parents, that wasn't a part of their relationship.

"I guess I considered her better than me, and she was, but my pride kept me from relaxing around her. We went to the same church. I tried to ignore her even though I felt drawn to her. She befriended me and slowly won me over. I think she even had the pastor and his wife helping get the two of us together."

Harold didn't really see what this had to do with his relationship, or lack thereof, with Charlsey.

"When we married, she was glad to live in a tiny cottage with me. She did things servants had always done for her, working beside me as we built the first horse farm into a thriving enterprise. Her father became sick, so we moved back to Boston to be near him. He brought me into the bank, and I was able to take over when he died. Your mother took her place in Boston society, but I still remember her helping me deliver foals. And she didn't wear dresses when she did it either."

That was a new image for Harold. His mother wearing trousers to help her father on a horse farm? Maybe she *would* accept Charlsey.

"Son, don't miss a chance at what God might have planned for you." He stood. "I'm going up to join your mother. It's been a long day."

That it had, but Harold knew his day wasn't over. He had to spend time with the Lord.

Chapter 8

Over a week since Charlsey had seen Boston, and finally she was coming to grips with all that happened. The man didn't understand what it took to run a ranch. Her father had taught them to do whatever it took to finish the job. No one else who knew them would *ever* consider her indecent. Boston had the problem, and she wouldn't let it affect her anymore.

She spent the morning in town buying supplies and visiting with friends. After helping Bess store everything, she changed into work clothes so she could get out on the range. She was heading toward the back of the house when someone knocked on the front door. *Must be a stranger; friends would come to the back or even to the barn this time of day.*

She retraced her steps down the hallway and pulled the door open wide. Frozen in surprise, she stared into the dark brown eyes she'd thought she would never see again.

After a moment, she started to slam the door.

A scuffed brown leather boot prevented it from closing. Boston pushed the heavy wooden door as if it were hollow. She stepped back and crossed her arms, then stood tapping her foot.

"What do you want?" Anger and bitterness dripped from each word.

Pain glistened in his eyes, almost like the sheen of tears. "I am so sorry, Charlsey." His deep voice carried conviction.

"Sorry won't cut it with me." She let her upper lip curl in scorn.

How dare he think he could just waltz in here and say he was sorry and everything would be all right? He'd delivered a heart-deep insult that still ached even though she tried to put it out of her mind. Him standing there in her face brought all the pain back. . .full force.

He studied her as if she were the most interesting thing in the world, making her uncomfortable. "How could I not have known you? You're the essence of femininity."

She glanced down at the loose trousers and shirt, belted tight at the waist. *I look like a sack of potatoes. That's not feminine.* She opened her mouth but didn't know what to say, so she snapped it closed.

"I know I don't deserve your forgiveness." He moved a hand toward her shoulder, but she pulled it back out of his reach. "I'm here to prove how sorry I am and to earn your forgiveness."

"When h—" She knew he'd really think she was indecent if she said that out loud. "When it snows in August, Boston." That was the first time she'd actually used her derogatory name for him to his face.

He smiled. "Then get ready for a blizzard." He turned on his heel and headed back out the door.

She slammed it behind him. *How dare you!*

Harold hurried toward the barn, a smile tickling his lips. A woman wouldn't have that much fire if she didn't feel something for him. He looked forward to spending time around her while he broke down her defenses. No matter how long it took, he'd stay till the end. And the only end he would consider was Charlsey as his wife.

Since the door of the office was closed, he realized Mr. Ames must be out on the range. Unhitching Sunshine, he jumped into the saddle and headed across the open land toward a cloud of dust. The cowhands had to be moving cattle.

Before he topped the hill, a lone rider headed toward him. Mr. Ames must be on his way back to headquarters. Harold rode Sunshine right into his path.

He knew the moment the ranch owner recognized him. The man slowed his horse to a walk the last few feet before he stopped in front of Harold.

"So, Miller, you did come back. I thought you might." A twinkle lit his eyes. "And you didn't stay away very long."

"No, sir." Harold rested both hands on his saddle horn. "I couldn't."

Mr. Ames took off his Stetson and swiped his bandanna across his brow before resettling his hat. "It's already a scorcher today."

"Yes, sir."

"So are we going to dance around each other all day, or are you going to tell me what's going on?"

Nothing like getting right to the point. "I need to explain something to you, sir." Harold swallowed and tried to decide where to start.

"I know my Charlsey's unhappy. And I figure you're a big part of it. You want to explain that? Go ahead." A stern mask settled over the man's face.

"I was an idiot, sir."

"Stop calling me sir and tell me what you did to my daughter. I don't like to see her hurting." The man's horse shifted and his saddle creaked.

"Yes, s—I don't know how it happened, but I never realized that Charlsey is also Charlie. I know I was stupid, and when I found out, I said some things I regret."

"Why did you leave?" The stern expression didn't change.

"I went to talk to my father. I value his opinion, and he helped me straighten out my thoughts."

"What are you going to do about it?" Once more his eyes twinkled, and he gave a slight smile.

"I've already apologized to Charlsey, but she won't

accept it. I just want a chance to prove to her how much I mean it."

"Is that all?" The man could see right through him.

"Actually, I'd like your approval to court her when she realizes I don't intend to repeat my mistake."

Mr. Ames stared out across the land for long moments before turning back. "If you can get her to forgive you, you have my permission to court her." He lifted his reins, and his horse danced in place. "But if you hurt her again, I'll nail your hide to the barn door. Understood?"

"Yes, s—Mr. Ames. I won't hurt her again." *I just want to cherish her.*

For the next week, Harold hardly caught sight of Charlsey, except at dinner with the whole family. She was more elusive than gold in a worked-out mine. And after the meal, she didn't come into the parlor to visit.

Before going to dinner tonight, Harold pulled out his Bible and thumbed through it. He read several short passages from Proverbs. They all pointed toward patience. *Are You trying to tell me something, Lord?*

Go slow, son. Don't spook her.

Harold chuckled. Out here in Texas, God sounded like a cowboy to him. But he decided right then to be the most patient man in this large state.

Over the next few weeks, circumstances changed. Maybe because of the commitment he made to the Lord, Charlsey started staying after dinner and visiting with him along with her father and sisters. Soon hope filled Harold's heart, but when he studied Charlsey's face as she talked, a slight hesitancy toward him shadowed her eyes. That had to go away before he could proceed with wooing her.

For the first few weeks after Boston returned, Charlsey felt wary of him—waiting for him to make one wrong move. When he didn't, she relaxed more and more.

Besides being the handsomest man she'd ever seen, he'd also become immensely more interesting. As the whole family came to know him better, she liked who he really was—neither Dr. Jekyll nor Mr. Hyde. Just an interesting man who loved the Lord and wanted to be a good rancher. He was already a good accountant. That combination spelled success in all the ways that mattered.

This year, August was more of a scorcher than usual. After she finished helping Bess can a couple of bushels of tomatoes, sweat dripped off Charlsey's face and saturated her clothing. All she could think about was taking a dip in the river. Nothing was as refreshing as that, not even a tepid bath.

She tied a bundle of clean clothes to her saddle and headed Dancer to Charlsey's favorite spot. Knowing the hands were working in a different pasture made the slow-moving river a good choice. Since she'd grown up, Pa didn't want her swimming anywhere near the men.

Leaving Dancer grazing in the shade of a clump of weeping willow trees, Charlsey stripped down to her un-mentionables and dove in. She stroked through the water, then turned on her back and floated. All her cares washed down the Guadalupe.

Finally, she dressed in her clean clothes before leaving the shelter of the bushes. Dancer raised her head and ambled over to nuzzle Charlsey's neck.

Soon she and Dancer were sailing like the wind across the prairie grass. Charlsey imagined it would feel like this to be a bird.

Abruptly, Dancer went down, and Charlsey sailed through the air, landing hard on her left ankle before her whole body slammed into the ground. Her breath whooshed out of her, and blackness descended.

When she once more became aware of her surroundings, everything hurt. Only a prairie dog hole could make Dancer go down like that, and she hadn't seen any in this area before. If she had, she would have been more careful.

Charlsey gingerly pulled herself into a sitting position with her knees close to her chest, and her surroundings began to swirl. She laid her head on her knees and took several deep breaths. Her ankle throbbed, and she wasn't sure she could put her weight on it.

Dancer stood a few feet away. She gave a whiffling sound with a whine attached. Charlsey studied her horse, noticing that Dancer kept lifting one foot.

"Come to me, girl." She gave a clicking sound that usually brought her horse to her side.

Instead, Dancer sidled over, keeping as much weight as she could off that one leg. No way could Charlsey ride her back to the barn, and Charlsey couldn't stand up. Here she sat in the hot sun, and no one knew where she was. *Lord, I need help right away.*

Dancer nudged her. Charlsey used the reins and saddle to pull herself up on her horse's good side. She untied the canteen then hugged Dancer's neck.

"Go home." She gave the horse a slap on the rump and watched her limp away.

The farther the horse moved, the lonelier Charlsey felt. She took a sip of the lukewarm liquid and recapped the canteen. She might need this water to last a long time.

Her thoughts kept returning to Harold. Why hadn't she let him know that she forgave him? More than forgave. All she wanted was to be with him the rest of her life. Hopefully, she wouldn't die out here before she could let him know. With the intense August heat and no shade nearby, death was a real possibility.

Harold closed the ledger and stretched his back. He'd offered to make sure the books balanced for Mr. Ames. Since the older man didn't really like the bookwork, he was glad to get out with the cowboys.

Harold heard a horse with a strange gait approaching. He went to the open door and saw Dancer struggling toward the barn.

"Bart, get out here." His shout echoed in the large building. "Dancer's coming in without Charlsey."

The stable hand ran toward him. "That horse is hurt." He grabbed the reins and led the limping animal into the shade.

"Was Charlsey riding Dancer when she left?"

"Yeah. Wonder where she is."

"We've got to find her, but how?" Harold hurriedly saddled Sunshine.

"Larry is over at his house. I saw him come in a while ago." Bart started cooing at the tired mare. "And he's good at tracking."

"Saddle up his horse. I'll go get him."

Tracking was a slow, tedious business. Harold wanted to ride fast and find the woman he loved, but the foreman studied the grass and dusty ground, taking it slow and easy.

They made their way across a vast sea of dry prairie grass like that stupid dime novel described. The grass was so tall that Charlsey could be lying on the ground hidden, so Harold held in his impatience and followed the foreman's lead.

An eternity later, Harold spied Charlsey's head above the waving grass. With her head resting on her knees, she looked wilted in the heat. His heart almost broke, seeing her that way.

He turned toward Larry. "You go on back and have them get a bed ready for her. I'll bring her."

He raced Sunshine across the intervening space. Charlsey raised her head when he leapt from the saddle to crouch beside her.

"Charlsey, are you all right?" He gathered her into his arms and held her tight, her head resting on his chest, a canteen clutched in her hands. *Please, God, let her be okay.*

"Harold." She looked up at him and ran the tip of her tongue along her dry lips. "You came for me."

"Of course I did." He let her feet slowly slide to the ground, but she groaned when one landed. "You're hurt."

She leaned into his embrace. "I think my ankle is broken or at least sprained."

"Do you need a drink?"

"Yes, I was saving the water in case it took a long time for someone to find me."

Still holding her with one arm, he opened the canteen with the other hand. She tipped it up and drank deeply.

"Not too fast." He pulled it away from her. "Don't want you getting sick."

She clung to the front of his shirt with both hands and gazed up at him. "My hero."

"Are you delirious?" He didn't want to believe it, but that could explain her smile.

His attention settled on her lips, no longer dry, but soft and inviting. He tentatively touched them with his own. She didn't pull back, so he settled his on them more firmly.

Her hands slid up his shoulders and clasped behind his neck.

He pulled her closer and lost himself in a world he

never knew existed. A place where two hearts meet and intertwine and soar above the mundane to the sublime.

An eon later but much too soon, she pulled away and nestled her face against his neck. Her soft breath both tickled and soothed him.

"Charlsey, I love you, and I want you to be my wife."

She stiffened, then relaxed. "I'd like that."

"You would?" Surprise, then delight, shot through him. "You'll marry me?"

"Yes, Harold. I love you, too."

She sounded so meek, he laughed. "What happened to Boston?"

"That was my bad name for you." She chuckled.

"I like it. You can use it when we're alone. A secret between us."

He lifted her and set her on Sunshine. After mounting, he pulled her back against him.

"Do I see clouds laden with snow on the horizon?"

She twisted and looked up at him as if he were crazy. "This is the hottest day of the year, and I don't see any clouds."

"Ah yes, but a blizzard is coming, my dear, because you have forgiven me."

Their laughter intermingled in a cloud around them. He'd never felt this happy. *Thank You, Lord.*

Epilogue

Charlsey's eyes shot open. Today was her wedding day. Christmas Eve 1890. A day she'd never forget. While her sisters had been busy decorating the house for the holiday, Charlsey couldn't keep her mind on that. Too many other things had captured her attention—all of them connected to the man she loved and her upcoming wedding. While her sisters made bows and popcorn and paper garlands for the tree, she worked on her wedding dress of blue velvet with white lace.

So much had happened since that day in August. Harold's parents came to Texas at the end of October. Charlsey loved her future in-laws, and they welcomed her into the family. They accompanied Charlsey and Harold on a trip to the new ranch, which had a two-story house. Mrs. Miller took her shopping in Fort Worth and Dallas to replace the worn furniture while the men caught up on the financial security of the enterprise.

Their new home on the Miller ranch would keep her close enough to her own family to visit often. After all, in this modern day and time, the railroad could take her there so much faster than by wagon or on horseback. And they could go to Boston or Chicago whenever Harold needed to for business. A very exciting arrangement. In addition, the railroad was going to take her and her accountant on a wedding trip to Galveston.

Life was wonderful. But it was going to get even better this evening when she and Boston exchanged their vows. Thinking about all that would usher into her life sent delicious shivers up her spine and stirred a longing deep within her.

By tonight, she would be Mrs. Harold Miller III. Mrs. Boston to her and her new husband.

 **Lena Nelson Dooley** is an author, editor, and speaker. A full-time writer, she is the president of DFW Ready Writers, the local Dallas–Fort Worth chapter of American Christian Fiction Writers. She has also hosted a critique group in her home for over twenty years. Several of the writers she's mentored have become published authors, too.

Lena lives with the love of her life in North Texas. They enjoy traveling and spending time with family and friends. They're active members of their church, where Lena serves in the bookstore, on the Altar Ministry team, and as a volunteer for the Care Ministry and Global Ministries.

The Dooley family includes two daughters, their spouses, two granddaughters, two grandsons, and a great-grandson.

You can find Lena at several places on the Internet: www.lenanelsondooley.com, lenanelsondooley.blogspot.com, and her monthly newsletter is at lenanelsondooleynewsletter.blogspot.com. You can also visit her on Shoutlife, Facebook, and Twitter.

LUCY AMES, SHARPSHOOTER

by Darlene Franklin

To the best Christmas present I've ever received—
Jordan Elizabeth Franklin, who arrived on December 11,
2008. Jordan, God gave me hope in a difficult time as
I anticipated your birth. May you, like Lucy, pursue
God's calling on your life, wherever He leads you.

Chapter 1

April 1891
Horsefly, Texas

OPEN AUDITION

Can you ride? Rope a calf? Shoot a nickel at fifty paces? Major Paulson's Wild West Show is seeking skilled cowboys and cowgirls. If travel and adventure appeal to you, we want to talk with YOU. Come to the picnic grounds on the Guadalupe River on Thursday morning prepared to showcase your skill.

Lucy Ames clutched the ad from the weekly *Horsefly Herald Gazette* in her hand. She'd read and reread the page until the ink had smudged. Could her dreams at last be coming true?

She smoothed her skirt with her free hand, wishing it resembled the short skirt with a fancy blouse and bead-work that Annie Oakley wore in posters from Buffalo Bill's Wild West Show. Anxious to get started, she fingered Ranger, a Winchester rifle, named after a favorite dog from her childhood. "The gun that won the West" would hit anything she aimed at.

"Lucy Ames." A man called her name.

Hands trembling on Ranger, she stepped forward. "Here I am." She hoped nerves wouldn't prevent her from doing her best.

A young man of twenty-five or twenty-six greeted her. "Pleased to meet you, Miss Ames. I'm Gordon Paulson, Major Paulson's son. I'm helping out, but he will make the final decisions." Sympathetic warmth radiated from his brown eyes. "There's no need to be nervous."

Lucy nodded and breathed deeply. Peace descended on her. If God wanted her in Major Paulson's show, He would steady her hands the way He had the first time she brought down a buck.

"What do you want to show us today?" He didn't express any surprise that a *woman* was here to audition, and she liked him for that.

"I'm a good shot." *I'm mumbling.* She cleared her throat. "The best in Gillespie County, in fact."

The man nodded, unimpressed. "Shooting acts are always popular." He made a note on a pad of paper. "Step this way, please. I'll ask you to wait until we see if anyone else is interested in shooting."

Her stomach twisted in knots as she moved to the waiting area. Who else was auditioning? She was the best shot she knew, but what about competition from the other hundred-plus counties in Texas? Major Paulson took only the best of the best.

While she waited, she studied the dozen or so hopefuls present at the auditions. She knew most of the people by sight. Tess Gardner could give Lucy's sister Sarah a run for best horsewoman in the county. Of course, Sarah wasn't auditioning. Baby sister Charlsey would have impressed the Paulsons with roping and branding, but she had married her accountant, Harold Miller, last Christmas and moved north of Fort Worth. Billy Baumgartner could always get people to smile, but he wasn't much good at ranch work. Maybe he hoped to become a clown.

Another acquaintance, Rupert Schmidt, waved at her and came over. "I might as well go home now if you're auditioning." He bowed. "I never thought. . ."

"We don't know what they're looking for." Lucy reassured her friend, the person who'd provided the closest competition at the county fair. "Perhaps they will take *both* of us."

"Rupert Schmidt?" Gordon Paulson surveyed the group.

The lanky Texan walked toward Paulson. "I'm Schmidt."

A few minutes later, those present had been divided according to their interests. An older man and woman joined Paulson in the center of the circle. "If we could have your attention." The young man had a pleasant voice that carried well. It would resonate with audiences. "Let me introduce my parents, Major and Mrs. David Paulson."

A smile creased the older man's weather-beaten face. He lacked the flowing locks of Buffalo Bill but shared his large mustache. Happy memories returned when she saw the familiar figure. The visit of Major Paulson's Wild West Show was a highlight of the year in Horsefly. She had never seen him so close. Father and son shared the same strong chin and crooked smile, but Gordon's curly blond hair had surely come from his mother. They looked like good people to work for.

The older man stood at attention. "The Major Paulson Wild West Show prides itself on providing wholesome entertainment for the entire family. We come here today seeking both ensemble members as well as specialty acts. In a few moments, we will ask you to demonstrate why you believe *you* qualify. My wife and son will help me judge your skill. If you pass the initial trial, we will ask you to return before tonight's performance for a further audition. Thank you, and may God be with you."

Lucy's heart tightened in her chest. Now that the time had come to prove her skill, she calmed down. Who would judge the sharpshooters? Three of them waited together: herself, Rupert, and a petite redhead with long curly hair. Men might pay money just to look at her. Lucy didn't consider herself plain, but she knew she was no beauty like this woman.

Gordon Paulson strode in their direction, and Lucy relaxed. The few minutes she had observed him speaking with the crowd let her know he would be fair. In other circumstances, she would have liked to get to know him better. A breeze stirred the hair around his face. He walked with the ease of a true Texan, but judging from the pallor of his skin, he hadn't seen much of the Texas sun in recent months.

"Come this way." He led them to a distant circle, where a series of targets had been arranged. The setup reminded her of the Gillespie County Fair.

Gordon stopped them beside a flag. "Please forgive the formality, but Major Paulson engages only the best. We wish to test your skills before we proceed. For this round, we will provide you each with matching weapons and ask you to shoot at the targets you see in the field from a standing, kneeling, and prone position."

Use a weapon *they* provided? Lucy's fingers tightened on Ranger, so familiar that it felt like an extension of herself. She couldn't imagine using anything else. Reluctantly, she let Gordon take the familiar rifle from her and hand her another Winchester, a model from a different year. She tested its weight and sighed with relief—a quality weapon. He did the same with Rupert and the other woman.

"You each have separate targets. You will fire at the closest target three times. After I replace the target, you will kneel and then lie down. We will repeat the procedure for the two farther targets as well. Any questions?"

They all shook their heads then took their places.

"Fire at will."

God, if this be Your will. . . Lucy breathed a prayer and took aim.

Gordon Paulson watched the three hopefuls shoot. He didn't need to study the targets; he could gauge their accuracy when they finished. For now, he wanted to study their poise and comportment. Did any of them have the makings of a performer?

Although he needed to consider all three equally, Lucy Ames drew his attention. In spite of her obvious reluctance to give up her treasured rifle, she looked perfectly at ease with the shotgun. The late morning sun glinted like diamonds where it beat down upon her dark head. He liked the way she carried herself, her self-confidence, her ease with the weapon. If she caught an audience's attention the way she caught his, she would be an asset to the show. Depending on her ability, she could even star in her own act.

He forced himself to study the other two contestants. Schmidt handled his weapon well, but he treated the entire experience as a joke. Regardless of his skill level, Gordon wondered if Rupert would leave the show after a few weeks in order to help his family with spring planting. Nothing about him stood out.

After all three completed the first round from a standing position, he replaced the targets. "Fire!" He squinted through the smoky haze but gave up the effort. Instead, he marked their names on the sheets and returned to studying the applicants.

The third contender, Annie Ruprecht, also had audience appeal. That red hair stood out in a crowd, and she looked comfortable in her clothes. If she could shoot as well as she looked, he would invite both women back. *Unlikely,* he felt, shaking his head. Even in Texas, where everything was bigger and better, he doubted they would find two Annie Oakley pretenders in a single town.

While Gordon replaced the targets for the third round, his mind wandered to the question that had troubled him ever since he finished seminary in December. *Am I supposed to be here?* Whether his first season back would also be his last, he didn't know. He prayed the Almighty would make His will plain over the course of the next few weeks.

From the time he was a boy, the Paulsons left their West Texas ranch behind in early spring in order to tour the country. Gordon had started and ended every school year on the road, under Mom's tutelage. The major had toured with Buffalo Bill's Show for a few years after the War of Northern Aggression, but then he struck out on his own.

What set the major apart was his desire to share the good news of Jesus Christ in addition to entertaining the audience. Gordon learned his love for evangelism at his parents' knees, and after finishing high school, he went to seminary to train for the ministry.

The Paulsons started touring earlier than usual this year to find new acts for the show. Last fall, his sister Melinda had married and stopped performing. Her shooting had always drawn crowds. Who could replace her? They had advertised in towns from Plainview to Longview and had picked up some fine additions for the cast. But they still lacked that one special act, and they were running out of time. Their departure for Arkansas, St. Louis, and points east loomed on the first of May. The family prayed continuously that *this* would be the day they found that special someone.

Looking once again at Lucy Ames, Gordon hoped, *prayed*, they had.

Chapter 2

Lucy finished shooting from her prone position on the ground a moment before her two competitors. She stood and dusted herself off.

"Hold. I'll check your targets." Gordon Paulson put away the weapons loaned to them and walked into the field.

The first target troubled Lucy the most. Adjusting to a new weapon took time, and she didn't feel certain of her aim until she had spent several shots. But the others operated under the same disadvantages. She only hoped they had struggled as she had.

Gordon wrote something on each target—their names?—and removed them from the easels. When he returned with a thick sheaf of papers in hand, he looked at them one by one.

Oh God, please let me have done well. What a silly prayer. God couldn't change the outcome of shots already fired;

and besides, the others also wanted to succeed.

After his perusal, Gordon lifted his head and a genuine smile lit his face. "This is some of the best target shooting I have seen this year. You have all done well enough to return this afternoon for a further audition."

Lucy's insides clapped and danced, but she waited demurely. Rupert grinned. "Well, I'll be. Thanks, Paulson."

"In fact, two of you did so well, we may consider using you in individual acts in the show." Gordon's face didn't give anything away. "Bring your best stuff."

Am I one of them? Lucy wanted to scream.

"I'm sorry, Schmidt. You did well, but both the ladies earned a near perfect score."

Lucy did clap at that news. Beside her, she heard the other woman's sharp intake of breath. She wondered again where the stranger had come from.

"Congratulations to all of you. Come two hours before tonight's performance prepared to show us what you've got." Gordon shook their hands and bid them good-bye.

Fireflies danced in the stranger's green eyes. "I am *so* excited. My father happened to bring home the *Horsefly Herald Gazette* after his last delivery at Kofka's Mercantile, and as soon as I saw the ad, I begged him to let me come." She nodded at a man waiting by the corral.

"So you're not from around here?"

"No, we live in Austin. I'm Annie Ruprecht."

"And I'm Lucy Ames. I live outside Horsefly, on my father's ranch." The two women shook hands.

"I guess we'll see each other this evening."

Annie's father had brought her with him so she could audition. What on earth was Pa going to say when he learned how Lucy had spent her morning? She would find out soon.

On her way home, Lucy stopped at the spot where Pa first taught her how to handle a weapon. She sighted a dead branch dancing from the top of a tree but laid down her weapon without firing a shot. What kind of trick would impress the Paulsons? Maybe if she shot a feather from a hat at thirty paces. . . She pondered the question while she shot and dressed a pair of rabbits.

Once she arrived home, Lucy carried the meat into the kitchen. Pa had a liking for rabbit stew. Maybe her gift would sweeten her request.

Her oldest sister, Bess, stood at the kitchen table, rolling out piecrust. "A brace of rabbits. Wonderful! I'll use that instead of the ham bone I was planning on." She cut the meat into chunks that would cook quickly. "I don't know what we'd do without you to bring in fresh meat."

"And what would we do without you?" Lucy loved all her sisters, but as the two eldest, she and Bess shared a special bond. "Can I tell you a secret?"

"Lucinda Lee Ames, what have you done this time?" Bess used her full name in a mock reprimand.

Lucy showed her sister the ad in the *Horsefly Herald Gazette*. "I tried out for a part in Major Paulson's show. And they want me to come back for a second audition tonight." She grabbed an oilcloth and set to work cleaning her rifle.

Bess stopped rolling the crust. "You *didn't*."

"They had a shooting contest, like we do at the county fair every year. I did so well that they want to see if I know any tricks." She found herself humming. *Buffalo gals, won't you come out tonight*. . . . So she wanted to be a buffalo gal, did she? Maybe this was her chance. "Will you help me, Bess? I want to do something that will make Major Paulson want to hire me."

"What do you have in mind?" Sensible Bess wanted to know before she agreed.

After Lucy explained her ideas, her sister broke into a wide smile. She patted the crust into pie tins and added the chopped meat. "Then I'll have to make the rabbit pie extra special today, so Pa will listen to what Major Paulson has to say."

Come five o'clock, Gordon was pacing the entrance to the arena. During the afternoon, he had made arrangements with Annie's father, a wholesaler working out of Austin, for fresh provisions when they arrived there the following week. Setting up for the evening kept his hands busy but allowed his mind to wander back to Lucy Ames. The major hadn't seen anything special among the variety acts, but Mom thought that one barrel rider, Tess Gardner, might work.

His gaze returned to the road from town. The four

invitees should arrive at any moment. He told himself his eagerness resulted from the discovery of new talent and had nothing to do with his desire to see the dark-haired beauty again. That assurance held about as much truth as a prediction of snow at an Independence Day parade. He wanted her to do well.

A swirl of dust suggested horses coming down the road. As they neared, Gordon saw a buggy filled with a family. Lucy had returned with two other dark-haired women who looked so much alike they must be her sisters, and an older gentleman he took to be her father.

Mr. Ames stepped down from the buggy, but the sisters remained seated.

Even at this distance, Gordon could read the pleading in Lucy's eyes.

He approached. "Miss Ames." He smiled encouragement at Lucy. "This must be your father. Pleased to make your acquaintance, Mr. Ames. And these lovely ladies?"

"My sisters. Bess Ames and Sarah."

Lucy's father had had enough of pleasantries. "Are you Major Paulson?" The man, whose hair must once have been as dark as that of his daughters, tensed with every muscle hardened by years of hard work under the Texas sun.

"I am his son." Gordon exercised every bit of control he had to keep his voice even. "You want my father." He headed in the direction of the tent where his parents took a bite of refreshment before the auditions.

Ames pushed past him. "Major? Are you responsible

for filling my daughter's head with this nonsense of traveling the country with your show?"

"You have me at a disadvantage, sir. I am Major David Paulson."

"This is Lucy Ames's father," Gordon offered by way of explanation.

"Miss Ames's father? Are you the person who taught your daughter to shoot so well? You must be proud, yes, proud indeed."

Ames's posture relaxed a hair. "I've taught all my girls. Lucy always was good with a rifle. But that doesn't mean I want her to become a sideshow at some carnival."

"Of course you don't. But we are not a carnival, as you put it. We seek to entertain, 'tis true, but we also want to teach our fellow countrymen about their heritage. And we seek to share our Lord and Savior with them while we're about it. Are you a Christian man, Mr. Ames?"

"Of course! Went forward when I was but eight years old."

"Then why don't we see what *God* has for your daughter before we continue this discussion?"

Gordon could never get over his father's ability to sway people's thinking in a matter of a few words.

They exited the tent. A couple dozen of the ensemble gathered around the arena. While the final decision lay with the major, he valued the input of the other performers. How well would the man or woman hold up under the pressure of a live performance?

The other two women had arrived while they were in the tent, and Rupert Schmidt dismounted at a minute past five. "I have a confession to make." His face turned brick red. "I came on a lark. I didn't think you'd invite me back."

Gordon could hear the excuse coming.

"I believe I'll decline your offer for a second audition. But I'm mighty proud you asked me."

Gordon shook his hand. "I hope you'll stay for tonight's performance?"

"I wouldn't miss it for the world. May I stay and watch?"

"Anywhere you like."

First up, Tess Gardner rode a roan gelding into the ring. She swung a lasso around a flyaway tumbleweed and darted her horse in between barrels faster than a coyote running away from a wasp. Gordon didn't think she qualified as solo act material, but she'd make a solid addition to the cast.

Annie Ruprecht followed, wielding a weapon that looked as though her father ordered it straight from the factory. She sailed through a few simple tricks—splitting an apple in half, creating the letter *A* in a wooden board with six bullets. Unfortunately, the performance lacked the spark that great entertainers had. Annie Oakley made audiences feel at home with her ready smile and friendly presence. This Annie's mouth puckered as though she was eating sour apples, but she also looked totally confident in her ability. Give her a few weeks with the show, and she might make solo act material.

As Gordon had expected, the major offered her a position with the show.

Last of all came Lucy Ames, and Gordon's insides twisted in anticipation. He hoped she would do well. Why he should care so much for a woman he had met only hours before, he didn't know. But he sensed God had something to do with it.

Lucy rode bareback into the arena on her Appaloosa, Misty. That way, she figured more people could see her. Over lunch, Pa had reluctantly agreed to let her return for the second audition. She and Bess had spent the afternoon practicing tricks to show the Paulsons. *Lord, help me to do well. Let this be Your will for me.*

Bess placed a three-pronged candlestick in the center of the arena. Lucy lacked the equipment to match Annie Oakley's famous trick of shooting out the flames of a revolving candelabra, but she thought this would work as a substitute. Bess lit the candles and walked to the edge of the arena.

Lucy galloped around the arena once before urging her mare toward the candles. She leaned sideways in her saddle until she was almost perpendicular to the horse. At the last minute, she shot out all three flames with a single bullet. She righted herself in the saddle, and Misty sprung over the candelabra.

Applause broke out among the spectators. She hadn't expected such a large crowd, but she shut out their presence.

She had thought about drawing a house with bullets in the sand, but she didn't want to imitate the previous performer. She skipped that trick and went to one she and Bess had devised that afternoon. Bess planted her favorite Sunday-go-to-meeting hat on a stand. Lucy didn't have an opportunity to practice the routine; Bess only had one hat. Once again, Lucy spurred Misty into motion and cantered toward the center ring. She pulled out Ranger and shot the flower clean off the hat. Bess picked up the hat and twirled it around her finger to show the bullet hadn't even grazed the straw. An appreciative murmur spread through the crowd, but Gordon Paulson's smile meant more to her than anything else.

Last of all, Lucy borrowed another trick from Annie Oakley's book. Bess waited in the center of the ring.

Smile. She remembered Bess's advice. *Even if you're unsure, keep on smiling.*

Lucy urged Misty into a full-fledged gallop. On the third flying circle around the arena, Bess tossed a penny in the air. Lucy drew Ranger out of her holster and shot the coin before it hit the ground.

There was no mistaking the crowd's reaction this time. Loud cheers went up from the crowd, hooting and hollering and expressing their pleasure.

Lucy dismounted and bowed low with her hand at her

waist. Then she gestured to Bess and clapped for her.

Major Paulson jumped over the woodwork forming the arena and met her in mid-circle. Gordon followed, a smile lifting the edges of his lips, like the smile her teacher gave when she won the spelling bee.

"Miss Ames, that was stupendous. Amazing."

Did Major Paulson always speak in superlatives?

"I believe I speak for everyone here when I say we hope you will join the show as a solo act."

God had opened the door.

Chapter 3

Mr. Ames's face registered shock, and Gordon saw the elation on Lucy's face turn to doubt. She might not join the show after all. No matter what Lucy wanted, the major would not act against her father's wishes.

"Please come this way, you and your family." The major led them toward the tent that housed the Paulsons' private quarters, where he had spoken with Mr. Ames before the auditions.

They settled on comfortable chairs while his mother poured them each a glass of lemonade and offered cookies. Ames stared at a cookie as if taking a bite equaled accepting defeat. Lucy took a small sip of her drink but set the glass down when her hand trembled. Relief at the end of a good performance—he had seen it dozens of times.

"Your daughter has a God-given talent, Mr. Ames." The major made the first move in the discussion.

"May I join you?" Ruprecht entered the tent without waiting for an answer, his daughter Annie following behind.

"I'll not deny Lucy's skill with a rifle." Ames's long fingers twined around the glass, and he took a deep drink. "But I am concerned for her well-being. She has lived a sheltered life on the ranch."

The major pushed his back against his chair. "I told you earlier that I am a Christian man, Mr. Ames. Women have been in our cast from the beginning, and never a one has been compromised. Why, we care for the young ones as if they were our own."

"The ladies never go anywhere without a chaperone." Mom refilled their glasses. "We insist on a strict curfew whenever they leave our camp. I promise you no harm will come to your daughter."

Gordon could almost see visions of faraway places dancing in Lucy's eyes. He wondered how far she had traveled from home. Had she ever left Texas? Given the extent of the state, it was unlikely.

"In fact, I would like to invite your lovely daughters to join us. The charming lady who assisted Lucy in her act would be a welcome asset." He nodded at Bess. "And perhaps your other daughter has skills she wishes to demonstrate."

Gordon nodded. Bess had shown a definite flair during the performance. A dreamy look passed through Sarah's eyes, and he wondered what dreams she held.

"Oh, I couldn't." A mixture of panic and something less well defined—a desire to escape, perhaps—crossed Bess's face. "Lucy is the one who wants to go. My place is with the family."

"And I'm needed with the horses at the ranch," Sarah demurred.

"I'm sorry to hear that." The major tapped a gloved hand on the end of the arm of his chair. "But you're welcome to join us at any time if you change your mind."

Which option would Ames prefer? Would he feel better if Bess went along as a kind of chaperone? Or would he be less willing to part with two of his daughters at the same time? Gordon wanted very much for him to allow Lucy to join the ensemble.

"If I may say a word." Gordon wanted to say whatever he could to convince Lucy's father to let her come along. "My parents not only claim to be Christian; they live their faith every day of their lives. They have never broken a promise. I met men at seminary who could not say the same for their minister fathers." He lowered his voice, hoping the sincerity of his words would shine through. "And my father remains eager to share his faith with others. To that end, it has been my privilege to hold a chapel service for everyone in the cast each morning. We bring each day's concerns to God. You couldn't ask for a safer place for your daughter, sir, other than your own home." He nodded at Lucy. Both he and his father would give their lives to protect the women in their care, this one in particular.

"I've known Major Paulson for nigh on twenty years, and I can testify to his character myself." Ruprecht spoke up. "I'm allowing my Annie to join the ensemble, and believe me, I wouldn't do that if I had any doubts about him whatsoever."

"Then I guess only one question remains." Ames looked at his daughter. "Do you want to join this company?"

A spark glittered in her dark eyes. "Oh yes, Pa. With all my heart." She looked at Gordon, and something inside him fluttered open.

"You're leaving in the morning?" Lucy's younger sister Sarah repeated her question.

"Isn't it wonderful? Why, by this time next week, she could be anywhere." Bess folded some unmentionables and tucked them in Lucy's trunk.

"What will Mr. Lutz say?" Sarah mentioned the widowed rancher who had expressed an interest in Lucy.

"We're not promised." Lucy hid a grimace. No man had caught her eye since her childhood sweetheart died of influenza. "Major Paulson gave Pa a copy of the itinerary. You'll be able to follow our progress, and I promise I'll write every week." Lucy studied her dresses and chose two to pack in the trunk.

She didn't need much. Mrs. Paulson had taken her aside after their conference and taken her measurements. "To make you a costume, dear."

"Now, Sarah, if you're not going to help. . ."

At Lucy's words, Sarah leapt to her feet. "How many pairs of hosiery will you need?"

Clothing and other necessities soon filled the trunk. After Lucy added her Bible, room for one more item remained. A book? She decided on a volume of Shakespeare's historical plays. She loved history, and Shakespeare was the undisputed master of the English language. That left a small space.

"How about *The Pilgrim's Progress*?" Bess extracted a well-worn paperback copy of the classic from Lucy's nightstand.

"Excellent." Christian's adventures through the Slough of Despond might encourage her if she got homesick.

"I can't believe I won't see you two again until September." The magnitude of what Lucy intended to do hit her. Leaving home and everyone she had ever known? To travel with strangers and perform in front of hundreds of people six days a week?

Then she thought of Gordon Paulson, his reassuring smile and his confidence in her. Everything would be all right.

Two weeks later from his spot in the wings, Gordon watched Lucy bow to the audience. She had done it again. Her natural charm, humility, and skill won the hearts of audiences at every stop. Every girl wanted to grow up to be like her, and as for her popularity with the lads. . . the number of young men seeking a moment to speak with her exceeded the admirers of anyone else. Several nights he chased them away when he noticed her tiring.

Tomorrow they would leave Texas for Arkansas, Missouri, and other points east. Tonight the major intended to share a surprise with Lucy. Gordon hoped she would be pleased with the news.

After they had all changed from their performance duds, Lucy joined Gordon and his parents in their tent. "You wanted to speak with me, Major?" Her face still reflected her post-performance glow. Making people smile energized her.

"Definitely." The major offered Lucy a chair and then sat opposite her. Mom poured glasses of cool water—always the best restorative after a night's performance, she said—and Lucy drank it down gratefully. She looked a little nervous. Didn't she realize her value to the show by now?

"Miss Ames, have you enjoyed your time with us?" The major leaned forward.

"Oh, it's been *wonderful.*"

"No regrets?"

Lucy shook her head. "Not a one."

"I'm glad to hear it. Because the truth is. . .we want to move your act up in the show. To give you top billing." Now his father relaxed, a smile crinkling the corners of his eyes.

Rarely had Gordon seen Lucy speechless, but she was now.

"You'll be the star of the show." The major beamed.

"But I just joined. . . . There are so many others more talented. . . ." Lucy stumbled over her words.

"You've earned it, dear." Mrs. Paulson sliced through a loaf of date pecan bread. "Have a slice."

Lucy ate a bite and recovered her composure.

"Of course you will receive an increase in salary."

Gordon enjoyed watching Lucy's eyes widen at the figure his father mentioned.

"We'll be calling you 'A Texas-Born Annie Oakley.' Given time, you will become even more famous than she is." His father's eyes twinkled. "Because of course, anything from Texas is bigger and better than from anywhere else."

Lucy's lips formed the syllables *Annie Oakley* in speechless astonishment. "I never imagined such a thing. Miss Oakley is a *legend*."

"And so will you be, in time. You don't realize just how talented you are. That's part of your appeal." The major rubbed his hands together. "That's settled, then. We're having new posters featuring your portrait printed in Fort Smith. But your new position will start in a week, to give you a few days to develop some new material. I'll announce it at chapel tomorrow. I'd appreciate it if you didn't say anything before then."

"No, of course not."

A few minutes later, Lucy left the tent. She looked so dazed anyone could tell something significant had happened with a glance.

"Do you think she can keep it secret?" Gordon asked. "She has the moon shining from her eyes."

"So you noticed?" The major slapped Gordon on the back. "She's a fine woman."

"Yes, she is." Gordon wasn't ready to discuss his feelings for Lucy.

He had promised Mr. Ames that she would not form any inappropriate attachments during their summer tour. He never expected to have to protect her from himself and his growing attraction to the sharpshooter. He moved toward his sectioned-off area of tent, the one spot that afforded him some privacy.

"Before you retire for the night. . ." Mom lifted an envelope from her side table. "This letter caught up with us today. It's from West Texas Christian College." She handed him the envelope. "We're praying with you, son."

Upon completion of his seminary studies, Gordon had sent an inquiry to the college about a teaching position. The school, only three years old, sought to prepare men for ministry. Few Texans had the resources to travel east for education.

The board met with him before the family left on tour. Gordon wasn't sure how the interview had gone. His education had impressed them—perhaps he even struck the men as *overly* qualified—and he knew they shared his passion for evangelism. His greatest lack lay in actual experience in the pulpit.

Gordon prepared for bed. He did preach at the chapel service every day. Surely that counted for something. *Your will be done.* He took his penknife and opened the missive.

Chapter 4

"We have prayed about your interest in West Texas Christian College. . .pleased to offer the position of professor of theology and evangelism. . .term starts in September."

Gordon had the job! So why didn't he feel elated? Did it have anything to do with a certain brunette about to become the star attraction of Major Paulson's Wild West Show?

God rarely answers our prayers early, but always right on time. A bit of Mom's wisdom passed through his mind. *Well, God, I confess I don't understand.*

After wrestling with the question all night, Gordon still didn't have an answer. He hadn't prepared as much as usual for the chapel service and prayed while the major made his announcement about Lucy. Since attendance was mandatory, they always made announcements at that time.

The gasps and spontaneous applause told Gordon

that Lucy had managed to keep her news secret.

"Miss Ames, I'm sure we'd all like to hear from you." The major motioned her forward.

Gordon saw a moment of panic flit through her lively brown eyes, but then she stood to her feet and put on her happy face—the one she presented to the audience night after night.

She was a born performer, that was for sure.

He wants me to speak to everyone? Put Ranger in her hands, and Lucy could pretend she was still back on the ranch. But ask her to talk. . . *God, show me what to say.*

Lucy considered the major's advice before her first performance as she walked down the aisle to the front. *Look for one friendly face.* She scanned the assembly, and her roommates, Annie and Tess, smiled encouragement.

"I am honored to be part of Major Paulson's Wild West Show." Some people in the back leaned forward as if to hear her better, and she raised her voice. "I remember how much I looked forward to your annual appearance in Horsefly. Every year I learned something new about our country, our heritage." She bowed in the Paulsons' direction. "But since I joined the cast, I have observed their faith at work. Now I learn something new about my Lord and Savior every day at chapel, instead of the rare times you come to town. It is my privilege to be in your midst." What else did she want to say? "I pray that my act will glorify God. That matters the most to me."

Eager to hear what Gordon would share for the day, she took a seat in the front row. His messages encouraged her to live for the Lord every hour of every day. She had never met a Christian who loved the Lord as much as he did.

"Lucy has already touched on what I wanted to share this morning. Tomorrow we will leave Texas for St. Louis, Chicago, Washington, and New York, as well as points in between. I don't know about you"—that endearing, crooked smile broke out on Gordon's face—"but I am always nervous before we start on tour. I thought it wise to remind us of who is really in charge of our success. I am reading today from the third chapter of Ephesians, verses 20 and 21."

Lucy knew the verses. They were among her favorites. She closed her eyes and recited the verse silently with Gordon. "Now unto him that is able to do exceeding abundantly above all that we ask or think, according to the power that worketh in us, unto him be glory in the church by Christ Jesus throughout all ages, world without end. Amen."

How had the middle of May arrived so quickly? The stop in St. Louis for a few days offered an opportunity to send and receive mail, do some shopping, and maybe, God willing, spend time visiting the sights with Lucy.

"Gordon."

At the sound of Lucy's voice, he jerked and turned

around. She must have read his thoughts.

"Yes, Lucy?"

"We wanted to let you know that we are heading into town to do some shopping." Tess and Annie waved at him from the waiting wagon. "But we will be back before the evening's performance."

Gordon swallowed past the disappointment in his throat. "Who is accompanying you? You know the policy." Maybe he could. . .

"I am." Jacob Haas, one of the experienced cast members who seemed sweet on Tess, joined them. "I will take good care of them, sir; you can count on that."

"Very well." Gordon decided to speak before he lost his nerve—or opportunity. "I have work-related business to attend to today, but I would love to escort you—and your friends, of course—around the city tomorrow. There are several interesting sites."

Gordon loved the way Lucy's brown eyes sparkled with excitement. "Wonderful! I can't wait to see the Mississippi." She waved good-bye and headed with Jacob toward the wagon.

The next day, as soon as chapel ended, Gordon met Lucy and her friends outside the ladies' tent. Since they had to return for a matinee performance, he wanted to leave as early as possible. He wished he could accompany Lucy alone, but his parents prohibited such behavior, and rightly so. Jacob would also join them.

All three women had dressed for their trip to town, but Gordon only had eyes for Lucy. She had combed her hair in some kind of updo, perhaps a style she had seen in a magazine they brought home from their shopping trip. In her frock the color of a spring day, she was a bluebonnet, and Annie and Tess mere dandelions.

"The three of you do Major Paulson's show credit. I am honored to escort you today." He bowed to all three ladies, refusing to let his preference show. "I thought we would ride a trolley to the river embankment. It's easier than trying to maneuver the streets."

"A trolley! How fun." Lucy invited adventure. Tess looked a little less certain. Bells announced the arrival of their ride.

Jacob helped Tess onto the vehicle, while Gordon assisted Annie and then Lucy. Lucy gave a little gasp when the trolley car started moving, and he steadied her with his arm. Her bright brown eyes looked up at him, laughter shining in their depths.

"It's a bit like riding a boat. It may take a moment to find your bearings." The car lurched forward, cutting off the rest of Gordon's warning.

Annie clung to the railing like it was a life preserver; Tess leaned into Jacob's broad chest. Lucy did neither. She held the railing lightly and planted her feet solidly on the swaying floor, bending her knees slightly with each jolt.

"This is *fun*." She let go of the railing but stumbled at the next stop—into Gordon's arms.

Right where he wanted her to be. He held her a moment longer than necessary, and something passed between them. Then she grabbed a pole and pulled away.

"Goodness, if I can't keep my balance any better than that, I'll have to give up my plans for a new act." She was practicing Annie Oakley's trick of riding her horse at odd angles, to increase the difficulty of her shots.

"Look, there's the river!" Tess squealed. The woman could ride a horse, but her high-pitched voice drove Gordon to distraction. Jacob didn't seem to mind.

"Where?" Lucy swiveled her head in bewilderment.

Gordon clasped her hand in his and pointed in the right direction, as if it was the most natural thing in the world. He marveled at how her delicate fingers could work such magic with her Winchester.

The mighty Mississippi disappeared from view. "That's all there is?"

"No, indeed." Jacob spoke up. "We're getting closer though."

A small café Gordon had visited before sat near the next stop, and they disembarked. After buying pastries, they walked down to the wharves.

"It's so *huge*." Lucy's thrill at new experiences was contagious. How old was he when he saw it for the first time? Nine, ten?

"Things have changed here since I was a boy. Not nearly as much river traffic. The railroads have taken over the country. Faster, perhaps, but not nearly as scenic."

"I think it's *fascinating*. I can't wait to see the ocean."

Every stop on the tour represented another first for Lucy, and Gordon hoped to share each one with her. "Wait until we get to Minneapolis. Mark Twain said the lower Mississippi from St. Louis south was very uninteresting. That we tend to ignore the bluffs and islands and prairies along the upper Mississippi."

"I don't recall reading that." A small frown furrowed Lucy's forehead.

"He was quoted in an interview in the *Chicago Tribune* a few years back. Dad read it to us." Gordon leaned against the parapet overlooking the river. "I can't say I agree with him, however. I look at the river and think what a great country we live in." He glanced at the woman beside him. *Especially with someone like you.*

The morning couldn't last long enough to satisfy Lucy. She wanted to walk down every wharf and learn about every boat, skiff, and tug, especially when Gordon was the one describing everything. Somehow, without ever singling her out, he made her feel special. Under his protection, she felt free to appreciate the wonder of new experiences. He didn't perceive her as a simple country girl who had never seen anything beyond her beloved Texas hill country.

She missed her sisters dreadfully, although a letter from them waited at every stop. Her new friends helped distract her from her loneliness. Tess shared her dreams of seeing the wide world beyond the confines of Horsefly.

· Lucy didn't feel as close to Annie. Although she tried to hide it, Lucy knew Annie resented her quick rise to stardom. Lucy shook her head. She still couldn't believe the billboards mounted all across town: MAJOR PAULSON'S WILD WEST SHOW FEATURING LUCY AMES, SHARPSHOOTER, A TEXAS-BORN ANNIE OAKLEY. ANYTHING FROM TEXAS IS BOUND TO BE BETTER. But the biggest barrier between them remained Annie's lack of faith in God. She attended daily chapel as required, but she had told Lucy she didn't understand the fuss. Everyone attended church. What was the nonsense about a daily personal relationship with God? Lucy prayed that the Lord would open her eyes.

All too soon, the morning passed and the sun fast approached the apex of the sky. If they did not leave now, they would arrive late for the matinee. Nonetheless, she wished they could linger. Her hunger for new sights seemed insatiable. There was so much to see.

Gordon's hand lightly touched Lucy's arm, and he guided her around a horse patty on the street. *Gordon*. He was the other reason she didn't want the morning to end. She welcomed the first opportunity to spend time with the young preacher away from the show, and she had enjoyed every moment of it.

On the trolley ride back, the bell rang in time with the beating of Lucy's heart. The things nearest and dearest to her echoed with every beat. God, Gordon, home, Gordon, the show, Gordon, Tess, Gordon.

Had God brought love into Lucy's life, as well as fulfilling her wildest dreams?

Chapter 5

Lucy swung Misty around and cantered toward the center of the arena. One of the ensemble members, a veteran named Mary Parsons, pumped an old-fashioned spinning wheel. Lucy rode around her in ever-tightening circles, firing with each lap. She took out first one, then two, then all the spokes of the wheel. She dismounted and bowed deeply. The enthusiastic applause of the audience drowned out the jingle of the bells on her shirt.

"Another round of applause for Miss Lucy Ames!" Major Paulson pronounced in his loudest voice. People stamped the stands with their feet. A few whistled.

Lucy bowed in all four directions, took off her hat with a smile and a wave, and then departed through the cast entrance. Tess rushed past her with the ensemble of trick riders.

"Good luck!" Lucy called. She settled Misty and then

retired to their tent. The Paulsons had offered her a private tent after her promotion, but Lucy didn't want preferential treatment. She preferred to remain where she was. Tess's and Annie's presence made the nights away from home less lonely.

She changed into a red, white, and blue outfit for the final parade, eager for tonight's show to end. Ten days had passed since they had left Chicago, and tomorrow morning Gordon promised to accompany anyone interested on a hunting expedition. Indiana boasted of wildfowl like turkey, grouse, and doves as well as white-tailed deer.

Gordon warned they might encounter more dangerous animals and advised they bring at least two weapons—a shotgun and a high-caliber rifle. The fiercest beast she had ever encountered in Horsefly was a wild boar, unless you counted rattlers, and she could usually avoid them.

The hunters hoped to supplement the show's canned supplies with fresh meat. How strange—Lucy never expected to miss hunting for food when she left Horsefly. But she did.

Shooting at unimportant targets for the sole purpose of entertaining an audience grew tiresome after a while. For this morning, she could put her skill to practical use.

The next morning, Gordon awoke before the sun rose. He had arranged with the major to postpone the chapel service until after lunch; the best time for hunting was early morning.

He knelt by his bed and offered his daily prayers. After praying for safety for those involved in today's expedition, he returned to the choice pending before him. Should he accept the teaching position, stay with the show, or seek something else? His recent visit with Dwight L. Moody in Chicago had only magnified his confusion.

"Lord, I feel torn. In my heart of hearts, I know you have called me to evangelism. And You confirmed that calling through Mr. Moody. Yet the door You have opened for me would keep me bound to a single place for most of the year." He paused, unwilling to voice his innermost feelings. How foolish. God knew his heart better than he did himself. "And now I have a desire to remain where I am, at least as long as Lucy is here."

A few minutes passed in silent waiting. When at last he rose from his knees to read his Bible, no answer had come. He hoped God would reveal His will soon; the college needed an answer by the end of June.

After his quiet time, he joined the group waiting at the corral. Mom was serving coffee to all who wanted it. She had wrapped ham and biscuits the cook had prepared for them to take on their journey. "We look forward to today's catch."

Even dressed in sensible dark colors, Lucy and Annie stood out like red bows on a Christmas tree in the crowd of men. All of them were experienced huntsmen. Still, he gave them the usual warnings. *Stay downwind. If someone is in danger, fire three shots into the air.* They rode an hour by horseback until they approached the edge of a dense wood.

From there they dismounted. Gordon loved getting away from the dust and dirt of the cities where they performed night after night. Breathing the fresh forest air, hearing the crunch of needles underfoot, tasting crystal clear water of untouched streams all refreshed his spirit. Soon a sparkling blue lake appeared. "We've had success here in the past," he informed the group.

A cry from one of the men announced their quarry had been spotted. With a ruffle of feathers, three or four flocks of ducks and geese took to the air. Pistol shots rang out. Soon their bags bulged with as much meat as they could use before it spoiled.

The group settled by the riverbank to enjoy the meal the cook had packed. Gordon found a seat near Lucy. She pushed her hat to the back of her head and sat with her face upraised to the air, cool this deep in the woods.

"Have you enjoyed your morning's outing?" He smiled.

"Ever so much. I haven't seen this many trees since we left home. And never trees like these." She gestured at the heavy canopy overhead, tall enough to house a cathedral, dense enough that in most places you couldn't see your own shadow. She breathed deeply and sighed.

"Homesick?" Gordon asked sympathetically.

Were those tears he saw in Lucy's eyes? She wiped them away. "I don't want to seem ungrateful. I love traveling with the show. But today has reminded me of home.

And I've wondered how my family is faring, and whether Pa gets his favorite rabbit stew whenever he wants it."

"I know the feeling. The first year I was away at school, I worried about how our clerk would manage provisions. Whether Mom would have her favorite brand of tea and cookies. That kind of thing."

"What a blessing to know that God is there with them and here with us. I've always known God is everywhere, but the farther I travel from home, the more I understand." She ate the rest of her sandwich with precise bites, bent over the water, and filled her canteen.

With such simple yet moving words, Lucy expressed her faith. She had a gift, if only she would realize it. The more time he spent with her, the more he liked her.

A sharp cry pierced the air. Gordon sprang to his feet. *Annie.*

Why did she wander so far from the group? He reached her side in a few seconds. What he saw froze him in his tracks; then he yelled, "Lunch over! Head back!"

He raised his eyes to the very thing he feared. A hulking, four-hundred-pound black bear wanted his food.

"Get away," he whispered to Annie.

He felt rather than heard her retreat. The rifle he carried might bring down a bear, but he did not have the skill. He used the only weapon left in his arsenal. Stretching his body to his full height of six feet two inches, he spoke in his "crowd" voice, loud, authoritative.

"We mean you no harm." He took one step back; the

bear lumbered toward him with surprising speed.

Grass rustled to his left, and in the periphery of his vision, he saw Lucy. She walked without pausing, holding her rifle at her shoulder. *Foolish woman.* She should have gone with the others. *Brave woman.* The best shot in the company, she wanted to protect them all.

The bear had crossed half the distance between them when three shots rang out in rapid succession. The bear was within a hundred yards of Gordon when it fell, head first, onto the ground. Gordon's limbs quivered with relief. As soon as he had himself under control, he ran to Lucy.

"You foolish, brave woman." He took her into his arms and kissed her, soundly, on the lips. He ran his hands over her silky hair. "Don't ever do anything like that again."

Chapter 6

*G*ordon kissed me? He was reacting to the situation, *our brush with death, nothing more.* As much as she reveled in their closeness, Lucy removed herself from Gordon's embrace before the others returned. She drew in a deep breath to steady her nerves. "That was a close call."

Gordon was frowning. Did he regret kissing her? Lucy hoped not. Her lips still burned where they had met his.

"We're late. We don't have time to dress the carcass."

At least he didn't apologize. The major's son was back in control, responsible for the smooth operation of the show.

"It wouldn't take much time to make a travois." Lucy followed his lead in changing the topic, although she didn't know whether to be relieved or disappointed. "I would really like to keep the fur for a rug, and they say bear meat makes good eating."

"I've never had any. No one's ever brought down a bear in all our years on the road." Gordon flashed an admiring smile at her. "That was one incredible shot."

"Maybe we should change your billing to Lucy Ames, bear killer. Replay the famous feat in the show." The other hunters had returned.

"Yeah, and *you* can be the bear." The men laughed. None of them could have made the shot, and they knew it. Their acceptance warmed her heart.

Gordon instructed the men to build a travois, and two of the show's strong men hoisted the poles on their shoulders. The burden slowed them down a little while they walked to the edge of the forest, but the weight didn't seem to bother the horses on the way back to the arena.

Lucy took one last look at the trees. As much as she loved doing the show, she had reveled in the morning in the wild. Even if it was the Wild East. She giggled to herself. Relief of tension, she supposed.

Annie didn't join in the conversation on the ride back, nor did she add her congratulations to the accolades the men showered on Lucy. She hadn't even thanked Lucy and Gordon for the quick action that saved her life. *You should be ashamed of yourself, Lucinda Lee. The pleasure of Your heavenly Father should be enough.* Still, Annie's reticence struck Lucy as odd. Perhaps her fellow sharpshooter was in shock.

The news of Lucy's exploit spread across the camp almost before they reached it. Mrs. Paulson wrapped the carcass in heavy canvas and put it up out of the reach of predators. They would have to dress it as soon as possible.

Lucy floated along, the excitement of the kill thrilling along her nerves. The crush of well-wishers prevented her from retiring to her tent before they gathered for chapel.

Major Paulson welcomed the hunters to the service like returning warriors. "We can thank the good Lord for sparing your lives today. Lucy Ames proved that she is indeed Texas-sized in bringing down the dangerous beast, the bear."

As so often, the major sounded like he was announcing an act at the show. But Lucy knew his heart's devotion to the almighty God. She kept her eyes downcast, not wanting to appear boastful. The constant praise had worn on her nerves, and she turned to private prayer to shut out the applause.

Silence fell across the group, and Lucy sensed she was the center of attention. She opened her eyes. Gordon smiled at her, as if he was aware of her short mental absence from the hoopla. "Lucy, would you like to share a few words?"

Speak? The possibility of speaking to the group still frightened Lucy. She sent up a quick prayer.

"Come up front."

At least Gordon's invitation gave her a few moments to think about what to say.

She looked across the group of people who had

become her second family over the past six weeks. Gordon nodded his encouragement from his seat in the front row, and she found the courage to speak.

"I guess y'all have heard I shot a bear dead today."

Laughter and applause greeted her words.

"To my way of thinking, I didn't do anything special. I've always known I'm good with a gun." She smiled shyly. She searched for the words to turn the credit back to God. "But I'm only good with a gun because God gave me that gift. Now, my sister Charlsey can rope and brand a calf faster than any hand on the ranch. And Sarah has the sweetest hands on working with horses. And Bess, well, she keeps the house running and is an expert tracker. God gave Pa four daughters, but each one of us does something different around the ranch.

"But lately I sensed God had something else for me to do, and Major Paulson invited me to join his Wild West Show." She nodded at the couple, signaling her thanks. "Today was just another one of those things. Maybe God brought me all the way from Texas to Indiana so I could be there to shoot that bear today."

Gordon tilted his head, as if eager to listen to whatever else she had to say.

"I guess I'm saying that nothing happens by chance. God has a plan for every one of us. And whether your part in the show is setting up the stands or cooking food or"—now she allowed herself to grin—"shooting a nickel out between two fingers, the most important thing is that we're all exactly where God wants us to be. Even those among us who have not yet claimed Jesus as their Savior."

Gordon had always known Lucy shared his faith, but he had never heard her speak so passionately. If she were a man, he might have called that *preaching*. Instead of puffing herself up, she had shared her testimony.

Lucy's confidence faded, and she shuffled her feet. "If you want to find out how to invite Jesus to be your Savior, you can talk to Major Paulson or his wife or Gordon."

Or you. After listening to her testimony, Gordon believed she could share the plan of salvation with anyone. He wanted to talk with her about it.

Gordon pushed aside his plans for the day's sermon. Instead, he invited the congregation to join him in singing "I Love to Tell the Story" and "Jesus, Keep Me Near the Cross." A hush fell across the group as the last note of the chorus died away, and Gordon began to speak.

"An old adage says simple stories are best. And why is that? Because we know them. No matter how many times we hear about Hansel and Gretel, we hope the witch won't eat Hansel and we smile at Gretel's scheme to keep her brother safe. We enjoy the story because we know there will always be a happy ending, not like our everyday lives where evil often seems to get the upper hand. But the cross—the symbol of the horrible death Jesus endured— is the best story of all. Listen to these words from the fifth chapter of Romans: 'But God commendeth his love toward us, in that, while we were yet sinners, Christ died for us. Much more then, being now justified by his blood, we shall be saved from wrath through him.'" He explained the gospel in the simplest terms he could find, and at the end, he felt God telling him to offer an invitation. Three cast members came forward, including Tess's beau, Jacob Haas.

God had used Gordon to lead people into His kingdom before, but euphoria always sizzled through his body and mind. His heart still soared when the evening's performance started. Force of habit moved his body at the right times, and the show went down well with the audience.

By the final curtain call, the elation had faded to the same perplexing question. *Which is my calling? Teaching—or evangelism?*

The answer eluded Gordon.

Lucy's insides felt all jumpy. The last time she had seen the Holy Spirit work as He had today was during a tent meeting in Horsefly the year her baby sister, Charlsey, received Christ.

What a day. From shooting down a bear to sharing her testimony to welcoming new people into God's family. Needing time alone, she excused herself early and retired to the tent she shared with Tess and Annie. The adrenaline that carried her through the night's tricks and curtain calls drained away with the face paint she removed.

Annie slipped into the tent a few moments later. She looked drained, an exhaustion born of something beyond the physical. She joined Lucy at the dressing table and applied cold cream to her face.

Lord, give me patience. Lucy didn't want Annie's foul mood to spoil the wonder of the day.

Neither spoke for a few minutes. *Maybe she'll let me be.* Lucy turned her back on Annie and prepared to slip into her nightgown.

"Lucy. Please wait." Annie twisted the cloth she used to freshen her face in her hands. "I never thanked you for saving my life today."

"You're welcome. I'm thankful God gave me a good shot." Lucy shivered. The bear could have attacked any of them. Annie, yes, but also Gordon or even herself. "I admit I was frightened."

"*You* were frightened? You never act scared at all." Annie removed a last dab of face paint, turned, and looked straight at Lucy. "I could have died out there."

Speak to her. God's Spirit nudged Lucy. "If you had died, where do you think you'd be right now?"

Annie's eyes widened and her forehead creased. "I've always thought that once somebody died, that was it. But after today, I'm not so sure."

"The Bible says, 'It is appointed unto men once to die, but after this the judgment.' We're all going to have to face God someday." *Lord, open her heart.* Lucy couldn't believe she was witnessing like this.

"I'm a good person." Annie looked insulted. "I'm not a murderer or a thief."

"The Bible also says something about everybody having sinned. None of us is good enough for God. I know I'm not."

"You? You're as good as they come." Annie sounded disbelieving.

"Oh, but I've envied my sisters. I've been angry with them, too. And felt bitter when my sweetheart died. Jesus said if we even *think* angry thoughts, we're as bad as a murderer."

Annie's mouth snapped shut. "Then no one is good enough."

"That's why God sent Jesus. Jesus lived a perfect life, and God accepted His sacrifice on the cross. When we believe in Him, God wipes our slates clean. Do you know John 3:16?"

"I'm not sure."

"It's one of my favorite verses. 'God so loved the world, that he gave his only begotten Son, that whosoever'—that means you, Annie—'believeth in him should not perish, but have everlasting life.'"

Annie waited a moment before replying. "Everlasting life. I'd like that."

"All you have to do is pray and invite Jesus into your heart. Do you want to do that?"

"I do!"

Lucy led Annie in the sinner's prayer. The two women

embraced each other, tears of joy spilling down their cheeks. "The Bible also says you need to confess Jesus before men. Tomorrow it would be a good thing for you to tell the Paulsons about what just happened. I would say tonight, but it's getting late."

After Annie's decision to cap off the amazing day, Lucy doubted she could fall asleep, but God shut her eyes. She fell asleep dreaming of the day to come.

Chapter 7

orning. Gordon jumped to his feet, the ground cold under his soles in these northern climes. He sped through his morning ablutions and rushed from the tent to breakfast. He wanted to visit with Lucy today, to relive yesterday's events, and to assist in dressing the bear.

Lucy and her tent mates were talking with his parents when he arrived. All of them wore wide smiles, excitement and joy evident in their faces. He took a plate from the cook and walked toward them.

"Oh, Gordon." Mom spoke first. "The most wonderful news."

Tess is engaged. She did have the look of someone over the moon in love.

"Tell him, Annie." Lucy flashed her trademark grin at Gordon.

"I—I asked Jesus to be my Savior last night." The

normally outspoken girl sounded shy.

"Praise the Lord!" He refrained from embracing her and instead took her hand.

"We have been praying for you every day since you joined us, you know." Dad's mustache quivered slightly. "We do, for everyone on our cast."

"And I praise God for that. I was thanking Lucy, telling her I realized how close I came to dying yesterday. And she explained how without Jesus, I wasn't ready to die." Annie pulled in a deep breath. "So she showed me how to invite Jesus into my life."

Yes! I knew it! Gordon looked at Lucy and saw the excitement written on her face. He recognized it, because he had experienced it himself from time to time.

The women joined Gordon and his parents at the table. Eggs and flapjacks disappeared quickly, and they hurried to the big tent for the morning's chapel service. Gordon invited each of the new believers to share their faith. Two others came forward at the end of the service. Revival had broken out in Major Paulson's Wild West Show.

All too soon, the service ended and everyone returned to their regular duties. The bear carcass would not wait. They had one more night's performance scheduled, and tomorrow they must travel to their next destination. Gordon, Annie, and a few of the other hunters joined Lucy in the task.

"I've never skinned a bear," Lucy confessed. "Has anyone else?"

"You're the only one here who could bring the beast down." One of the men laughed. "But skinning it can't be that different from skinning a deer."

"I want to keep the fur for a rug, so I'd like to do a neat job."

"I'm good with a knife," one of the younger men offered. When no one else volunteered, he set to work. As good as his word, he removed the pelt in one clean piece.

"I know a tanner in town who can prepare it for a rug. And he can ship it back to Horsefly if you like." Gordon had used his services on previous trips. Lucy agreed, and soon the pelt was on its way to her family.

They carved out a few bear steaks. Gordon's mother had promised a feast they would not soon forget. The rest would go to a butcher in town.

"What does bear meat taste like, anyhow?" Annie wrinkled her nose, much like she had when she first ran across the bear's cache yesterday.

"They say it tastes kinda like pork. You'll like it." Gordon repeated his mother's description.

"Have you ever had it before?" Lucy's brown eyes challenged his.

"Well, no," he admitted. "But Mom always tells the truth."

"People's tastes differ." Lucy's tone held a hint of teasing challenge.

"True." His eyes darted to Tess and Jacob walking hand in hand to the corral, and he lowered his voice. "Some people like blue-eyed blonds who can ride a horse."

"But you?"

"I have a preference for brown-eyed brunettes who can bring down a bear with a single killing shot." Had he said that out loud? Gordon felt heat rise to his cheeks.

He needn't have worried about whether Lucy had noticed his blush. She was too busy averting her own rosy cheeks. Her response emboldened him to continue. "I especially like brunettes who know how to share their faith and lead others to our Savior. You are a special woman, Lucy Ames."

Lucy lifted her eyes to meet his. "If I shared my faith, it's only because you inspired me. I've learned so much listening to you. I just repeated what I've heard you say in chapel day after day. I wanted to get away from the ranch to see the world. Now I wonder if God wanted to teach me something new. Or maybe both." She glanced away.

Did she see him as teacher? Mentor? Hero? Nothing more. . .personal? Gordon swallowed past a disappointed hope he didn't realize he harbored. He slipped into the role she had assigned him. "I'm sure you will succeed, whatever direction God leads you."

"As will you." Gordon barely heard her words as he carried the bear steaks to the waiting cook.

"Lucy!"

Lucy jumped at the sound of the major's booming voice. She left the tasty stew made from the bear meat, cooked with potatoes, mushrooms, and carrots, to join the Paulsons at their private dinner table.

"Yes, Major?"

"Sit down and let me talk with you."

Have I done something wrong? Lucy fought back panic that exceeded even her fear when facing the bear. Then she didn't have time to think, only act. *Did I offend Gordon somehow with what I said to him this morning?* She had never been so forthright with a man before.

"The missus and I are tickled pink that you led Annie to Christ last night."

"The Holy Spirit did the leading. All I did was point the way." Lucy shifted her feet, uncomfortable with the praise.

"He used *you*. Out of all the Christian young women in our company."

Lucy relaxed a little bit. She didn't think the major would reprimand her for leading her fellow sharpshooter to the Lord.

"And of course we heard the remarkable testimony you shared at chapel. God has given you a gift, young lady, and I'm not talking about your ability to shoot a feather off a cap."

Lucy remembered her training. *Lift your head and look him straight in the eye.* "I suppose God did give me the words to speak."

"Ah, I'm glad you see it that way." The major leaned forward so that the ends of his mustache brushed the tabletop. "I believe God wants you to use *both* your gifts as part of the Major Paulson Wild West Show. I'd like you to share your testimony as part of your act."

It took every ounce of Lucy's willpower to keep her composure. Speaking to a group of friends, people who had become her substitute family, was one thing. Speaking to total strangers was entirely different. She didn't mind the audience during her performance. She went out, concentrated on her target, and forgot about the onlookers.

Mrs. Paulson must have sensed her discomfort. "You don't have to make a decision today. Please pray about it." She sent the affectionate smile she usually reserved for her husband Lucy's way. "But I agree with him. And so does Gordon."

Gordon had come up behind them while she was talking with his parents. "I concur wholeheartedly." Something warm and welcoming shone from his eyes, something that made her feel accepted, special, accomplished. She remembered their kiss in the forest, and she crossed her fingers to keep her hands from touching her lips where they had met his. The memory tempted her to say yes without further consideration, but she held back.

"I will pray about it, as you have asked," Lucy promised. "I will have an answer for you before we reach Columbus." Perhaps she shouldn't restrict God to a specific timetable, but as Pa had said more than once, God can move fast as well as slow. The longer she hesitated, the more likely she was to let fear get the upper hand. Since tomorrow was a travel day, she had a couple of days to find her answer.

Lucy paid little attention to her surroundings for the remainder of the afternoon. In the morning, they boarded the eastbound train. Ordinarily she sought a window seat to take in the changing scenery, no matter how grimy the glass. But today she took a seat toward the front of the passenger car, a single seat most people avoided because of the roar of the engine. She shut her eyes as if sleeping, but behind her closed lids, she prayed constantly. *Lord, give me a sign.*

The ensemble members sensed her desire for privacy and left her alone. Only Gordon interrupted her. "I won't presume to tell you God's will." He spoke only loud enough for her to hear him above the engine's roar, their own private conversation. "But I want to repeat that I believe you have a gift for evangelism. God will use you to bring others to Himself, whether you share your testimony during the show or not."

Tears sprang to Lucy's eyes. "I don't know about that. I do know God has given *you* a tremendous calling. Whether you preach or teach or. . ."

"Run a Wild West show?" He smiled humorlessly.

"Well, yes. You honor God in all you do."

"I am only a servant." He tapped the tiny Bible in her hands. "I'll leave you to your argument with God. You might try reading the sixth chapter of Judges." He straightened and made his way back down the car.

How kind. Gordon had offered his thoughts without

telling her what to do. But what did any of the judges have to do with her dilemma? Deborah, Gideon, Samson . . .they seemed as far removed from the decision she faced as the distance from Horsefly to London. Curious, she turned to the sixth chapter. Soon Gideon's story enthralled her. *"The LORD is with thee, thou mighty man of valour."* Isn't that what she had said to Gordon, that God was with him whatever he did? And was that what the major was saying to her? She smiled a little at the thought of the mustachioed major in the role of an angel.

Lucy liked to think that if an angel appeared to her in person, she would jump to obey. But maybe Gideon's angel didn't look much different than Major Paulson, an ordinary-looking person with an extraordinary message. Like her, Gideon had doubts. *"If now I have found grace in thy sight, then shew me a sign that thou talkest with me."* Gideon's fleece. Confident that God had led her aright, she prayed silently. *Oh Lord, if You want me to share my testimony, Your testimony really, with the audience—then let someone else encourage me to do so.*

A few minutes later, the lunch bell rang and Lucy joined her friends in the dining car. Jacob sat with them, as had become his habit. Tess managed to tear her gaze away from her sweetheart long enough to quiz Lucy about the previous day's events.

"You've hidden yourself away all morning!" Tess complained. "Annie has told me all about your conversation last night. It's a good thing she spoke with you. If she had asked me, why, I wouldn't have known what to say."

"God gave me the words to speak," Lucy repeated. *God gave* me *the words to speak—not Tess or Gordon or anyone else. Is this the sign I asked God for?* A gentle peace settled over her spirit. God had answered her question.

Chapter 8

Where did the summer go? Gordon would leave within the week to accept the teaching position at West Texas Christian College. After much prayer, and with encouragement from Lucy, he had decided to take the job. God would have to work out the details of how he would practice evangelism working among people who claimed to be Christian already.

Major Paulson's Wild West Show would continue touring for a month after his departure, continuing its sweep through the Southeast en route to Texas. A part of him didn't want to depart. Most of all, he didn't want to say good-bye to Lucy. She had grown from a shy country girl to a confident young woman, a capable servant in God's hands. He couldn't, wouldn't, ask her to leave the place where God had brought her to become a teacher's wife on the Texas plains. It would be like asking a butterfly to become a caterpillar again.

As he prepared for the morning's chapel, he suspected he knew what Paul felt when he visited Ephesus for the last time. *"Therefore watch, and remember, that by the space of three years"*—or three months, in Gordon's case—*"I ceased not to warn every one night and day with tears."* At his final service with the troupe, he planned to preach from the relevant passage from the twentieth chapter of Acts.

That day had not yet arrived. Today the major had a special announcement to make, one that would thrill every member of the ensemble.

Except me. His father's news represented another reason to regret leaving the comfort of his extended family behind.

"The major has asked for the opportunity to say a few words." Gordon motioned his father to come forward.

"I am in receipt of a letter." His father waved the paper theatrically. *Always the showman.* When God gave gifts to people, that was the one doled out to his father, and he used it to the utmost.

"It comes from a Monsieur Jacques Colbert. Let me read from his letter. 'I have heard of the wonderful Major Paulson's Wild West Show'"—the major did a terrific imitation French accent—"'of the skilled horsemen in your troop, of the dangerous clown acts, but most especially, of the amazing Lucy Ames. *Mon ami,* how can *la femme* be the size of Texas?" He paused and winked at the ensemble. "These Frenchies can't understand hyperbole, can they?"

Gordon felt the breaths held across the gathering.

"'On behalf of the Service d'Arts et Culture, I invite you to come to Paris next summer. You will be our most honored guests. I know that Herr Gunter of Munich is equally interested in your exhibition.'"

The major paused for dramatic effect while he folded the pages. "That's right, folks. Next summer the Major Paulson Wild West Show will tour Europe!"

Squeals and applause greeted the announcement. "Not every newlywed couple gets to go to Europe for a honeymoon." He spoke to Jacob and Tess, who had announced their engagement after her parents joined them for a weekend in New York.

I wish that were me and Lucy. Gordon felt a pang. Lucy would remain where she belonged, with the show. God would use her to bring the gospel to "the uttermost ends of the earth." Perhaps through his students, God would use Gordon to reach the same world.

His eyes were irresistibly drawn to Lucy. As he expected, her face shone at the news. She had shared her dream of someday going to Europe, and now God had opened the door. Why was God leading them in different directions? *God never answers why.* Gordon pondered the inspired records of Job and Habakkuk's arguments with the Almighty and knew better than to ask. Perhaps someone better suited to be his helpmate waited at the college.

So why did his heart break at the thought?

"Y'all just watched me kill a pretend bear. A few months back, I killed me a real one."

Lucy brandished the rifle she used in the mock attack. The major's decision to reenact the hunt had proved wise. Tonight in Houston, during the last performance of the season, the audience roared as loudly as they had the first time they had tried the act.

"On that day, I learned that God is always with me. He guards the steps that I take. Now, you may never face a black bear. I hope you don't." She fought back a smile as the audience laughed. "But whatever happens, you, too, can know that God is always with you. As long as you've asked Jesus to be your Savior, why, God Himself lives in you." Over the months, Lucy felt more at ease sharing the gospel. She avoided saying the same thing twice—she didn't want her testimony to become rote memorization—but she always incorporated the basic ABCs. Admit you're a sinner, believe on Jesus, and confess it to others.

She spoke the words with all sincerity, her heart close to breaking. Tomorrow the troupe would head back to Austin, where they would break up for the winter months. The weight of the separation had grown on her the past few weeks—ever since Gordon had departed for school.

Get over it. God had called Gordon to the marvelous work of molding young men for ministry. Lucy had the best of both worlds. A loving family awaited her return home, and next spring she would leave for Europe. She didn't even have to wait all seven months to see her friends again; Jacob and Tess had invited everyone to their wedding in January.

If the months in between stretched out like the Mississippi River, why, she welcomed long hours with her sisters. She could spend days reacquainting herself with every tree and hillock on the Rocking A Ranch. What more could a girl want?

Their time on the train sped by in a blur. Every woman promised to keep in touch, and even the men promised to see her again next year.

"You will come to Austin to visit me sometime?" Annie pressed. They had become close friends in the months since her decision to receive Christ.

Lucy knew her friend feared her parents' reaction to her new commitment. A friend of a friend had recommended a church; that might well be the first battle. The Ruprechts were Christmas-and-Easter Christians, according to Annie.

"I hope so. I'll be praying for you. Every day," Lucy promised. "And you have to come to the ranch. Maybe we can practice some new tricks that we can do together."

The prairie gave way to buildings. Lucy wondered if they would pass the state capitol building, boasted to be "the seventh largest building in the world." Funny, after all the cities she had visited over the summer, but she wanted to see a Texas-sized capitol. Maybe she should have her picture taken for next year's posters. She chuckled to herself. After a night at the hotel with the Paulsons and several cast members, she would leave for Horsefly in the morning. Soon she'd be home.

The train chugged into the station, and Lucy gave her window seat to those expecting to see loved ones. She had refused Pa's offer to come get her. Ranch life kept him busy 365 days a year, and she felt confident she could get home on her own. Major Paulson had arranged for her to continue her trip in the morning. After that, she wouldn't leave the car unless necessary until they arrived in Horsefly.

Annie stood at the window, waving frantically. "You'll never believe who's here." Lucy stayed back so that Annie could have a private reunion with a childhood sweetheart she had mentioned more than once over the summer.

After the car emptied, Lucy walked through, touching the backdrops and props used for various acts. The once-offensive strong mixture of scents now struck her as natural as the earthy smell of a barn. She was leaving one home to return to another, and she wanted to say good-bye.

At last she tied her hat under her chin and moved to the stairs.

"Lucy! Miss Lucy Ames!"

She would recognize that voice anywhere. *Gordon.* Her feet almost skipped the bottom step as she descended to the platform, her gaze sweeping left to right. Gordon waited by the baggage. She wanted to run but instead maintained a ladylike pace. She had no control, however, over the smile that spread across her face. Would he sweep her up in his arms?

Folk wisdom said absence made the heart grow fonder, and Gordon now knew the truth of that proverb. After a month's separation, he had wondered if his memory had exaggerated the sparkle in Lucy's dark eyes, or added extra bounce to the curls in her hair, or widened the scope of her trademark grin.

They hadn't. Even in her practical beige traveling dress, she looked more beautiful than he remembered.

Stop gawking. Gordon resisted the urge to take her in his arms. Instead, he bowed and spoke words of greeting. "Welcome home, Lucy. The major delegated me to accompany you."

Did a shade of regret pass over Lucy's face? Too fast to determine. "I didn't expect to see you here. . . . Haven't classes started?"

"We don't hold classes on Monday. Students need time to return from the towns where they preach on Sundays." And he had made arrangements with another teacher to cover his Friday classes; he had hopped on a train early Thursday evening so he could meet Lucy at this moment.

"It's—wonderful—to see you again. How do you like teaching so far?"

"I love it." That was true. He enjoyed his classes, the light of comprehension that dawned in a student's eyes, the challenge of preparing the next generation of preachers for the Texas plains. If only he didn't think of Lucy every waking moment, he would be perfectly content. "But I want to hear about this last month. The major said you added the bear scene to your act?"

Lucy laughed, a hearty sound that matched her outgoing personality. "Yes, we did. Milton donned a bear suit and held its head high above his body. Somehow the audience believed the fantasy and gasped every time the bear threatened me and I shot him."

The largest, tallest, and broadest of all the stagehands, even Milton could not match a full-grown bear for size. Gordon grinned at the image. "The major also told me that your testimonies have been very effective."

"Only God knows." As always, Lucy shied away from praise.

Gordon pondered their role reversals after he retired to bed that night. God had given Lucy the outlet for evangelism that he craved. As much as he longed to court her, he didn't want to take her away from her God-given calling. He resolved not to bare his heart.

Chapter 9

Gordon insisted on traveling with Lucy to Horse-fly. "It's on the way." He admitted to himself that stretched the truth. Another line ran more directly, and the extra stop meant he would arrive back at the college only hours before his first class on Tuesday morning. But he wanted to squeeze every possible moment out of the weekend. He pled with God to open a door that appeared closed.

"So what do you think of the European tour next year?" Gordon approached the topic after they settled into their seats.

Girlish excitement raced across Lucy's features. "I have dreamed of Paris since I was a schoolgirl and first read *Little Women*. You know, when Amy went with Aunt March?"

God had given Lucy her dreams and, so far, denied Gordon his. *Your will be done*. He determined not to speak a word beyond sincere friendship. The second hand on his watch ticked away minutes and hours as they talked of common friends, strange cities, and his classes. He bid Lucy good-bye in Horsefly and vowed not to look back.

"Mr. Lutz is waiting for you in the parlor. He probably wants to hear the story about the rug." Bess urged Lucy into the room.

Lucy sighed. She had told the bear story so often that she began to think she should submit it to a magazine. She could picture the headline, printed in lurid ink: THE TRUE TALE OF HOW A BRAVE TEXAS WOMAN FACED DANGER. She paused at the door. The dark fur complemented the pine floor, and she had felt for herself how soft it was on her feet. The tanner had done a wonderful job.

Karl, the widowed rancher who had asked permission to court her earlier in the year, stood to his feet. He was in his early thirties, not an unreasonable difference for a woman of twenty three. Lucy adored his two children, and he presented himself well. With him her future would be safe, secure—boring. *I promised Pa I would listen.* Maybe her suitor would show unexpected aspects of his personality.

"Miss Ames." He said her name with a trace of a German accent. His parents were first-generation immigrants who made good in the Texas hill country. "How good to see you back in Horsefly again." He took her hand and kissed it.

Lucy waited for the expected thrill. None came. Why

did she suspect that she would feel much differently if Gordon had kissed her hand? *Forget Gordon.* On the train ride back to Horsefly, he had made it clear that he held no feelings for her beyond friendship.

Karl held a chair for her, a true gentleman. "Tell me about your travels."

No lady talks about herself. Bess's advice echoed in her head. "I had a wonderful time. But tell me about summer at your ranch. I understand conditions have been dry."

"Some have found it hard, yes, but I have had some success." Karl took the opportunity she offered and proceeded to give a day-by-day account of his ranch operations. Perhaps he hoped to impress her with his business acumen.

Lucy fought to pay attention. She interjected an occasional "How interesting" and "Tell me more" throughout his monologue. As little as she liked talking about the incident with the bear, Karl was the first visitor *not* to ask about it. She couldn't decide if that made her happy or sad.

"They say you shot the bear." He mentioned it at last, tapping the fur with his boot.

"Yes, I did. It attacked someone in our hunting group, and. . ." She outlined the story.

"I would never allow a woman to put herself in such danger. It is a man's duty to protect the weaker sex."

Lucy wondered what Karl would think of her act. No one in Major Paulson's show ever questioned her skill as the best marksman of the group, male or female.

An hour later, the widower said his good-byes. "May I have the pleasure of your company at church on Sunday?"

I promised Pa. "It would be my privilege."

The following morning, she arose early—early compared to her months on the road. Performances lasting into the late evening had encouraged a habit of sleeping late. By the time she reached the kitchen, Bess was cleaning up from the meal she had served to the hands.

"Good morning, sleepyhead." The smile on Bess's face took away the sting of her words. "I made some biscuits and gravy, if you're hungry."

Lucy helped herself to a plate. "I thought I would go hunting today. Maybe bring back rabbit for lunch for Pa."

Bess's face crumpled in a frown. "You don't need to do that. Johann has done all the hunting while you've been gone. After all, you're a star now."

During Lucy's six-month absence, ranch life had filled in the gap her departure had created. She didn't know how to spend her days. The family didn't need her to hunt, and she wouldn't kill an animal unless they needed the meat. She didn't have any other practical skills to offer.

Lucy missed the familiar routines of the show, even the daily chapel services. She read her Bible every day, but it wasn't the same as hearing Gordon's patient, clear teaching. She longed for opportunities to share her faith on a regular basis. Was it like a muscle? Would it weaken from lack of exercise?

Restless, Lucy took trusty Ranger and headed out to the hollow. She let her mare take the lead, and they plunged through the thicket to the refreshing water.

Misty drank greedily from the brook while Lucy refilled her canteen. There were lots of spots like this on the Rocking A—oaks, junipers, and redbuds crowding around a water source. This particular one had always been her favorite. She had spent hours crouching beneath the rock outcropping, hidden by trees, waiting for animals to come at twilight.

Today she wouldn't hunt game, but she could practice her shooting. April and the promise of Europe seemed further away than ever. She didn't feel like she belonged on the ranch anymore. But without Gordon, would she enjoy traveling with the show as much? She doubted it. She practiced splitting twigs and seeing how many leaves she could drop with a single shot. No new tricks suggested themselves to her.

Lucy returned to the ranch house and climbed the stairs to her room. Reaching into her desk drawer, she took out a package of sweet-smelling stationery she had purchased in New York. By suppertime, she had completed letters to Annie and to Tess. Would it seem too forward to write to Gordon? Would his fellow teachers tease him if he received a scented letter? She crumpled the page she had started.

She couldn't go on this way, without anything to do. Maybe she could learn to cook so she could give Bess a break once in a while.

Gordon paced his small room, housing provided by the college for its unmarried staff. If not for the books lining the walls, the room was spacious. An equal number of volumes waited in his office.

He picked up the page he had written earlier in the day. The major had begged him to complete this particular task, "since the two of you were such good friends." Gordon sensed his mother's presence behind the blatant matchmaking scheme. He wished they wouldn't interfere, but he could never refuse his parents.

"Dear Lucy." Was that too familiar? *No*, he decided.

"I pray this letter finds you and your family in good health, and that you are adjusting to life back on the ranch." Year after year, cast members mentioned battling boredom during the months the show rested. Lucy, with her outgoing manner, might find the change especially hard.

"This year, the Major Paulson Wild West Show is putting on a New Year's benefit in our hometown. All profits will go to the propagation of foreign missions. We are inviting as many of our summer cast as can join us to participate in this event. Because you are our star performer, the major wants to extend a special invitation to you. It is his sincere belief—as well as mine, I might add—that your presence will add dramatically to the draw of the show.

"If you choose to participate, all your expenses will be covered, as well as your standard performance fee. We await your reply."

Satisfied that the letter expressed his father's wishes, Gordon signed his name. Pen in hand, his fingers hovered over the page. He couldn't resist adding another note.

"It would be my great pleasure to see you again. Please say you can make the performance." Before he could change his mind, he blotted the letter and sealed it in an envelope.

Lucy read through Gordon's letter for the fifth time on Sunday morning. Pa had given his immediate consent. She read the final lines over and over again until she feared the ink would fade away. *It would be my great pleasure to see you again.* Did she dare hope Gordon felt something more than friendship for her?

For now, however, she had promised to attend the morning worship service with Karl Lutz. She donned a deep rose dress—one that she had custom-made for her in New York—and tied her hair back in a chignon. Of course a few curls escaped. Today the church was celebrating its twenty-fifth anniversary with dinner on the grounds after the service.

On the dot of nine, Karl appeared outside the door with his buggy. "My housekeeper is taking the children with her," he explained. Every eye on the ranch watched their

progress. She knew that people expected an announcement in the near future, "now that Lucy has all those fancy
thoughts out of her system." She planned to accompany
Major Paulson's Wild West Show next summer, and Karl
didn't appeal to her any more than he had before she left
in the spring. Out of fairness to him, she needed to make
a final decision soon.

The pastor's sermon swept Lucy's mind away from
her worries about Karl. He preached a clear gospel message, one that Gordon might have shared. Two seats down
from her, Hilda Strong, a young mother she had known in
school, took in every word. But when the preacher issued
the invitation, she didn't move. Praise God, two young
children went forward. Hilda stayed glued to her seat.
Lucy sensed her struggle and wondered if she should offer
to go up front with her, but the invitation ended before
she moved. Lucy determined to speak to her at some
point before they went their separate ways.

As soon as the pastor spoke the benediction, Hilda
took her children's hands and headed for the door.

"Excuse me," Lucy said to Karl. She hurried after
Hilda.

"Where are you going?" Karl called. Lucy didn't respond. She had a more important matter to take care of.

"Hilda, wait for me a moment, please."

Hilda turned, fair blond hair framing a tired face.
A smile lit her face. "Lucy! I've heard all about your
adventures. To think that someone I know has become a
celebrity!"

Lucy fashioned the compliment into the opening she needed. "It wasn't so much that I became famous, but Jesus showed me what He wanted me to do with my life." She paused. "Can you stay for a few minutes? I'd like to talk."

"Oh, but I didn't bring anything. I was just going to take my girls home and—"

"Nonsense. You know what the pastor says. There's always more than enough food to go around." Lucy noticed more than Hilda's tired face. Her dress had seen a few too many washings, and the children looked small and frail. While her fortunes had grown, Hilda must have struggled.

"If you're sure," Hilda agreed. Lucy spread out the quilt she had brought for the picnic and insisted on serving her guests.

When Lucy went through the line for a third time—this time for her own plate—Karl touched her elbow. "Lucy. I thought you were sitting with me today."

"I planned to. But Hilda. . . I knew her in school. God is working in her heart, Karl; I know He is. I feel I should talk with her some more."

"Leave that to the pastor. That's his job."

Lucy looked at the widower, kindly and dependable, but with no heart for evangelism.

"I'm sorry, Karl. I have to do this. Let's. . .talk later."

Karl wouldn't like what she had to say.

Chapter 10

Gordon stood to his feet. His end-of-semester interview with college president Peter Merton was completed. "I look forward to seeing you in January."

"We are blessed that you decided to join our faculty." Dr. Merton smiled. "I am thankful that we were able to resolve your concerns." He placed a hand on Gordon's shoulder. "My wife and I will be praying with you about the other matter."

"Thank you, sir." The two men shook hands, and Gordon walked out the door. Once he passed the threshold, he had to force himself not to skip down the stairs. Final exams finished by the middle of the month, and now he had a three-week break before the next semester began in the new year. He would need every moment of the vacation.

Gordon boarded the evening train for a quick trip to

see his parents. He had considered waiting for the benefit show to see Lucy again, but he had decided to make his move. Some business shouldn't wait.

This Christmas season, Lucy had less than usual to do. She had completed all of her shopping while on the road and had shipped presents ahead of time. In addition to a few trinkets, she had purchased and wrapped something special for each family member. What fun she'd had choosing presents: a hand-crafted leather saddle for Sarah, bought in Kansas City; a newly printed edition of all of Shakespeare's plays for Pa, found in Boston; a silk scarf and pearl hair combs for Bess; as well as presents for Harold and Charlsey should they come.

With no shopping to finish and no assigned job at the ranch, Lucy threw herself into preparations at church. Activities that would have frightened her a year ago—coordinating the children's Christmas pageant or giving a recitation of "'Twas the Night Before Christmas"—seemed like child's play after her months as the "Texas-Born Annie Oakley." Most precious of all were the opportunities to discuss the reason Jesus came to earth with the children. She prayed that some, if not all of them, would accept God's gift of salvation this Christmas.

Christmas greetings from members of the cast of Major Paulson's Wild West Show poured in. She checked every day for the one card she had not yet received.

"You'll need to add string all the way out to the barn if

you receive many more," Sarah commented as Lucy sorted the mail on Christmas Eve. "Everyone must have sent at least two cards apiece."

"Oh, quit teasing me." Disappointed, Lucy studied the garlands of cards that festooned their center hallway. She could give a lesson in Texas history from the variety of places people lived. The family had made a game of choosing a different card each night and demanding a story.

"Are you looking for something special?"

"Not really."

Bess shook her head as if she didn't believe her. Lucy hadn't told her much about Gordon, but her perceptive older sister had probably guessed. "Don't worry. Sometimes the mail is delayed."

From what Gordon had shared about his days in seminary, those papers and exams crammed the last few days. Now that he was teaching, he had to grade them. He must have been busy. *He'll write. Soon.*

Bess begged Lucy to hunt that afternoon. Pa had given Johann the weekend to spend with his family in a nearby town. The request gave Lucy an opportunity to do something useful and enjoy the brisk winter air. Tonight the children would stage their pageant; and by then, why, it would be almost Christmas. . .almost time to join the cast for the charity performance in January.

The door to the parlor was closed when Lucy returned from hunting. "Do we have company?"

Bess shrugged. "Pa answered the door awhile ago and took the guest into the parlor. I didn't see who it was."

While Lucy cleaned Ranger and washed up, Bess rolled out sugar cookie dough. Lucy had promised to help, since most of the cookies would go to the children taking part in the pageant. She dipped a bell-shaped cutter in flour and pressed it into the dough. An upside-side down jelly jar created a round circle. She pinched the sides to create a misshapen star. The children wouldn't mind, especially after they were coated with colored sugar. She struggled with transferring the cookies onto baking sheets without breaking the shapes, and soon tiny flecks of flour sprinkled her hair and powdered her dress.

"Lucy?" Pa appeared in the doorway to the kitchen.

"Yes, Pa? I found us some good rabbits for tonight." It felt good to contribute to the family's dinner table again.

"Ah, that's good news. But right now, please come into the parlor. You have company."

Please, let it not be Karl. Lucy sent up a silent prayer. The widower persisted in seeking her hand, even though she had told Karl of her lack of interest in his courtship. She looked down at her disheveled outfit. How Bess stayed so neat when she cooked evaded Lucy's limited skills. She shrugged. Better for Karl to see her at her worst. She opened the door.

Not Karl.

Curly blond hair that no comb could tame sprang from a well-shaped head, and warm brown eyes drank in her presence, as she reeled at his. *Gordon? Here at the ranch?*

Pa chuckled and shut the door behind them.

"Gordon." Lucy took in a deep breath. That was a mistake. The room reeked of the cedar-scented Christmas tree brought in that morning, and the air caught in her lungs.

"Lucy." In two long strides, Gordon crossed the room and took her hands in his. "You've been baking, I see." Laughter laced the molasses of his eyes.

"Oh." *Why didn't I take the time to change?* "I was helping Bess bake sugar cookies for the children at church. I'm helping them with the Christmas pageant."

"Of course. You would not miss an opportunity to use your gift to help others." Gordon lifted her hands to his lips. Once again Lucy swayed, and this time, she couldn't blame the cedar tree. She remembered her reaction to Karl's similar caress. She was right; he couldn't compare to Gordon.

"Shall we sit down?" She took a seat without waiting for his answer. He sat next to her, never letting go of her hands. Why was he here? She gathered her wits about her and asked a question. "Have you enjoyed teaching?" *You asked him that before,* she chided herself.

"I want to tell you something." Gordon's words drowned out her polite query.

Lucy's heart beat faster, pulsating in time with the dance of the flames in the fireplace.

"You know I felt I must choose between evangelism and teaching. You encouraged me to teach, and I have enjoyed the classroom very much. But. . ."

"You have another opportunity?" Lucy envisioned something that would take him far away. At least with him at the college, they remained in the same state.

"Dr. Merton, the president of the college, wants me to hold revival meetings during the summer breaks. He knows of my passion for evangelism, and he believes that I will also bring attention to the school as I travel. He has even gone so far as to arrange two months of meetings for me this coming year."

"How *wonderful*! Doesn't Paul say 'the gifts and calling of God are without repentance'? And now He's made both of your dreams possible. I'm so happy for you." Her heart split in two halves. Part of her rejoiced at this new direction for Gordon. Another part of her mourned the confirmation he would not travel with the show to Europe.

Lord, let her listen with favor. "I'll not only be touring Texas, but Oklahoma and Arkansas, too. It's not Paris. It's not even New York City. But God is opening doors." He searched her face for some hint of her reaction.

She looked as dazed, stunned, as she had when she first spotted him in the parlor. Had he just imagined the thrill that passed between them when he kissed her hands? Dare he hope she cared for him in the same way he cared for her? Mr. Ames thought so.

What was he going to say next? Oh yes. "But one thing is lacking from my plans. I want something extra for the revival services. Something—or should I say *someone*—who will draw people in, the way Ira Sankey and his music does for Dwight L. Moody. And I believe God has shown me the perfect answer."

A wild light appeared in Lucy's eyes, hinting at joy and hope she did not attempt to conceal.

"That's right. I want *you*, Lucy. You're not only the best entertainer I have ever seen; you have a heart wholly committed to the Lord, and a gift for evangelism." *I sound like I'm recommending her for a job.* "The truth is, I love you, Lucy. I have for months. But I couldn't ask you to leave the major's show. Not when I saw how God used you."

"You. . .*love*. . .me?" Nothing else he said had registered.

"I love you, Miss Lucy Ames." He dropped to one knee and once again lifted her hand to his lips. "Will you do me the honor of becoming my wife?"

"Oh yes, yes, yes! Today and always, Christmas and the Fourth of July and every day in between. *Wherever* God leads us. . .together." She lifted him to his feet.

Gordon maneuvered Lucy under the mistletoe and claimed a kiss. When their lips parted, he found his voice again. "God led our two searching souls together. He's given me the best Christmas present since the birth of our Savior." He chuckled as he slid a ring made of intricate sterling silver scrollwork adorned by a single luminous pearl on Lucy's finger. "With a God like that, who knows what tomorrow will bring?"

"I don't care." Lucy let the ring sparkle in the firelight. "As long as I'm with you."

Award-winning author and speaker **Darlene Franklin** has recently returned to cowboy (and cowgirl) country—Oklahoma. The move was prompted by her desire to be close to family—mother Anita, son Jaran, daughter-in-law Shelley, and three beautiful granddaughters. One daughter has preceded her into glory. Talia, a Lynx point Siamese, proudly claims Darlene as her person. Darlene loves music, needlework, reading, and reality TV.

She has published four books and one novella previously, all with Barbour: *Romanian Rhapsody, Beacon of Love,* and two mysteries, *Gunfight at Grace Gulch* and *A String of Murders. Dressed in Scarlet* appeared in the Christmas anthology *Snowbound Colorado Christmas.* Visit Darlene's blog at www.darlenefranklinwrites.blogspot.com.

A BREED APART

by Vickie McDonough

This story is dedicated to my parents, Harold and Margie Robinson. I was a city girl who loved horses, and my parents bought me several during my early teen years. I realize now what an expense that was for them, but I'm ever so grateful. Those experiences with my horses helped me immensely in my writing and have made my stories richer and more realistic. Thanks, Mom and Dad, for being such great parents, for training me up in the ways of the Lord, and for indulging your daughter in her fantasy to own a horse.

In all thy ways acknowledge him,
and he shall direct thy paths.
PROVERBS 3:6

Chapter 1

S arah Ames rubbed coal ash on her chin and jawline and studied her reflection in the mirror. All her life she'd tried to be the son her father never had, and today she actually looked like a teenage boy—if one didn't look too hard. With her index finger, she rubbed coal dust across her upper lip, hoping the black soot looked like a mustache. It didn't. But it would have to do.

She cleaned her hands then braided her long dark hair and coiled it onto the top of her head. With the braid firmly secured with hairpins, she set her western hat on top of her bun and pulled the brim down on her forehead. Her gaze narrowed, and she stared at her image in the cheval mirror. With a blue plaid flannel shirt untucked and hanging loose over her jeans, she might pass as a young man.

She had to. Her family's future depended on it.

Her lips tilted as she thought of how her two married sisters would laugh if they could see her now. Charlsey and Lucy had both been cohorts in crime at different times, but Bess and Pa were a whole other issue.

A knock sounded on Sarah's bedroom door. She jumped and spun around, her hand against her heart. Had she locked her door?

"Are you ready to leave for the big festival in town?" Bess pushed open the door, and her mouth dropped open. Her sister glared at her and ran her gaze up and down Sarah's long form. "Sarah Eleanor Ames, what in the world are you doing?"

Sarah blew out a breath. "You wouldn't understand."

Bess shook her head. "You've pulled a lot of stunts, but this is just plain crazy. Why would you want to look like a man?"

Sarah's heart jumped. "Do I?"

Bess set her hands on her trim waist. "Do you what?"

"Look like a man."

Her sister cocked her head. "I suppose, if one doesn't look too hard at your face—or your chest."

Sarah spun around and peered in the mirror again. "I bound my chest. Does it still look like a woman's?"

Bess shook her head. "It doesn't matter, because you're not going to town looking like that. It's just plain indecent."

Sarah lifted her chin, ready to do battle, and caught a

whiff of the apple pies and fried chicken Bess had made to take to the annual celebration of Horsefly, Texas, becoming an official town. Fortunately, this December first dawned warm with the promise of a bright, sunny day instead of with the chill that had daunted last year's celebration. She stared at her sister. "You saw how everybody laughed at Maggie Daniels before the race two years ago. I figured if I looked the part, nobody would pay any attention to me."

"Well, you look preposterous, and don't glare at me like that, Sarah. You have five minutes to get changed, or you can stay home."

Sarah crossed her arms. "You're not my mother. I'm twenty-two and don't need my big sister ordering me around."

Hurt laced Bess's brown eyes. She didn't deserve Sarah's ire, but backing down wasn't an option.

"How do you ever expect to get a husband when you can't act like a lady?"

"I don't want a husband to boss me around. Besides, I'm doing this for Pa."

Bess snorted. "Oh, he would be so proud to see his lovely daughter dressed like a ranch hand."

Sarah eyed the clock on the mantel. She had to get to town, register for the horse race, and allow her mare to rest before the start time. "Mr. Westbrook donated a blue roan quarter horse stallion as prize for this year's horse-race. I mean to win it for Pa. You know he doesn't have the money to replace the stud that died last month."

"Sarah!" Bess scolded and pressed her fingers to her forehead. "A decent woman shouldn't be talking about"—Bess coughed and turned red—"stud horses." She said the word *stud* as if her tongue was coated with castor oil.

Sarah dropped into her chair and attached spurs to her boots. She'd never use them on her mare, but they would add to her illusion. "I have to get going. I'll meet you and Pa in town."

Bess stood in the doorway, her arms against the jamb. "You're not getting out of this room looking like that. Stop this nonsense and get changed before I miss the pie judging."

Most times, Bess was sweet and congenial, but she had a stubborn streak, just like the rest of the Ames girls. But Sarah was more stubborn. She flashed a wicked grin at her sister and dove out the open window. Bess screeched behind her as Sarah rolled down the porch roof and landed on her feet, running.

"I'm gonna tell Pa, and we'll see who has the last laugh." Bess's loud shout followed her into the barn.

With the ranch hands either out working or already in town, the building was empty, except for Golden Lady. Sarah led her buckskin mare out of her stall and slapped the saddle blanket on her back. The mare nickered as Sarah grabbed her saddle and set it on the horse. She cinched it tight and bridled the mare; all the while her legs shook. If she didn't leave before Pa caught her, she didn't stand a chance. And without a stallion, they couldn't raise horses.

Sarah led Lady to the barn's open back door. She'd have to take the long way, but it was worth it to avoid Bess and Pa. Lady responded to Sarah's gentle knee nudge and broke into a trot and then a smooth gallop. The mare had the highest-quality breeding anywhere in a three-county area, and she was as fast as the wind.

The warm breeze whipped tears into Sarah's eyes, but she wiped them on her sleeve. She couldn't afford for the coal dust to smear. She just had to get into that race—and she *had* to win that stallion.

She pulled Lady back into a smooth lope and rode up a hill and down the other side. Golden Lady was made to run. The countryside passed almost in a blur as she headed for Horsefly. "Please, Lord, let me win today. I'm doing this for Pa."

A measure of guilt needled her. Yes, she wanted the blue roan stallion so they could continue to raise and train quality quarter horses, but she also wanted him for herself. She hated being inside and doing chores women were supposed to do. Training horses was all she was good at, and she had to prove that to her pa. All she'd ever wanted was his approval, but being the third daughter of four, she never seemed to fit in. She'd tried to be the son Frank Ames never had, but nothing she did pleased him or her sisters. She was the odd duck. Winning the race would prove to everyone that she could train winning horses. She had to win. Losing wasn't an option.

Sarah shifted from foot to foot. The line to register barely moved, and she feared Pa would arrive before she got signed up to race. The deception made her stomach churn. She didn't like tricking folks but was afraid they wouldn't let a woman ride. As far as she knew, there were no laws against women racing, but only one had ever done it, and she'd caused three horses to fall, ending up with one horse having to be put down.

She felt like a child, cocooned between the taller and much broader men, but her size would give her an advantage. Though tall for a woman, she was thin and probably weighed a good seventy-five pounds less than most of the men entering.

"Hey, boy." The man behind her nudged her shoulder. "Why don't you sign up for the sheep riding? It's more your size."

Chuckles sounded behind her, but she ignored them. The man in front of her stepped away after registering, and now it was her turn. Her heartbeat quickened. Old man Kaiser glanced up, looking over the top of his spectacles.

"Name?"

Sarah caught her breath. She hadn't thought of that, but she wasn't going to lie. "S. E. Ames," she said, making her voice sound deeper.

Mr. Kaiser pushed his spectacles up. The whole town

knew he couldn't see past his nose.

"You kin to Frank Ames and his bunch?"

Sarah's hands trembled, and she shrugged one shoulder. "Could be."

"Seems like you ought to know who you're related to." The man chuckled and looked down as he wrote her name on the list. "Got your fee?"

She swallowed hard and slid five silver dollars toward him. She'd earned that money training a cutting horse, and it was all she had.

He took it and held out his hand. "Good luck, young man."

She resisted blowing out a breath of relief and shook his wrinkled hand. One hurdle crossed. Keeping her hat pulled low, she swaggered away, spurs jingling.

The town was filled with people from all the outlying ranches and farms. Golden Lady was well hid, and all Sarah had to do was stay away from Pa and Bess until the race.

A trio of schoolgirls sat on a bench outside the Eberhardt Emporium. One looked up shyly at Sarah then said something to her friends. The girls giggled and stared at Sarah. She wasn't sure if she'd been found out or if the girls were making eyes at her, thinking she was a young cowboy. Looking back at their grinning faces, she ran smack into something—a solid wall of man.

She bounced off him, and if he hadn't grabbed her arms, she would have fallen on her backside. She looked up into the darkest eyes she'd ever seen, and they were laced with humor. The man was evidently part Mexican by the bronze of his skin and his black hair. One of his brows shot up, and he released her.

"Watch where you're goin', *boy*." He said "boy" as if he knew her secret. He stepped around her, and Sarah turned and watched him go. The three girls turned their noses up even though he tipped his hat and smiled at them.

Sarah walked on, her thoughts still on the handsome and solidly built man. She shook her head and focused back on the race. She knew the route like the back of her hand, which gave her another edge. All she needed was a quick start, and Golden Lady would pull away from the group. She just knew it.

Her limbs felt weak from excitement, and her stomach swirled like the waters of a flash flood. She leaned against the café wall and stared at the crowd, all the time watching for Pa and Bess. She missed Lucy and Charlsey. What were they doing today? Did they like being married?

Sarah's mind wandered back to the man she'd run into, but just as quickly she cast that thought aside. She'd never seen him before and knew nothing about him, not that she wanted to. Bess desired to marry, but Sarah had never considered it, even though Charlsey married the Christmas before last and then Lucy had become engaged this past Christmas. All she wanted was to work with the horses on their ranch. She hated cooking and cleaning and wished she'd been born a boy.

A bell sounded, indicating that riders should begin lining up. Sarah pushed away from the wall, a tornado of nerves swirling her emotions in all directions. She glanced up at the sky as she crossed the street and headed for Golden Lady. "Please, God, let me win today."

Chapter 2

Carson cast a glance over his shoulder as the young woman dressed as a man sashayed away. He knew the moment he grasped her soft, feminine arms and looked into eyes the color of coffee with just a drop of milk that she was a female. Her surprised expression, mixed with a touch of wariness, couldn't hide her heart-shaped face behind the dirt on her cheeks. He grinned and shook his head. Whatever her game was, she wouldn't fool anyone unless they had bad eyesight.

A man and woman walked toward him. The elderly man nodded at Carson, but the woman scowled and made a wide arc around him. Why couldn't people see past the color of his skin? He'd heard Horsefly was a friendly town and would reserve judgment until he encountered more of its citizens.

Arriving in town on the day of a big festival could make finding work easier since so many ranchers had come to Horsefly; but if they all had celebrating in mind, they might not want to talk business. He was tired of drifting, but he wasn't ready to return home yet. One of these days he'd have to go back to his ranch and face his problems, but today wasn't that day.

Carson purchased an apple strudel some German women were selling, leaned back against the hitching post where his horse was tied, and enjoyed the sweet confection. A man wearing a badge walked toward him, and Carson tensed.

"Howdy, stranger." The sheriff tipped his hat, but no welcoming smile draped his face. "Don't believe I've seen you in these parts before."

"Haven't been here before." Carson tried to relax and look casual. This wouldn't be the first time he was run out of town because he was a half-breed. Although his mother was Scottish, he bore his father's dark hair and black eyes. His skin may be lighter than a full-blooded Mexican's, but that didn't matter in the eyes of most white folks. Character mattered little if your skin was too dark. At least God saw his heart.

"You here on business?"

"Looking for a job and to ride in the race. I've got a hankering to win that blue roan stallion."

The sheriff nodded. "You and two dozen others, I reckon."

Carson finished his snack and dusted off his hands. He held his palm out. "Carson Romero. Pleased to make your acquaintance, Sheriff."

The lawman looked at his hand and then shook it. "Ben Kleberg. I run a clean town here and don't want no trouble."

"I don't mean to cause any, sir. You'll notice I'm not wearing a gun."

The sheriff's lips twitched. "I noticed. What kind of work you looking for?"

"Ranching. Working with horses would be my preference."

"I heard Otto Ackerman and Frank Ames may be looking for hands." The sheriff scanned the crowd. "There's Ackerman over there, but I don't see Ames yet. He'll be here though. Just ask around for him. Tall fellow with gray hair and a couple of pretty gals on his arm."

"Thank you, sir. I'll go talk to Mr. Ackerman now."

The sheriff nodded. "Good luck to you."

Carson heaved a sigh of relief, feeling as if he'd just passed his first test. At least he hadn't been told to leave town. The war between Texas and Mexico may have ended decades ago, but some folks just couldn't seem to put it behind them. Maybe in this town he could find peace and a fresh start.

Half an hour later, he sat in his saddle, waiting for the race to begin. The sheriff had been right; there looked to be a good two dozen riders. He'd need a quick start to win. *Lobo Rojo*, Red Wolf, danced beneath him, picking up on the excitement surrounding them. Horses whinnied. One on his left reared up, and another bucked off his rider. The crowd near the man laughed as the cowboy dusted himself off and climbed back on the agitated horse. Carson's horse was fast, and winning that stallion could mean a whole new life for him.

He studied his competition. Most horses looked like regular saddle mounts, and they'd be little match for Red Wolf. His gaze landed on a sleek buckskin off to the side with a skinny man on its back. Suddenly he felt a punch to his gut. That was no man. That was the woman in disguise whom he'd run into. Surely she didn't mean to compete with a group of rowdy men.

Shaking his head, he nudged Lobo toward her. She stayed off to the side, her gaze scanning the crowd as if she was looking for someone. She had no business riding in a race like this one.

A man with a megaphone stood on a tall platform. "Gentlemen, if y'all will line up your horses, we'll get this race started."

Carson cast aside his concern for the woman and refocused on the race. She'd probably be left behind by the first turn.

Excitement surged through him. The horses to his right and left snorted and stomped their feet. He studied the man on the platform. The man held a watch in one hand and a gun pointed to the sky in the other. Carson watched his trigger finger for movement.

The gun blasted. The horses jumped, and in that second, Red Wolf lurched forward. Out of the corner of his eye, he saw the buckskin also get off to a quick start. Good for her.

He hunkered down and rode all out. The sound of hoofbeats let him know the others were right on his heels. One mistake, and he would lose.

The rocky hill country of central Texas whipped by. Carson kept his focus on the road, making sure there was nothing that could harm Lobo. Suddenly the foolishness of this venture hit him full force. Where would he be without his horse?

A cowboy on foot.

He rounded the bend indicating the halfway mark of the three-mile ride and glanced to his left as his horse made the turn. The rider on the buckskin was second, with a man on a black mount right on her tail. The rest of the crowd was a good three horse-lengths back.

"Heyah!" The rider on the buckskin eased closer until they were neck and neck. Carson tore his gaze away from the road for a split second to weigh his competition. Surprise, like an Indian's arrow, pierced his mind, causing him to lose focus. That female was his closest competitor, and she looked as if she planned to win.

When their gazes collided, the surprise was just as evident in her eyes. Who was she? And why would she go to such lengths to win a horse?

Carson touched his heels to Lobo's side, and the gelding shot forward, taking the lead again. The girl hunched down like him, becoming one with her horse. Neck and neck they raced toward town. Carson's horse, longer legged than the determined buckskin, managed to take the lead again as they thundered into Horsefly.

Main Street was lined with people, all cheering and some waving colorful pennants. A wall in Carson's heart cracked as he felt welcomed and wanted. He crossed the finish line a mere head in front of the buckskin, with the black two strides behind them. Carson slowed Lobo gradually as the cheers subsided.

The gal on the buckskin eased her mare to a walk and glared at him. "My family needed that stallion."

The hurt in her eyes as she turned and rode away stole his pleasure at winning. She didn't know he needed the horse, too. That stallion would be the start of a new beginning for him. As soon as he gathered the courage to return home.

Disappointment weighted Sarah down as if she carried a blacksmith's anvil. She was so close—but that man—that stranger had stolen her horse. Why were strangers even allowed to race? Shouldn't it just be the townsfolk? She knew every rancher around here and knew that Golden Lady could beat any of their horses, but she hadn't factored in a stranger. It wasn't fair.

How would they get a new stallion now? And without a stud, there wouldn't be any foals next year. She'd have no new horses to train, and then what would she do?

She dismounted and walked Lady until the horse

cooled then turned back toward town. There was a wealth of food to eat today, all made by the women of Horsefly and the area ranchers' and farmers' wives. In spite of her loss, her stomach growled just thinking about it.

As she reached the outskirts of town, Bess and Pa were waiting. "Uh-oh."

Pa, mild-mannered man that he was, looked madder than a newly branded longhorn. He stood with his hands on his hips and glared at her. Suddenly her idea of riding didn't seem as good as it had earlier.

"Sarah Ames, just what are you thinking coming to town dressed like that and riding in a race with men?"

"She wasn't thinking." Bess had to get her two bits' worth in.

"I was, too, Pa. I wanted to win that stallion for you."

His mouth twitched. "I reckon you wanted that horse more for yourself than me."

She wouldn't lie to him, so she kept silent.

"Go home and get out of those clothes. I'm pressing the rules of propriety allowing you to wear trousers at the ranch, but I won't have you wearing them to town. You go get cleaned up and come back when you look like the woman you are. Am I clear?"

She toed the dirt with her boots. "Yes, sir."

"And don't ever jump out your window or off the roof again, unless there's a fire. You could break a leg."

She nodded, mounted her horse, and turned toward home. The heat of Bess's glare singed her, and she felt like a schoolgirl instead of the twenty-two-year-old spinster she was. Her sister was just concerned for her welfare, but at times like this, she wished she were an only child instead of the third—inconsequential—daughter.

If only she were the youngest and had golden hair like Charlsey. Or if she could cook and tend house like Bess, then maybe she'd earn her pa's respect. Even Lucy had carved a niche for herself by riding in that Wild West show and making their pa proud.

Sarah heaved a sigh. Wallowing in self-pity never got her anywhere. She nudged Lady into an easy canter, and the wind cooled Sarah's sweaty body. She still had a pasture of yearlings to work with, and horses always took her mind off her troubles.

Training horses was the only thing she was good at. What would she do next year when there weren't any yearlings?

"Congratulations on your win, Mr. Romero. That was one fine ride. I'm sure you'll enjoy owning this exceptional horse."

Carson accepted the stallion's lead rope and certificate of ownership from the judge. "Thank you, sir. This is an honor, to be sure."

The crowd quickly dispersed after the awards ceremony, and Carson took his time examining the stallion. He was young, probably only five years or so, but his lines were good, and his black head was finely chiseled, with a wide forehead and smart, alert eyes. His black legs were strong and sturdy, typical of a quarter horse, and his shoulders and gray haunches were heavy and muscular. Carson patted the horse's neck, still unable to believe he owned such an exceptional animal. "You are a fine specimen of horseflesh, my friend."

The blue roan would make a good saddle horse and could be used for breeding. Carson looked up at the bright sky. "Thank You, Father, for this blessing."

Behind him a man cleared his throat, and Carson spun around. The older man was taller and thinner than him with thick gray hair. Carson suspected he was only the first in a long line of people who would offer to buy his stallion.

"I was wondering if I might talk with you for a moment."

Carson nodded. "*Sí*, of course."

The man's gaze drifted to the blue roan. "Mighty nice horse you won there."

Carson kept silent, waiting for the man to state his business. Behind him, hordes of people crowded Main Street, eating, mingling, or looking at the booths of wares for sale. Fragrant scents of all manner of food reminded him all he'd eaten today was that pastry. Somewhere nearby someone started playing a fiddle.

After a minute the man returned his gaze to Carson. "First-rate race your horse ran."

"Thank you, sir. There was some excellent competition."

Something like a smirk passed over the stranger's face. "Yes, that's true, but then you beat them all. I could use a man who is good with horses. Are you interested in a job, by chance?"

Carson's heart skipped a beat. The man wasn't interested in the stallion but in him. "Sí. Yes, I am interested. What did you have in mind?"

"My name's Frank Ames." He held out his hand, and Carson shook it. "I own a ranch about five miles from town. I need someone to work with the horses. I noticed how well you handle yours. I've. . .uh. . .had someone else working them, but have something else in mind for her. Have you trained horses before?"

Her? He had a woman working his horses? For a brief moment Carson's thoughts returned to the fiery young woman who almost outrode him in the race. "Yes, sir, I have trained many horses, including the one I rode today."

"All right, then why don't you come home with me, and we'll get you settled. I'll hire you for a month and see how things work out."

Chapter 3

S arah ate the last bite of her eggs and set the fork on her plate. She dabbed her lips with a napkin, looking first at Bess and then at Pa. He'd been especially quiet during breakfast, and Sarah knew he had something on his mind. After the race yesterday, she'd returned home, grabbed something to eat while the others were still gone, and spent the evening in her room—moping.

God hadn't answered her prayers—again.

Pa sipped his coffee and stared at her over the top of his cup. Sarah resisted the urge to squirm. She didn't want another lecture and snatched her plate and cup from the table and set them in the sink. Bess's mouth alternated between an irritated pucker and a smirk. A chill tickled the back of Sarah's neck. What did her sister know?

Sarah had to get out of there before Pa uttered something that would change her life. He cleared his throat, and she scurried toward the door.

"Hold your horses, Sarah." Pa set his cup down. "I have something to say."

Sarah stopped and closed her eyes. Here it came. Was he sending her away?

"I want you to start dressing like a woman and helping your sister more. She no longer has Lucy and Charlsey to assist with the household duties, and besides, one day you'll run your own home and will need to know how to do all those womanly chores."

Sarah grabbed hold of the door frame, her heart sinking. "But, Pa, you know I'd much rather be working outside than in the house. I love working with the horses, and I can't cook, clean, do the wash, and still have enough time to train them. The ranch hands are too busy with the cattle and their other chores, and Bess can ask Martha if she needs help." The foreman's wife was always delighted to assist them and enjoyed the female companionship. "Besides, if I did all that, what would Bess do?"

Bess crossed her arms over her chest and shook her head. Sarah knew she disappointed her oldest sister, who'd done her best to raise her after their mother died when Sarah was only two. But she was different. More like a son in her heart than a daughter, and she had tried so hard to be the son her father never had.

Pa stood and rubbed the back of his neck. "About the horses—"

Sarah glanced out the window. The sun had already been up a good two hours. "I've got to go, Pa. I'm way behind from taking off the past few days."

Pa cast a look at Bess that curdled Sarah's stomach. "Sarah, I need to tell you—"

She backed out the door. "Tell me tonight, Pa. I've got to get to work right now."

"Sarah!" Her Pa's voice took on a stern tone she'd rarely heard, and it was enough to make her feet move faster.

She grabbed her hat and duster and ran out the back door, relishing the slam that surely made Bess jump. She shouldn't ignore her father, but she wasn't ready to hear what he had to say. She needed time to prepare herself. Her breakfast churned in her stomach. She almost returned to the house but continued on. Instead of preparing to hear what Pa had to say, she'd probably fret all day.

As she neared the barn, she waved at Larry, their foreman, and Bart, one of their ranch hands, who were shoeing a stock horse in the corral. Golden Lady nickered to her as she entered the barn. Dust motes floated on the sunbeams that had found their way through the cracks in the walls like little fairies dancing in the air. Sarah loved the smell of fresh hay, leather, and horses. "Morning, Lady. Ready to go for a ride?"

She made quick work of saddling her horse, half expecting her pa to come and find her. But he was more a peacemaker than a disciplinarian and would probably wait until tonight to approach her again. She sighed, feeling guilty for her rudeness. Pa was a nice man and a loving father, but he'd never seemed to know how to handle her. Why couldn't he let her live life as she saw fit?

On Golden Lady, she rode north toward the pastureland of their large ranch. She'd turned the yearlings she'd been training out to pasture several days ago while she got her horse ready for the race. But what a disappointment that had turned out to be.

Rocky hills rose to her right, and as she topped the next rise, a wide valley spread out before her. The horses generally stayed in this area, with the river north of them and the ranch to the south. Leaning on her saddle horn, she scanned the herd of horses but didn't see Starburst, the yearling she first wanted to work with today. She named him that because of the splotch of white on his forehead. She turned west to check another valley where their herd of Hereford cattle normally grazed. Starburst's mother was one of their more recently acquired horses and sometimes wandered away from the others.

The cool wind whipped her face, but the sun warmed her body. She loved Texas winters, because they gave a welcome relief from the heat of summer and weren't too cold, at least most of the time. By noon, she wouldn't even need her duster.

Her thoughts drifted back to Pa, and a wave of uneasiness washed over her. What had he been about to say? She had an odd feeling that it might change her life.

Half an hour later, she crested another hill. Nearly a

hundred head of Hereford cattle grazed quietly on the yellow-brown grass. A movement snagged her attention. A man on horseback rode out of a copse of trees. Behind him he led two horses, and Starburst trotted along beside them. Her gaze narrowed as she studied the horse closest to Starburst. Why, that was his mother! Was the man a horse thief?

In the past few months, the Rocking A had lost two dozen head of cattle and several horses. Could this man be responsible? But he was riding bold as he pleased in the light of day. How brazen was that?

Her hand drifted to the stock of her rifle. She rarely used it and wasn't as good a shot as Lucy, but she always kept it handy. One never knew what they might encounter in the Texas hill country. Her gaze pulled from Starburst's dam to the rider's horse, and her heart skipped a beat. That was the stallion she'd wanted to win, and the rider was the stranger who'd beat her. She remembered the moment her gaze had connected with his during the race. Something in his black eyes had reached out and touched her in a way no man's gaze ever had. Had he been trying to distract her? To purposely cause her to lose her concentration?

She pulled out her rifle and laid it across her lap. The man had already cheated her out of one horse, but he wasn't about to get Starburst and his dam.

Carson lifted his face to the sun and closed his eyes. He

was bone weary from helping the bay mare get loose from the muddy bog that had held her captive. Her colt's frantic cries had snagged his attention as he rode around the Ames ranch, and it had taken a solid hour and a half to free her. But she looked none the worse for all her troubles, once her trembling had stopped. Still, he decided to take her up to the ranch house to clean off the mud and make sure she had no injuries.

He whistled a tune and hoped this new job would work out for a few months. Maybe by then he'd be able to return to his own ranch and face the empty house. He cracked his neck and put the thoughts of his parents' deaths from his mind. He didn't want to remember that awful day.

He'd been pleased to learn the blue roan was already saddle broke and was enjoying the stallion's smooth, easy gait. He would have enjoyed training the animal, but with his new job, he'd be busy. He looked around, taking in the scenery of the hill country. Gentle hills rolled across the land, sprinkled with dried yellow grass, rocks, and prickly pear cactus. There were a few trees, but most hugged the river. This countryside was more pleasant to the eye than the flat lands of his ranch, but it made watching the livestock more difficult with all the nooks and crannies where the animals might take a notion to hide.

He'd decided to make a circle of the Rocking A before reporting for work. That way when Mr. Ames talked about the area, he would already have a picture of it in his mind. Good thing for the mare that he had. If she'd been stuck overnight, she might have become wolf or coyote food.

As he crested the next hill, he saw a rider sitting on a palomino—aiming a rifle in his direction. His heart shuddered. He recognized the animal and his strongest competitor in yesterday's race. He studied the rider as she watched him. It was the same woman. She still wore denim trousers, but her shirt was tucked in, revealing her pleasing feminine form. He tugged his gaze to her face. Free of that ridiculous blackening she'd worn the day before, he discovered a very pretty face, albeit an agitated one. A western hat sat low on her head, and a thick braid of dark brown hair hung over one shoulder. Her brown eyes snapped, making him feel like a schoolboy caught pulling a prank. What was she doing on the Ames ranch? And why was she holding a rifle on him?

He touched the end of his hat. "Morning, ma'am."

"That's my mare and yearling you've got there, mister."

Carson nodded. "Guess that makes you an Ames?"

She narrowed her gaze. "What are *you* doing on our land?"

So much for taking the friendly approach. He leaned back in his saddle, trying to look casual. If he had to, he could probably wrestle the rifle away from her, but he couldn't risk himself or one of the horses getting shot. He forced a grin. "Reporting for work, ma'am."

Confusion softened her glare for a moment. "What do you mean?"

"Mr. Ames hired me yesterday and told me to report for work today."

"More likely you're a fast-talking rustler. In case you didn't know it, the ranch house is back that way." She nudged her head to the south. "And the town is five miles further. You've got no reason to be out here unless you're up to no good."

He opened his hands in surrender. "Just trying to acclimate myself to the lay of the land before I start work. I find it helps me when my boss starts talking about the area to have visited it first."

She harrumphed. "Well, we'll see, won't we? Since you're so familiar with our ranch, just head toward the house, and we'll see who's telling the truth."

"You gonna keep that rifle on me the whole time?" He nudged the stallion forward.

"Just ride, mister." She fell in behind him.

"My name is Carson Romero, ma'am."

She kept silent. Carson's back burned as if he had a target on his jacket. He sure hoped she wasn't as good a shot as she was a rider.

Sarah wrestled with her thoughts as she followed the rustler back to the ranch. What troubled her was his gaze—and those obsidian eyes. They'd looked too nonchalant, too guiltless to belong to a rustler. But then, maybe he was just crafty. She'd heard plenty about men who could shoot a person in the back but had the innocence of a child in their gaze. She'd never been one to easily hide her guilt, and she'd done plenty wrong. Putting up a bold front wasn't always easy, but she'd done her best. It was in the dark, when she was alone in her room, that guilt needled its way into her heart and doubts loomed bigger than nightmares.

Reddish-brown mud coated the legs and belly of Starburst's mother, giving credence to Mr. Romero's story. Maybe he was telling the truth.

But still, why would Pa hire another man? They had enough ranch hands to handle their workload, especially with her doing the bulk of the horse training. She shook her head. That much of the man's story just didn't ring true.

She looked at his back, taking note of his wide shoulders and the straight black hair covering the collar of his denim shirt. His shoulders tapered to a narrow waist. She licked her lips, unable to deny that he was the handsomest man she'd seen in a long time, and he was obviously good with horses. But being comely or treating animals decently didn't mean he had a good heart.

She squared her shoulders, taking pride in her catch as she rode back into the ranch yard. Larry straightened up from nailing a shoe on a horse and looked her direction. She held up her rifle in salute, and he stepped onto the fence, watching her. Pa strode out of the house and looked her direction. She couldn't help grinning. Maybe catching a rustler would be the thing that made her pa proud of her.

Mr. Romero rode straight toward her pa and stopped at the porch. Pa's gaze traveled from her rifle to Mr. Romero and back. "What's going on here?"

"Caught me a rustler, Pa." A grin twitched on her lips.

Her pa scowled. "What's she talking about, Mr. Romero?"

Sarah's heart did a somersault. How did Pa know this man's name?

Her captive casually leaned on his saddle horn. "I rescued this mare from a bog, but this lady seems to think I was trying to rustle it. I just thought since I was headed this way, I'd bring in the mare, clean her up, and make sure she didn't have any injuries."

"Well, go ahead and dismount. I'll make sure my daughter doesn't shoot you in the back." Her pa had the audacity to chuckle and waved at her to lower her rifle.

She scowled as her captive dismounted. He cast a wary glance at her; then an ornery gleam sparked in his eyes. "Daughter, huh?"

"Yep, this is Sarah. She's number three of my four girls, and one of the two still living here at the Rocking A."

Sarah sheathed her rifle, wincing at how he described her. Not "Sarah, my daughter who's the best rider in the county," or "Sarah, my daughter who is a master at training horses," but rather "one of two still left at home." Kind of like the runt of the litter.

Mr. Romero touched the end of his hat again. "It's a pleasure to officially meet you, Miss Ames."

Pa jogged down the steps and slapped Mr. Romero on the back as if they were old friends. Sarah winced at the familiarity. How did they know each other? She'd never seen Mr. Romero before yesterday.

Her pa glanced up at her, his lips puckered. *Uh-oh.* She knew that look. She wasn't going to like what he had to say.

"I've hired Mr. Romero here to take over the horse training."

Sarah's eyes widened, and her heart hammered. "B–but, Pa. . ."

Mr. Ames held up his hand. "We'll discuss this later, Sarah."

Mr. Romero's surprised gaze darted from Sarah to her father. Pa just shrugged. "You heard what I said at breakfast. I tried to tell you about Mr. Romero, but you ran off and wouldn't listen."

A knife to the chest couldn't have hurt more. Tears blurred her view of the men. Larry cast a stunned glance at Bart. Even the ranch hands were shocked. Her own father had hired a replacement for her. How would she ever earn his respect now that he'd taken away the only thing she was good at? She spun Golden Lady around and raced out of the ranch yard. She hadn't cried since her dog died when she was fifteen. She'd learned long ago that tears only made you seem weak and gave you a runny nose and a headache, but for the life of her, she couldn't stop the tears gushing down her cheeks.

Chapter 4

Carson shook hands with Mr. Ames while the dust settled from his daughter's quick retreat. He didn't know if she was upset that he'd come to work on the ranch or was still angry that he'd won the stallion. Or maybe she just didn't like Mexicans. He'd hoped that once she learned he wasn't a rustler she might relax and accept him, but judging by her hasty exit, that wouldn't happen anytime in the near future. Trying to forget the hurt in her eyes, he patted the stallion. He'd have to name the animal soon.

"C'mon with me, and I'll give you a tour of the place." Mr. Ames claimed the lead rope for the muddy mare, and her colt followed behind prancing and kicking up his heels. He was a fine animal and would make a good riding horse after he'd grown some more.

"We run Hereford and some longhorns here, as well as raise and train stock horses." Mr. Ames eyed Carson's stallion. "My stud horse died last month of swamp fever. Maybe we could talk about using the services of your horse one of these days."

Carson nodded, wondering if that was why Mr. Ames had offered him the job in the first place. Half a dozen men had offered to buy the stallion last night and this morning before Carson had ridden out of Horsefly.

As they approached the corral, two men stood there, leaning on the rails. "This is Larry, my foreman, and Bart, my ranch hand." Mr. Ames held his hand out toward Carson. "Men, this is Carson Romero, and I've hired him to train our horses."

Both men's brows lifted, and they looked at each other as if it was odd for Mr. Ames to hire someone. Maybe they'd both been the only employees the man had ever had. The two men eyed Carson, and for a moment, he held his breath. Would they accept him as an equal or shun him, as was often the case?

Larry, a tall, thin cowboy, pushed away from the wooden rails and reached out his hand. "Nice to meet you."

Carson shook hands and nodded. Bart was a bit slower to follow, but he did. He, too, shook hands, but didn't offer a greeting.

"Larry can show you where to put your gear and horses. We got a nice herd of quarter horses, 'bout fifty head. Once you get settled, feel free to ride out and find a couple you think would make good saddle horses and start breaking them in. My daughter has been working with some of the yearlings, and you'll find them all to be halter broke and easy to handle."

Carson followed Larry to the bunkhouse. "You can room in here with Bart. He's been alone in here for a while, so let me know if he gives you any trouble. We have two more hands, but they're staying at the line shack keeping an eye on the longhorns." The small room had beds for twelve men, but only one was currently occupied. He tossed his gear on a bed in the corner, as far away from Bart's as he could get.

"Don't you stay here?" he asked Larry.

The foreman shook his head and grinned. "I live in that little house just east of here with my wife, Martha. She don't snore as loud as Bart does and smells a whole lot better."

Carson grinned and followed the man outside.

"There's a smithy on the other side of the barn that we use when needed. As Frank said, we run Hereford and longhorn and raise quarter horses. Why don't you clean up that mare you brought in and check her over? If she's all right, you can return her to the herd when you go out to select the horses you want to break."

"You don't want to choose them yourself?" Carson was surprised the foreman was giving him so much freedom. Normally when he started a job, the ranch hands would watch him like a cougar eyeing his prey, just waiting for him to slip up.

Larry shook his head. "Frank put you in charge of

training the horses. I don't envy you that job."

Carson scowled, wondering what was so hard about the job. "Why? I love working with horses."

Larry kicked at a rock, sending it skittering across the dirt, and then looked at the big house. "It seems you've just stepped into a family feud."

"How so?"

Larry scratched his chest and shook his head. "Sarah's the one who's been training horses at the Rocking A for as long as I can remember. She's good, too."

Carson studied the comfortable two-story rock house. "Why would Mr. Ames make her quit now? Obviously she is capable if she trained that mare that nearly beat me yesterday."

"It seems Frank's wanting to make a lady of her. They go through this about every six months, but he's never hired a replacement for her before. Sarah doesn't take to inside chores much."

"No wonder she was so mad." Unease tightened Carson's gut. That was twice in two days he'd taken something Sarah Ames wanted. She had every right to dislike him, and for some reason that didn't sit well with him.

"There's a tack room in the barn, and you'll find anything you need in there. Some of the stalls are empty if you want to use them for your horses, and there's feed in a couple of barrels. Bart and I are going out to check fences. Frank will be here if you have any questions."

Carson nodded and walked into the barn while Larry

joined Bart at the corral and the two rode off. The big barn had doors on each end to allow air to circulate and sunshine to illuminate the area. There were stalls for ten horses, as well as all the equipment one normally found in a barn this size.

He put Red Wolf and the blue roan in stalls and fed and watered them. After he tended the bay mare, he'd come back and brush down both animals. Outside, the colt hung his head, as if the excitement of the day had worn him out. Carson grabbed a curry brush and tied the muddy mare near the trough and poured buckets of water on her, scrubbing until the mud came off her coat.

How was he going to handle the situation with Miss Ames? He'd never wanted to steal her job, but he could understand her father wanting her to act more ladylike. He tried to imagine the spunky gal in a pretty dress with her hair fixed. Grinning, he shook his head. It didn't fit her. He'd never known another woman who wore britches, but on her they looked good.

He tossed another bucket of water onto the mare, rinsing off the last of the mud. If only soothing Miss Ames would be so easy. He didn't know why it mattered that she accept him, but it did. Glancing skyward, he muttered a prayer: "Lord, show me how to be Miss Ames's friend. Help her not to be angry with me for taking her job."

Sarah tossed another rock into the river, watching the ripples spiraling out in circles, just like her life was spiraling out of control. Why had her father hired that cowboy to take her place? What would she do with her time now?

Staring across the river and through the trees at the winter barren landscape, she longed for the colorful flowers of spring. Fields of brilliant bluebonnets mixed with bright red Indian paintbrush. She couldn't help wondering how much her life would change before she saw the wildflowers again.

Maybe she *should* learn to cook in case Bess ever got married. They couldn't eat Pa's scrambled eggs saturated with hot sauce all the time. She shuddered at the thought of eggs three times a day. She could barely tolerate them at breakfast. Why couldn't things stay the same?

When Lucy and Charlsey were still at home, things flowed well. Each girl did what she liked most and pitched in to help when someone else needed an extra set of hands. But now both were married and gone.

Sarah rested her arms on her knees. She thought about Lucy and Gordon together, hugging and stealing kisses. Charlsey and Harold were the same last time she saw them, even though they were no longer considered newlyweds. What would it be like to have a man stare at her with such love in his gaze? What would it be like to be married?

She grabbed another rock and threw it into the river. She'd never marry. What man would want a grumpy woman who preferred pants to dresses and horses to cooking? Why, she could barely sew well enough to mend the frequent tears in her clothing, much less make a shirt. No, there wasn't a man alive who'd want such a woman.

A pair of black eyes in a handsome face peered into her thoughts. Carson Romero had to be part Mexican, but she didn't care about things like that. Oh, he was comely, no doubt about that, but she was sure he was an outlaw. Could be he just wormed his way into a job so that he could spy on their operation.

Sarah rolled her neck from side to side to rid it of the kinks. Stewing about things took so much energy. She had to keep an eye on Mr. Romero, and how was she supposed to do that if she was in the house?

A horse's whinny pulled her from her thoughts. Golden Lady answered back. Sarah stood, dusted off her pants, and walked to the edge of the tree line. The horses that had been grazing peacefully moments earlier were trotting off in different directions. She moved toward her rifle when something snagged her attention.

Carson Romero stood in the middle of the pasture. He had a black two-year-old mare on a rope and was slowly moving toward the skittish horse. The mare reared then eyed Carson with a wary stare, her nostrils flaring. Sarah hadn't worked with the older horses for a while since she'd been concentrating on the yearlings, and they'd had time to go a bit wild.

She couldn't hear what the ranch hand was saying, but he continued to roll up the rope and move closer to the horse. Why didn't he just take the mare back to the ranch and put her in the corral? If she managed to get away, she could get seriously injured with that long rope trailing behind her. Did the man even know what he was doing?

The gentle wind blew in Sarah's face, and she caught the sound of humming. The mare settled and held her ears up, listening. Mr. Romero continued to move closer, winding up the rope as he went. When he was within three feet of the mare's head, he pulled something loose from the back of his belt that had been hanging there like a blue tail. She took a step closer, squinting her eyes. What was that?

He let the horse sniff it; then he ran the cloth over the horse's nose. The mare shook her head free and sniffed it again. The man kept humming—at least that's what Sarah thought he was doing—and rubbing the cloth all over the horse. Finally, the mare dropped her head and started grazing.

Mr. Romero laid his arms on the back of the horse and gradually put his weight on the mare. Sarah thought for a moment he might leap on top of the horse, but he didn't. He ambled back toward the front of the mare, reached into his pocket, and pulled out something. The mare sniffed it and then ate it.

He looped the rope, making a sort of halter, and led the black mare around the field. Sarah half expected her to balk, but she followed the man around as if she'd known him forever. Flummoxed, Sarah leaned against a tree.

She'd never been one to break a horse by saddling it

and riding until it quit bucking, but she'd never seen any-thing like what she'd just witnessed. Obviously, Carson Romero knew what he was doing. And that made her all the more concerned about her job.

"No! I'm not about to touch that dead chicken." Sarah backed away, not wanting to get blood on her boots. She'd never plucked one of those nasty birds yet, and she didn't intend to start today. Peeling potatoes, cutting up carrots, and scrubbing pots until her hands turned red was her limit. She eyed the beheaded hen Bess held out. Sarah loved all animals, although chickens did try her patience. They were such dumb birds. But she didn't think her stomach could stand plucking the poor thing, and if she did, she certainly couldn't eat it.

Bess turned up her lips. "How have you managed to live twenty-two years and not pluck a chicken?"

"Because the one time Pa tried to make me do it, I vomited all over him and the bird." Sarah grinned at the memory of his stunned expression. "I'd rather brand cattle or castrate horses any day."

Bess went white. "Sarah Eleanor Ames. I've half a mind to wash your mouth out with soap."

"Well, having half a mind is better than no mind at all."

Bess gasped and threw the chicken in her direction. Sarah lurched sideways and took off at a dead run, thank-ful the bird had gotten her out of kitchen duty. Pa would probably make her wash all the dishes after dinner, but at least she wouldn't have to touch that icky chicken skin.

Carson was in the corral, riding a sorrel gelding. Sarah had green broke the horse a few months ago, and he was responding well to Carson's handling. Two weeks had passed since he'd arrived, and Pa still wouldn't let her help with the horses. Of course, she rode off each morning and worked with her yearlings out in the field. Guilt nibbled at her for going against him, but he simply didn't know that she'd die without her work. It was the only thing she was good at. The one thing that gave her any satisfaction.

She'd proved to Bess that she couldn't sew when she'd capitulated and helped her sister stitch a quilt she was making. After thirty minutes, Bess had shooed her from the room and had already started ripping out her stitches. Sarah glanced up at the bright blue sky. Oh, why hadn't God let her be a boy? Everything she loved to do was man's work, and nobody understood.

Maybe if she could prove that Carson Romero was a rustler in sheep's clothing, then she'd make Pa and Bess proud. She'd watched him from afar at first, but curiosity had drawn her closer; and the closer she got, the less she believed the gentle horse trainer could be a thief. He smiled at her as she climbed up on the corral railing. "Afternoon, Miss Ames."

Sarah heaved a sigh. "How many times do I have to tell you to call me Sarah?"

He just shrugged and grinned, making her insides do

funny things. A tiny part of her still thought he was a horse thief, if for no other reason than he'd stolen the blue roan stallion from her grasp. But she couldn't deny she liked him. Each day that she watched him work the horses, her admiration grew. He was gifted, no doubt about that. And he never mocked her or poked fun because of her love of horses.

"Why don't you give him a try and see what you think? Seems to me that he's about done with this part of his training."

"Really?" Her shoulders lifted. He'd never before asked her opinion.

He nodded and dismounted. Sarah hopped down from the fence and climbed through the rails. Carson held out the reins to her as she walked toward him. She reached for them, touching his hand in the process, but he didn't let go. She glanced up, and her breath left her as her gaze collided with his. Something sparked in his eyes, and his stare felt as gentle as a caress. Then his lips tilted up in a grin, and he released the reins.

He clasped his hands together, waiting to boost her up. Sarah shook her head. What just happened? She'd felt a connection with Carson that she'd never had with another man. Had he noticed it? Felt the same?

Obviously not, because he stood there waiting to help her up. Well, she didn't need his assistance and batted his hands away. His brow creased and he stepped back. Sarah grabbed the saddle horn and swung herself up without so much as touching the stirrup. He tipped his hat to her and grinned again. Sarah stuck her nose in the air, guided the gelding to the gate, and flipped off the latch. She kicked the gelding, and he responded, bursting into a canter as if he, too, was anxious to be away from Carson Romero.

Chapter 5

The next day, Carson watched Sarah take the horse through its dry work. Pretending to be separating a calf from the herd, she reined the gelding to the left and then swiftly cut back to the right. The smart three-year-old would make an exceptional cutting horse and was just about ready for training with cattle. Sarah had the horse trained before he arrived, and all Carson had to do was soften a few of the gelding's rougher moves.

He leaned his elbows against the corral fence and kept an eye out for any inconsistencies or errors in the gelding's training. There were none. He'd quickly come to realize that Sarah knew her stuff. She may not be a decent cook, as evidenced by the charred biscuits she'd brought to the bunkhouse, along with the stew Bess had made for last night's dinner, but she was a master with horses.

Carson caught himself watching Sarah instead of the horse. Her brown waist-long braid swung back and forth like a pendulum on a mantel clock as she put the horse through his rounds. Her posture was in control but as relaxed as that of someone accustomed to riding all her life. She was beautiful, except for that trigger-finger temper. He lifted his hat and ran his hands through his hair. He was in trouble.

Women had caught his eye before, but none had managed to sneak her way past his outer wall. Something about Sarah—the anger, or maybe the vulnerability in her eyes when her father told her she was being replaced—touched his heart. But she hadn't given up her dreams. Sure, she helped in the house when forced to do so, but she'd spent plenty of time outside, too. At a distance at first, but then her curiosity had compelled her to come closer, to ask questions about his training methods.

"What do you think?" She rode the gelding up close and pulled him to a quick stop.

"You did a good job training him. I was thinking about trying him on some cattle." Carson patted the gelding's neck.

Something flickered in Sarah's eyes. "I say he's ready. Let's do it."

He smiled at her enthusiasm. He'd never met a woman quite like her. The man who married her could well starve to death, but he'd sure have a capable partner to help him with his livestock.

"What are you grinning at?"

Carson schooled his expression and climbed on his

horse. "Sure is a nice day."

The gelding pranced in a circle as if excited about the chore ahead. Sarah scowled at Carson, making him want to laugh out loud. She sure was a touchy thing, but he admired her gumption and skill.

They rode side by side through the ranch yard. A door slammed behind them, and Sarah jumped. Carson looked over his shoulder to see Bess stomping toward them. "Just hold on there, Sarah. You're supposed to be helping me make pies this morning."

Sarah shrugged. "Carson needed my help." She kicked the gelding, and he lurched into a run as if he'd just burst out of a rodeo chute.

"Sa—rahh!" Bess shoved her fists to her waist. "I declare, that girl should have been a boy."

Carson grinned again and turned Red Wolf loose to chase after the gelding. He'd been smiling a lot since he'd come to the Rocking A, and it felt good after being in mourning. Miss Feisty Sarah Ames was the one responsible, and he, for one, was very thankful that his heavenly Father had chosen to bless Frank Ames with four daughters. Watching Sarah find excuse after excuse not to work in the house had become comical. She probably needed to learn those womanly skills, but he couldn't deny her when she wanted to help him. Not that he needed the help, but he enjoyed her company.

Once the ranch house was out of sight, Sarah reined the gelding to a walk. Her tanned cheeks were stained a rosy hue, probably from the wind whipping her face. His heart bucked as he pulled alongside her. The gusty breeze had snatched some hair from her braid, whipping it across her face. She reached for a long strand and stuck it behind her ear. Her cheeks looked as soft as a horse's muzzle, and her nose turned up a speck on the end.

She turned to face him. "What?"

He looked away, realizing she'd caught him staring. He'd never planned to be anything more than a hand on the Rocking A, but at some point they'd become friends. In the dark of the night when his thoughts strayed to Sarah, he wondered if there was any chance she might come to care for him. He was afraid she already owned a part of his heart. She was like a proud mustang fighting for its freedom, one that didn't want to be forced into being a riding horse when it could run wild.

But the truth was, Frank Ames might have hired him to work on the Rocking A, but he'd never let a half-breed marry his daughter.

Marry? Where had that idea come from?

He needed a diversion from his thoughts. "Tell me about your sisters—the married ones, I mean."

Sarah's brows dipped as if she thought it an odd question, but she complied. "Lucy is a sharpshooter. She joined a Wild West show a year ago last summer and ended up marrying the son of the show's owners."

Carson knew surprise shone in his eyes. What was it about these Ames girls?

"Lucy and Gordon got engaged at Christmas and married last spring. They're now living in West Texas, where Gordon is teaching. Charlsey is the baby of the family and the only one of us girls who is blond. The Christmas before last, she married a city slicker-turned-rancher named Harold. They've got a ranch north of Fort Worth."

"Must be hard to have them so far away."

Sarah shrugged. "You got any siblings?"

Carson shook his head. He didn't feel like talking about the babes his mother had lost before they reached full term or the little sister who died of scarlet fever.

"And then there's Bess. You know all about her."

He didn't really, other than she was a fine cook and not as pretty or spirited as Sarah. Bess would probably make some man a great wife, while Sarah would be branding cattle or rounding up strays. His lips twitched, but he held back a grin. Sarah would just get upset if she knew his train of thought.

He wanted to tell her that he now owned the ranch that had belonged to his parents in West Texas. But that would mean he'd have to explain why he was here, working for her father instead of tending his own place. His ranch was in the capable hands of his foreman, Adam, but one day soon Carson would have to return home and accept his responsibility. He had toyed with the idea of selling the ranch because he found it hard to live there after his parents died, but he just couldn't let go of the land that had meant so much to his father. Would Sarah look at him in a different light if she knew he wasn't just a drifter?

As the cattle came into view, a thought popped into his head. One of Sarah's sisters had gotten engaged and the other married the past two Christmases. As far as he could tell, Bess didn't have a beau. His heart jolted just thinking of marrying Sarah under the mistletoe with a Christmas tree off to one side.

He shook his head, drawing Sarah's gaze. *Lord, help me not to think such thoughts.*

He would be heading home one of these weeks, and Miss Sarah Ames would be staying on her family's ranch. But he had to face the bigger truth. No man in his right mind would let his daughter marry a half-breed.

The gelding took to cutting cattle as if he'd been doing it his whole life. Sarah held on tight as the young horse made a game of keeping the unlucky calf away from its mother. And if the mother got too close, the horse would chase after her, keeping her away from the rest of the herd.

"Looks like he's a natural," Carson said as Sarah reined her mount away from the cattle.

She smiled. "Yep. He should be with his pedigree. His sire was one of the best cutting horses in Central Texas."

"A good bloodline can definitely make a difference with a cutting horse."

Sarah headed toward the river. Both she and her mount could use a drink. "Where did you learn so much about training horses?"

"My father. When he was young, he was a *vaquero* at a large *hacienda* in Mexico, as was his father before him." He shrugged, as if it was no big deal. "What about you? It is unusual for a woman to be so good with horses."

Sarah straightened her shoulders at his compliment. "Pa had no sons, so we all pitched in and did whatever we were best at. Each of us eventually discovered an area we excelled in. Lucy is a sharpshooter, and Charlsey is a great ranch hand and especially likes tending cattle." She caught his gaze and lost her breath for a moment. Why did that keep happening?

"Believe it or not, Bess is a great tracker. We used to test her skills when we were younger. We'd all hide and make her find us. Of course, Bess is good at a lot of other things."

Sarah fell silent, not wanting to brag about her horse-training abilities. It was the only thing she was good at, and if her pa hadn't relented some, she'd have been at a loss as to how to fill her time. She could only do so much cooking and cleaning in a day.

"And you are very skilled with horses." Carson's smile warmed her deep within.

At the river, he dismounted quickly and came to help her down. She stared at his outstretched hands, unable to remember the last time a man had helped her dismount.

She was tempted to ignore him, but something pulled her in his direction. Placing her hands on his shoulders, she allowed him to pull her off and set her on the ground. But he didn't let go. He just stood there staring into her eyes, making her breath clog up in her throat. If he didn't break his stare soon, she might faint dead at his feet, and yet she couldn't look away.

He lifted one hand and gently tucked some loose strands of hair behind her ear. Finally, her breath squeezed out, but it came choppy and ragged. Her stomach swirled, and her knees wobbled like a newborn foal's.

What was wrong with her?

"You are a special woman, Sarah, and don't let anyone tell you different."

Just when she thought he might kiss her, he stepped back. She leaned against the gelding and held on to one stirrup to keep from falling.

Oh dear.

An hour later, Sarah moseyed into the kitchen and sat down. Bess wasn't around, and for that she was thankful. Her thoughts were filled with Carson. How handsome he was. How gifted he was with horses. And how he made her go all limp.

The sweet scent of apple pies cooling in the pie safe tickled her nose and made her stomach growl. Bess would have a fit if she stole a piece. Instead, she buttered a slice of bread and poured herself a cup of milk. Just as she finished her snack, Bess entered the kitchen, her rose-colored dress swishing around her slender form.

"Wow, Sarah's in the kitchen and it isn't even meal-time." Bess held her hand over her heart. "To what do I owe the honor of your presence?"

"Cut it out, sis. I do live here, you know." Sarah wished she and Bess were closer, but then, Sarah had never been truly close to any of her sisters.

"You need a bath. You smell like a horse."

Sarah sniffed her shirt. "So? What's wrong with that?"

Bess shook her head and pulled out a chair. "You'll never catch a man like that."

Sarah's lips curled. "I told you I wasn't looking for a man." Instantly her thoughts veered to Carson, and she wondered if maybe things had changed. She could easily come to care for a man like him who loved horses so much.

"What about Mr. Ro–mer–o?" Bess stretched out the man's name and batted her eyelashes. "Seems to me my little sister has found her Romeo."

Sarah lurched to her feet, sure her cheeks were bright red. "What? No! Why, that's ridiculous."

Bess lifted her brows in a knowing stare. "I've seen how you look at him."

"What do you mean?"

"You can't wait to get outside to see him each morning, and it's 'Carson said this,' or 'Carson did that.'" Bess hugged her hands to her chest. "Why, you sound just like Lucy and Charlsey when they first met their husbands."

Sarah gaped at her sister. "You don't know what you're talking about. I just respect Mr. Romero. That's all."

Bess crossed her arms. "Uh-huh."

Swirling away from the table, Sarah marched out of the room with Bess's soft chuckles sounding behind her. Just because Bess was the oldest didn't mean she knew everything. But even as Sarah tried to deny her feelings for Carson, she knew she couldn't. She liked him and admired him, but that was all. Wasn't it?

Chapter 6

Sarah pushed back her plate of food after dinner. The platter in the center of the table still held a goodly amount of pot roast, potatoes, and carrots, but it no longer looked as appetizing as when she first sat down. The scent of fresh-baked rolls still hung in the air.

"We need to talk about Christmas. It will be here before we know it." Bess tucked the final bit of her dinner roll into her mouth.

"Are Lucy and Charlsey going to be able to make it home?" Sarah glanced at her father.

He pursed his lips and shrugged. "I don't know. I hadn't even stopped to think about Christmas." He glanced at Bess. "What have you heard from them?"

"Charlsey and Harold won't be able to come this year because of duties at their ranch." Bess stared into her lap. "It just won't be the same without her here."

"What of Lucy and Gordon?" Pa spooned another

potato onto his plate, smashed it with his fork, and then covered it with brown gravy.

"They may be able to come but weren't certain in the last letter I received. Gordon's family wants to spend the holidays with them since they were here last year for the wedding. It may just be the three of us."

Sarah fingered the handle of her coffee mug. She missed the camaraderie of her noisy sisters, and not having them here at Christmas made her almost wish she could forget the holidays. She and Bess had gotten along better when all four sisters had been here. Charlsey and Lucy helped calm the waters and gave Bess someone other than Sarah to boss around.

Pa continued to shovel food in as if he hadn't eaten in a week. Bess stared into her coffee cup, and Sarah pushed a lone carrot around on her plate. She hadn't thought about Christmas presents before now. She'd spent all her money on the race, and she couldn't make anything worth giving to someone else. How was she going to come up with a present for everyone?

Her father finally pushed back his plate. Bess stood and carried both her plate and Pa's to the kitchen counter.

"Maybe we could invite the Widow Vonheim to Christmas dinner. With her son gone so much, it would be the neighborly thing to do."

Sarah exchanged a glance with Bess. Their pa had taken to visiting the widow lately and helping her when she needed something repaired.

"That's a fine idea, Pa." Bess poured some more coffee into his cup.

"There's something else we need to talk about." Pa leaned back in his chair, brows furrowed.

What now? Sarah put her silverware on her plate and took it to the sink. She wanted to be close to the door in case she didn't like what Pa had to say. He was quick to erupt, like a volcano she'd read about in a book; but once he spouted, he was just as likely to never mention the topic again. She found that if she disappeared when he was spouting, then he usually didn't follow through with whatever it was that concerned him.

An arrow of guilt stabbed her. It wasn't that she purposely meant to be disrespectful of her father, but in one way, she was like him and avoided conflict whenever possible.

Pa worked his mouth as if he had something stuck in his teeth. Finally, he looked at her. "There's been some more rustling."

Sarah grabbed the back of her chair, her first thoughts racing to Carson. At some point she'd turned loose of the notion that he might be a rustler. When had that happened?

"How many this time, Pa?" Bess asked.

He heaved a weighted sigh. "I'm not sure. Maybe a dozen of the Herefords."

"What are we going to do? The rustlers hit so sporadically that we can't set a trap, and yet we can't allow them to continue stealing from us."

Pa leaned his elbows on the table, tucked his fingers in his hair, and scratched his head. "I don't rightly know."

"If Sarah can wash the dishes, I'll go out and see if I can pick up their trail." Bess removed the platter from the table and set it on the counter next to the dirty dishes.

Pa stood. "Good idea. I'll grab my rifle and get Bart, and we'll ride along with you."

Sarah's thoughts swerved back to Carson. She didn't want to believe the gentle man would steal from her family, but the fact was, his being here gave him the perfect opportunity to learn their schedule. If he was working with some other rustlers, Carson would be able to tell them the best time to strike, because he would know where she, her pa, and the other ranch hands were at most times.

Was his arrival just a coincidence, or could Carson have taken the job on the Rocking A simply so he could weasel up close to the family and rob them?

Her chest ached so badly she placed her hand over her heart. She'd spent hour after hour with the kind, talented man. He was a thief all right, but what he'd stolen was her heart, and she was afraid it just might break if her suspicions were to prove true. Sarah shook her head, receiving a strange look from Bess.

Surely Carson couldn't be a thief. *Please, Lord.*

Carson strode into the barn after having lunch with Larry, Martha, and Bart. Sarah rode out the back door as he entered, sending dust flying. Why was she avoiding him?

In the past three days, she'd been out to the barn less and less, and she hadn't spent any time with him. She'd either stayed in the house or ridden off on Golden Lady. He racked his brain trying to think of something he'd done to upset her and drew a blank.

Mr. Ames ambled toward the barn and soon stopped beside Carson. "Guess Sarah rode off again, huh?"

Carson nodded.

Frank scratched his chest. "If you ever have children, ask the good Lord to give you a house full of boys. Females are more difficult to handle than a bee-stung mule. Half the time something I say sets one of them off in a tizzy." He shook his head. "It's too bad children don't come with an instruction manual."

Carson grinned at Frank's last comment. Sarah was anything but a child. She had soft womanly curves, dark brown hair that sparkled in the sunlight, and eyes that gleamed with a good dose of orneriness when she wasn't overly worried about something. Yes, sir, that Sarah Ames was one lovely *señorita*.

"I guess we just need to pray for her."

Frank Ames stared at Carson as if seeing into his heart. A smile twitched on the old man's lips. "I reckon you're right about that. I tend to fret and not pray enough."

Carson snagged a currycomb and went into the stall that held his stallion. He'd neglected the animal because of the long hours that he'd been working with the Rocking A horses. The blue roan lifted his head and widened his eyes, wary of the man in his stall. Humming, Carson held out a handful of oats. After a moment the stallion stepped forward, sniffed, and lipped up the treat.

"He sure is a fine animal." Frank followed him and rested his arms on the stall gate. "Wish some of my mares were in heat. I'm hoping you'll be around long enough that I can breed them to your stallion. We'd sure have a fine batch of foals. 'Course, if those rustlers keep stealing my mares and cattle, I may have to turn to farming." Frank shuddered, as if the thought repulsed him.

Carson kept quiet. He'd like to help the man who'd been kind to him and treated him like an equal, but he couldn't promise that he'd be here when the time was right.

"Seen any signs of rustlers while you've been out riding?"

Carson shook his head. "No, sir, I haven't. Larry told me about the rustling. It is hard to believe the thieves would be bold enough to steal from a herd in the middle of the day."

"I may have to hire some extra men to help keep watch. I can't keep losing livestock like I have the past month."

Carson stopped brushing. "You don't suppose Sarah's in any danger riding off by herself, do you?"

Frank rubbed the whiskers on his chin. "Can't say as I've thought of that before. She could most likely outrun anyone who'd give her chase if she's on Golden Lady."

Staring at the older man, Carson had one thought. "But she can't outrun a bullet."

Frank scowled, and his lips puckered. "That's true. Maybe I ought to have her stay close to home until we catch them rustlers."

Carson shook his head. "Good luck with that, sir. You might just have better luck harnessing the wind."

Chuckling, Frank crossed the barn and opened the gate where his horse was stabled. "I think I'll ride out and have a look around the western valley."

"I need to exercise my stallion. If you don't mind, I'll ride in the other direction and see if I can find any sign of rustlers."

"Good idea, and both of us can be on the watch for Sarah."

Carson saddled the stallion and rode away from the ranch yard. "Heavenly Father, keep a watchful eye on Sarah. She is not always as careful as she should be. Sometimes I think she believes she's invincible."

He thought of Sarah's smile and how it transformed her face. She'd gone from being angry with him to almost partnering with him as they trained the horses. He missed her companionship.

Looking for her across the barren landscape as the stallion ate up the miles with his easy gallop, he missed the sparkle in Sarah's eyes as they worked a new horse and the animal responded. He missed her playful nudges and teasing comments. "Keep her safe, Lord. And help me not to fall in love with her."

The wind whipped his face, and he wondered if that last prayer had come too late.

Sarah wiped the sweat from her brow and ran the flatiron over Pa's shirt. How could it be so hot in December?

Between the oven, the iron, and Sarah's vigorous housecleaning, she'd worked up quite a sweat. No wonder Bess was so tired at night.

She lifted the iron and noticed a scorch mark. Gritting her teeth, she set the iron back on the stove and grabbed another one. At least the scorch was on the tail of Pa's shirt. Bess was brave to have Sarah do the ironing and then leave to go tracking. Sarah finished the shirt, hung it on a hanger, and stood back to survey her handiwork. There were still a few wrinkles on the arms and shoulders, but it looked better than when she started.

She wiped her brow again and snagged another shirt. What would it be like to wash and iron Carson's clothes? Why did such a tedious chore sound halfway fun when she thought of doing it for him? Determined to do better, she focused on the task at hand.

A loud knock sounded at the back door, and she jumped, touching the iron to her wrist. Wincing, she set the iron on the stove and opened the back door. Carson smiled at her, his arms loaded with firewood. With her heart bouncing around in her chest, she held the door open for him. He nodded his thanks and dumped the wood in the bin next to the stove. Dusting off his hands, he looked at her, a half smile pulling at his cheeks. "How are you?"

Sarah shrugged, suddenly conscious of how haggard she must look after an hour of baking and then ironing and cleaning before that. She pressed down her skirt. "I've been doing domestic chores."

"Have you, now?" Carson's gaze ran down her length and back up. His cast iron black eyes glimmered. "You look real pretty in a dress."

She huffed a laugh. "Uh-huh. I'm sweating like a bank robber in a room full of Texas Rangers, and I'm covered in flour."

He glanced down at his clothing. "At least you don't smell like sweaty horses."

"That sounds much better to me." They shared a laugh, and she suddenly became conscious of his nearness. A lump formed in her throat. "Would you, uh. . .like some pie and coffee?"

His gaze darted to the pie sitting on the stove. Sarah couldn't help grinning. "Bess made that one. Mine's still in the oven."

Something like relief softened his features. "Sí, I would like that. I was beginning to think you were avoiding me." He held up dirty hands. "Just let me wash up."

He ducked out the back door, and she averted the comment about avoiding him. It was the truth, though now she wasn't sure why she'd been so set on doing so.

She took down two plates from the shelf over the counter. She cut slices of Bess's dried apple pie and then poured a cup of coffee and one of milk. As she set the food on the table, Carson knocked and stepped back inside, his hair damp and shiny as a raven's wing.

Sarah waved at him to sit down while she grabbed the forks. Her hand shook. She leaned past him to set down the fork, and her arm pressed against his wide shoulder. He smelled of the outdoors, leather, and horses. But she loved it. Cheeks flaming at her thought, she sat across from him.

Carson smiled at her, his eyes shining with something that looked like affection. Was it possible that he cared for her in some small way? Or did he merely see her as a pesky intruder?

"Would you mind if I prayed?" He didn't wait for an answer but slid his hand across the table. Sarah reached out, forcing her hand not to tremble, and took his.

"Father, we thank You for this day and ask that You bless this food and the hands that prepared it. Help us to capture the rustlers so that the Ames family will stop losing their livestock and we won't have to worry about people being in danger. Amen."

Sarah took a bite of pie, considering his words. Surely a rustler wouldn't pray for rustlers to be caught. In fact, a rustler wouldn't pray at all, most likely. Something about that prayer erased her last traces of doubt. No man as nice as Carson Romero could be an outlaw. She'd been wrong to doubt him.

Carson finished his pie and pushed his plate back. He sipped his coffee, watching her over the top of his cup. Something about their being together like this felt so right to Sarah. She let her mind wander. If they were married, would he take time out from his day to spend with her like this? Her heart thundered. She shouldn't be thinking such thoughts. What man in his right mind would want a woman who could barely cook or sew? She ducked her head to avoid his intense stare.

"Sarah, there's something I want to tell you."

Her gaze darted up. He looked as if he was struggling to get the words out.

"I haven't told your father this yet, but I don't plan to be here more than a few months."

Sarah straightened. She'd just discovered her feelings for this man, and now he was telling her that he'd soon be riding out of her life?

His fingers tapped against his mug, and he looked up. "I own a ranch in West Texas."

Sarah's mouth opened, but her brain refused to cooperate. Thoughts swirled so fast it nearly made her dizzy.

He held up his hand. "Hear me out, please." He broke her gaze and stared off toward the window. "Six weeks ago my father was riding herd. He found a calf with his hoof caught in some rocks. From a distance, I saw him working and rode to help. Just before I got there, the calf went loco and started bucking. It broke loose but kicked my father in the chest."

Sarah listened, mesmerized with his story, sensing something awful was yet to come. "Was he all right?"

Carson's lips pressed together, and he shook his head. "No. As he fell backwards, he landed on top of a huge rattlesnake that had been under the rocks. It bit my father several times." Carson closed his eyes and breathed deeply, as if the painful thought was more than he could bear. "I got him back to the house, but he only lasted long enough to kiss my mother good-bye and to tell me to take care of her and the ranch."

Sarah's hand slid across the table, her heart aching. She and Pa might have had their differences, but she couldn't stand the thought of losing him.

Carson hung his head. "There is more. *Mi madre* couldn't be soothed. She was so distraught that her heart just gave out. I got up the next morning, and she, too, was dead."

Sarah couldn't help the tears coursing down her cheeks. She stood and walked around the table, resting her hands on Carson's shoulders. He sat with his head in his hands.

"I buried both my parents that day, beside my brother and sisters. I left my foreman in charge and rode off. I haven't been back since."

His shoulders trembled, and she knew he was struggling not to cry. After a moment, she stepped away from his chair. He pushed it back and stood. Sarah leaned against the counter.

"Why are you telling me all this?"

Standing a few feet in front of her, he shrugged one

shoulder. A melancholy smile tugged at his lips, and Sarah couldn't look away. Her breath caught in her throat. Her legs felt as rubbery as the last batch of bread dough she'd made.

"In spite of trying to keep them reined in, my feelings for you have grown, *cielito lindo*. I want you to know I am not a drifter. I have been grieving and had to leave my ranch for a time." He stepped closer and ran his finger down Sarah's cheek.

Her mouth was as dry as a West Texas summer. She leaned toward him, reaching her arms out, and he clutched her in his embrace like a desperate man. He'd been alone in his grief, and her heart ached for him. He was solid and strong, kindhearted and capable of caring for a woman. She felt him tremble and tightened her arms around him. *Take away his pain, Lord.*

Too soon, he pulled back and shot a hand across his eyes. "I am sorry for burdening you with my troubles." Before she could utter a response, he spun around, grabbed his hat off the back of his chair, and strode out the door.

Feeling as boneless as a bowl of pudding, Sarah leaned against the door frame. What did he mean that his feelings for her had grown? And what had he called her—little lindo?

An acrid scent taunted her nostrils, and she looked at the stove. Dark smoke swirled up from the edges of the oven door. "Oh no! My pie!"

Chapter 7

S arah took the charred pie outside and dumped it in the garbage barrel. She opened the windows and door and swirled a towel around, hoping to get the stink out before Bess and Pa returned.

Someone gasped, and she spun toward the door. Bess stood there with her hand over her nose. "What did you do?"

"I just wanted to show you I could bake a pie."

"Well, obviously you can't." Bess removed the jacket she wore when she was tracking and hung it on a peg in the mudroom. "Why can't you get anything right?"

Failure weighted down Sarah's shoulders. At least she was trying to obey Pa now and help Bess, but learning to cook wasn't easy for someone like her. She bit back a scathing response. Bess was tired from tracking since early this morning.

Her sister opened the oven door. "Oh, for heaven's

sake. What a mess!"

"It's just a little spilt sugar and apple juice."

Bess shoved her hands to her hips, her cheeks red, but Sarah wasn't sure if it was from the hours she'd spent in the sun or from anger. Sarah lifted her chin. Why did she even bother helping if this was the reaction she was going to get? "I just got distracted and lost track of how long the pie had been cooking."

Bess slammed the oven door shut and grabbed a towel, swirling it over her head. Sarah wasn't sure if she was trying to get the smoke out or warming up to lash into her.

Finally, Bess stopped her gyrating and glared at Sarah. "Don't you think it's about time you grow up, Sarah? I know you were little when Ma died, but I lost her, too. And I had to grow up immediately because I had three little sisters, a distraught father, and a house to run."

Sarah sniffed. "I don't even remember Ma. I was only two when she died. At least you have some memories."

"You think that makes it any easier?"

Sarah shrugged. She'd always been so caught up in her own worries that she hadn't really thought about Bess's side of things. It must have been hard on her, too. "I'm sorry, Bess. Sorry about the pie mess and about how hard things were for you."

Bess blinked, looking completely disarmed at Sarah's apology.

"I'll try harder to help you in the house, but I can't totally give up working with the horses. I love it too much."

"Well, at least you won't have to worry about learning to cook anymore. Pa decided to hire a woman from town to fix breakfast and dinner."

"Pa hired a cook?" Sarah couldn't help noticing Bess's smug smirk at the impact the announcement had on her.

"Fine." She crossed her arms. "I didn't want to do the hot, messy job anyway."

"Fine. I don't have time to teach you anyhow."

Sarah stomped out of the kitchen, ran upstairs, and changed clothes, but the stench of smoke still lingered around her like a gray cloud. She had honestly tried her hand at baking today, but she was a failure. No, that wasn't true. Her bread had come out of the oven golden brown and smelling delicious, although it did sag in the middle. And she was certain her pie would have been perfect if she hadn't been distracted by a handsome horse trainer.

Pa walked out of the barn as she marched toward it. They met in the yard. He lifted his head and sniffed. "What's that smell?"

Sarah sniffed her shirt, wrinkling her nose at the stench. "I burned the pie I was cooking."

"Smells like you burned down the whole kitchen." As if he wasn't certain she hadn't, his gaze traveled past her to the house.

"Don't worry, it's still there."

Pa cracked a grin then instantly sobered. "We lost some more cattle last night."

Sarah's mouth dropped as disbelief swirled in her mind. "How many?"

He shrugged. "Half dozen, maybe. Bess tracked them until they went into a rocky area in the hills. We lost them."

"Must be a small crew if they're taking so few at a time."

"Yeah, that's what I was thinking. I guess we're going to have to post some night guards. We may have to put a halt to the horse training for now."

Sarah straightened. "I can help."

Pa nodded. "It will take all of us. I wouldn't mind having Lucy and Charlsey back right now."

He walked past her toward the house. His steps were slow, like those of a man half defeated. She knew losing so many head of cattle was a big financial loss. Somehow they had to find the rustlers before the thieves sold the cattle.

Inside the barn, Golden Lady nickered to her, but Sarah stopped at the blue roan's stall. The poor stallion needed to be exercised. She'd only seen Carson ride him a time or two. Sarah looked over her shoulder, even though she knew Carson was out in one of the pastures, working the gelding. It wouldn't be long before the smart horse was ready to be sold. She nibbled her lip and looked back at the stallion. Surely Carson wouldn't mind if she rode him just this once.

Half an hour later, Sarah sat beside the Guadalupe River and tossed a rock into the smooth water.

The windy ride on the blue roan had helped drive the smoky smell from her clothes. She leaned back on the cool ground, put her hands behind her head, and stared at the sky. Her cooking was a disaster, and she was tired of fighting everyone. Bess. Pa. Her thoughts about Carson. And God. She clenched her fist, angry with the rustlers who caused her pa so much grief. Tears stung her eyes.

"Lord, I haven't been the best Christian. I know that, and I'm sorry. Forgive me for making Bess's life miserable, and help me to be kinder to her and more willing to help. Help me learn to sew and cook better. And show me what to do with my growing feelings for Carson."

She cared about him. Loved the way he handled horses, and the way his appealing lips tipped up in a teasing grin. He was handsome, kindhearted, and had a devotion to God that she admired. And he was leaving.

Standing, she stretched her back and then dusted off her pants. If Carson was leaving, he must not return her feelings. She thought about their hug. How good it had felt, and how she'd wanted him to kiss her. She'd never felt this way about a man before. What was she going to do?

She got a drink from the river, watered the stallion, and then mounted. "What say we go see if we can track those rustlers, boy? Maybe Bess missed something."

As she rode northwest, her thoughts warred in her mind. There wasn't much point in learning to cook if Pa was hiring someone for that job. Bess would be free to concentrate on keeping the house clean and doing the wash, so she wouldn't need Sarah's help. With Carson training the horses, there wasn't a whole lot left for her to do. Sure, he'd let her help him, but he didn't really need her. If only she had the guts to join the Wild West show like Lucy did last year, but she'd never had a desire to leave this ranch. It was her home.

But she wasn't needed here. Maybe it *was* time she thought of leaving. But where could she go?

The wind whipped her face as the stallion's smooth gait ate up the miles. A part of her wanted to just keep riding, but she couldn't—at least not on the stallion. Then *she'd* be a horse thief. She smiled at that thought. She loved the feel of the powerful horse beneath her. He reminded her of Carson, strong, sure of himself, in control.

Something whizzed past her ear and bounced off a boulder to her left. Sarah ducked down as another bullet zinged past her head. Someone was shooting at her!

She kicked the stallion hard, and he bolted forward. Making a wide turn, she headed back toward the river. Back toward home. If she got close enough, someone would hear the gunfire. Two men on horseback thundered behind her, but the gap between her and them widened. They'd never catch Carson's stallion.

As she neared the river, she had to slow her horse. She couldn't risk him being injured. But slowing him allowed her chasers to narrow the gap. Another bullet zipped by her head, exploding into a nearby cedar. The blue roan suddenly swerved to the right, and Sarah went left, flying through the air, straight for another tree.

Carson patted the gelding's neck as they rode into the ranch yard. He was eager to tell Frank that the horse was ready to be sold. He was sure the news would please his boss. The man needed some good news after all the cattle and horses he'd lost.

He dismounted and tied the gelding to the corral fence. Bart walked out of the barn leading Carson's stallion—his sweat-stained stallion. "What's going on?"

Bart shrugged. "Don't know. He came running into the barn a few minutes ago. I figured he'd bucked you off or something. I'm walking him—cooling him down; then I'd planned to put him in the corral and come looking for you."

Carson shoved back his hat. "I haven't ridden him today. Been out working this gelding." He moved forward and ran his hand over the stallion. The horse had been ridden hard but looked none the worse for his run. "Do you think Larry might have ridden him?"

Bart shook his head. "Frank sent him on an errand in town, and the boss said he had to fix some loose boards in the house, so I know it wasn't him."

That only left Sarah. Carson narrowed his gaze, irritated that she'd ride the stallion without asking his permission.

"Must have been Sarah." Bart shook his head. "Sometimes that gal ain't got the sense that God gave—"

Bart's words halted at Carson's glare. "I'll just keep

cooling him off, unless you want to."

Shaking his head, Carson headed for the house. He had to make sure Sarah wasn't there. It was possible someone had sneaked in and tried to steal the stallion. He hoped that was the case, because he didn't like the alternative.

He knocked on the door, and Bess answered. "Yes?"

"May I talk with your father, *por favor*?"

Bess smiled. "Yes, certainly."

Carson followed her to the stairs. The house reeked of something burnt.

"Pa, Mr. Romero needs to see you."

"Send him in." Frank was hammering a nail in the bottom step of the stairs that led to the rooms on the second story. He stood and rubbed the small of his back.

Carson marched straight up to him. "Is Sarah here?"

Frank's brows dipped down, and Bess halted near the parlor door. "No, she left a short while ago," Bess said.

Frank glanced at his daughter. A twinkle lit his eye. "Bess and Sarah had a disagreement after Sarah burnt a pie. Guess you noticed the stink in the house."

Carson nodded. "Do you know where she went afterwards?"

Frank's expression sharpened, as if he sensed something was wrong. "I imagine she went riding. As I came back to the house, she was headed to the barn."

Carson rubbed the back of his neck. Where could she be?

Mr. Ames's brows dipped. "Why? What's happened?"

"Someone took my stallion for a hard ride. The horse returned, but the rider didn't. I was hoping it wasn't Sarah, but she's the only person I can't locate."

"We argued." Bess stepped forward, a worried expression on her face. "I was upset she'd burned that pie and made such a mess in the kitchen."

Frank strode out of the room and grabbed his hat from the peg by the back door. "We'd better go looking for her. It's not like Sarah to get unseated from a horse, even one as strong as your stallion."

His words mirrored Carson's fears. Sarah was an excellent rider, and something must have happened or the stallion wouldn't have gotten away from her. He picked up his pace, jogging past his boss.

Somewhere along the line, he'd fallen in love with the spunky woman. He had to find her—to share his heart—and risk her rejection.

Please, Lord. Keep Sarah safe. Protect her. Bring her back to me.

Chapter 8

Darkness tried to suck Sarah under, but she clawed her way toward the light. She felt as if she was in a fog, and her head ached, as did the rest of her body. Heaviness weighted down her eyelids, but she forced them open. Where was she?

A man's raucous laugh rang out. Sarah froze. Blinking to clear her vision, she slowly turned her head, hoping she didn't draw attention. She tried to move her arms and realized her hands were tied together with a stiff rope.

Two men squatted next to a campfire, playing cards. A man in a dirty blue shirt tossed a coin onto a small pile. "I call you."

The other man, younger and leaner, slammed his cards down. "You cheater."

Both stood and glared at the other. Blue Shirt's hand eased toward his pistol. "You take that back before I give you another navel."

The younger man ducked his head. "Aw, I didn't mean anything by that, Jonas."

"Shh. . ." Jonas darted a glance at Sarah. She closed her eyes and hoped he didn't notice that she was awake.

"I don't want that gal to know our names."

"What does that matter when she's seen our faces?" The younger man scraped his hand across his whiskery jaw. "What are we gonna do with her?"

"I'll play you a hand of cards for her." Both men grinned. They squatted again and went back to their card game.

Sarah squinted at them. She had to get out of there. Moving her head as little as possible, she surveyed the camp. Now that she was fully awake, she heard the low of cattle nearby and could smell them. A horse whinnied. She moved her head back so she could see the horses. Her heart did a somersault. She must be in the rustlers' camp.

There was no sign of the blue roan stallion. He must have gotten away. *Please, Lord. Let him go back home. Let someone find him.*

But what if he didn't return home?

He could stumble on the reins and break a leg. Or he could get hung up in a bush and become wolf bait. She closed her eyes and laid her head down. *I'm so sorry, Carson. I pray nothing bad happens to your horse.*

A light wind cooled her cheeks. A cold chill worked its way through her. What were these men going to do? Would they kill her?

She couldn't wait to find out. She inched over to a

sharp-looking rock a foot away. Ever so slowly, she rubbed the rope back and forth over the jagged edge. If she could get free of the ropes, maybe she could make it to one of the horses, or if nothing else, she could hide in the hills until morning. Surely someone would come looking for her before then.

Once they found out she was missing, Bess would try to track Sarah. Her sister knew she often went to the river to sit and think. Bess would start there.

Please help her find my trail, Lord. Protect me from these rustlers.

Her arms soon cramped, and she rested them. The men were still hard at their game of cards. One had dragged out a bottle of whiskey from somewhere. If they drank enough, it would give her an advantage. Her reflexes would be quicker than theirs, and she could think more clearly.

But the rock wasn't cutting through the stiff rope. She couldn't help wondering if she'd see her family again. Would she see Carson again?

Please, Lord. I have to tell him how much he means to me. How much I love him.

Sarah rested again, blindsided by her prayer. When had she fallen in love with Carson?

She ached to see him. To be held in the comfort of his strong arms. Did he care for her at all?

One thing for certain, if she didn't get out of here, she'd never see him again. Cutting the rope was taking too long. The men sat with their backs to her. She eased to a sitting position and glanced at the horses that were tied to a tree. The men had neglected to bind her feet, probably thinking she wasn't much of a threat to them. Sarah rose to a squat, testing her legs. She hurt in places she'd never hurt before, but she'd only get one shot at this.

She stood. Like she'd been shot from a cannon, she sprinted toward the nearest horse.

"Woo-hoo! I won!" The younger man stood and turned toward Sarah. His feet went into motion. "She's getting away, Jonas!

Carson had a clear shot of the two men who held Sarah captive. She lay in a heap about a hundred yards away from her captors. His heart ached to go to her, to see if she was still alive.

But he waited. Frank and Larry were making their way around to the other side of the camp. Once they were all in place, they would attack.

Sarah's shoulders looked as if they were trembling. With her back to him, he thought she was crying, but as he watched longer, he realized her shoulders kept making the same repetitive movements. What was she doing?

She sat up and glanced toward the rustlers. Carson's gut clenched. Her hands were tied. She must have been trying to cut the ropes that bound her. He stared across the camp and saw that Frank wasn't quite in position.

"Lie down, Sarah. Don't try any funny stuff." He knew

she couldn't hear his whispers.

Suddenly Sarah bolted to her feet and took off running—away from him. The rustlers jumped up and chased after her. Carson fired at the dirt between Sarah and the men. Both men skidded to a halt.

Sarah reached the closest horse and vaulted onto it. She struggled to pull up the slack in the reins.

Carson stepped out from behind the tree, and the older rustler went for his gun. Carson fired, knocking the pistol from the man's hand.

"Ahh—" The wounded man fell to his knees, clutching his wrist. The younger thief tossed his gun to the ground and raised his hands.

Larry stepped out of the trees, keeping his gun aimed at the two rustlers. Frank hurried to his daughter, helped her down, and slit the rope that bound her hands. He hugged her tight.

Carson wanted to be the one hugging Sarah, but he walked toward the rustlers. At least they'd caught the men responsible for stealing the Rocking A's cattle. He and Larry tied up the two men and got them on their horses.

Carson looked for Sarah. Her father had doctored a wound on her forehead, and she now had a white cloth wrapped around her head. Her gaze locked with his. Frank eyed the two of them and nodded at Carson.

"I think I'll just help Larry get these rustlers back to the ranch." Frank stared at Carson. "Think you could bring Sarah home?"

Sarah took a long swig of water from Carson's canteen. Her father and Larry rode off, both leading one of the horses that held a bound outlaw. She swung around to face Carson. "Are we going to herd the stolen cattle back?"

Carson gawked at her as if she'd gone crazy. "Won't that be hard to do with just one horse between the two of us?"

Sarah glanced at the herd. She was going to argue the point that there were the horses the rustlers had stolen, but there wasn't another bridle or saddle. "It just seems prudent to take the herd with us since we're so far from home."

Carson took the canteen from Sarah and hooked it over his saddle horn. "The herd can wait. Right now all I'm concerned with is knowing if you're all right. Did they hurt you, Sarah?" Concern filled his onyx eyes.

She shook her head, realizing that it still hurt. "Only indirectly."

He scowled. "What does that mean?"

"They were shooting at me, and the stallion—oh, I'm so sorry for taking him, Carson. Is he all right? Did he return home?"

Carson placed his arm around her shoulders. "He's fine. Tell me what happened."

Sarah ducked her head. How could she tell him that she fell off a horse? It was so embarrassing. She closed her eyes. "The stallion balked when a bullet blasted a nearby tree. He went one way, and I went the other."

His grasp tightened. "The rustlers were shooting at you? Why?"

She shrugged. "I suppose they wanted the stallion."

He heaved a breath that warmed her forehead. "I could have lost you."

Sarah looked up. His concern was for her? Not the stallion?

Carson's expression softened. "Don't you know how much I care for you, cielito lindo?"

"How could I when you've never told me?" Sarah's heart soared. Did he care for her as much as she did for him?

He shook his head and grinned. "I love you, Sarah. I have spoken to your father, and he has given his permission. Will you marry me, cielito lindo?"

Sarah's eyes widened. "You want to marry me? Why, you'd starve to death."

Carson laughed out loud. He pulled her toward him, and his lips came down on hers. Sarah couldn't breathe, but she couldn't think of a better way to suffocate. Carson took a breath then explored her cheeks with his kisses. She pulled his mouth back to hers, showing him the depth of her love. All too soon, he stepped back.

"*Ai yi yi*, you set my blood on fire. Answer my question, Sarah."

She smiled and cocked her head, swinging from side to side. "I thought I just did."

"I don't care if you can't cook or do anything other wives do. I will hire a cook and housekeeper. Marry me, Sarah, and we will train the best cutting horses in the state of Texas." He grabbed her and pulled her close again. "Answer me, or I will kiss you again."

"Promise?" She grinned. "Of course I'll marry you."

She flung herself back in his arms, determined to make his blood boil.

Epilogue

Downstairs in the parlor, flickering Christmas candles decorated each window. A scrawny cedar tree sat in one corner, adorned with chains of popcorn and stuffed balls made from calico scraps. Presents sat around the bottom of the tree, just waiting for Christmas morning.

But today was Christmas Eve, and Sarah's wedding day. Any minute the pastor would arrive, the wedding would begin, and she'd become Mrs. Carson Romero. Sarah smiled at her image in the bedroom mirror. The new dark green dress felt tighter in the chest than her flannel shirt and made her legs cold, but it looked pretty on her and was sure to make Carson smile. Bess had been prophetic when she'd said Sarah had found her Romeo.

If only Lucy and Charlsey could be here to share this special day. Bess walked in, looking nice in her plum-colored church dress. She held something behind her back. "My, you look lovely."

Sarah glanced down at the dress. "Thank you for making it. I know Carson will love it."

A melancholy smile tugged at Bess's lips, and Sarah walked forward, giving her sister a hug. Ever since her capture, she and Bess had gotten along much better. And now they'd be losing each other. Sarah couldn't help aching for Bess. Her sister was the oldest and longed to marry, but instead she'd watched each of her younger sisters wed first.

Bess pulled away and handed Sarah a lovely bouquet of dried flowers tied with long, flowing cream and dark green ribbons. "Oh, it's so pretty. Thank you."

"I need to tell you something." Bess fiddled with the cuff of her sleeve. "What I told you about Pa hiring a cook wasn't true. I just wanted to make you feel bad. I'm sorry."

Sarah pulled her sister into her arms. "I'm sorry, too. For not helping you more and for irritating you on purpose so many times."

They both chuckled, and then Bess straightened Sarah's hair. "Carson won't be able to take his eyes off of you."

The front door banged shut. "I guess that's the minister. We'd better get you downstairs, Sarah."

Someone clomped loudly up the steps, and Bess and Sarah eyed each other with curiosity. Charlsey bounded into the room, her blond hair all a mess. The three sisters squealed and hugged.

"I can't believe you're home," Sarah said.

"When we got word of the wedding, I told Harold we had to come." They hugged again.

"You're beautiful. You should wear a dress more often." Charlsey smiled at Sarah. "The pastor is downstairs, and Pa said everyone is ready for you. Oh, and your Mr. Romero is quite handsome."

"Yes, he is that."

"Before we go, I wanted to share some news with you." Charlsey all but bounced on her toes. "Harold and I are going to have a baby come summer."

They all squealed and hugged again.

"Hey, what's going on up there?" Pa yelled. "We've got a wedding to start."

Sarah smiled and followed her sisters out the door. Carson waited at the bottom of the steps, dressed in a dark brown suit and a new pair of boots. He looked so handsome—but she still preferred him in denim.

As she made her way slowly down the stairs in the awkward dress, she thought about how much her life was about to change. They'd be moving to Carson's ranch in West Texas, but at least she'd be close to Lucy. Carson didn't care that she couldn't cook or sew, but he loved her for who she was—just like the Lord did.

She'd given up fighting everyone and decided to trust God with her future. God had formed her in her mother's womb and knew that she would grow up loving horses. And He had sent her the perfect husband—her very own horse trainer.

Vickie McDonough is an award-winning inspirational romance author. She has written sixteen novels and novellas. Her Heartsong books, *The Bounty Hunter and the Bride* and *Wild at Heart*, both placed third in the Top Ten Favorite Historical Romance category in Heartsong Presents' annual readers' contests. Her stories frequently place in national contests, such as the ACFW Book of the Year Contest and the Inspirational Readers' Choice Contest. She has also written book reviews for over eight years. Vickie is a wife of thirty-three years, mother of four grown sons, and grandma to a feisty three-year-old girl. When she's not writing, Vickie enjoys reading, gardening, watching movies, and traveling. To learn more about Vickie's books, visit www.vickiemcdonough.com.

PLAIN TROUBLE

by Kathleen Y'Barbo

*O praise the LORD, all ye nations: praise him, all ye people.
For his merciful kindness is great toward us: and the truth
of the LORD endureth for ever. Praise ye the LORD.*

PSALM 117

Chapter 1

November 12, 1893

He could still see the dead child, even in his sleep. Or what passed for sleep lately.

Ever since he'd stood on that side street in San Antonio and watched an innocent lad be used as a shield for the guilty, Texas Ranger Josef Mueller had found precious little reason to sleep.

A litany of if-onlys passed through his mind during the day, only to increase in volume when his head hit the pillow. The shooter was a known bank robber who went by the name of Pale Indian. Joe happened upon the scene by accident, practically tripping over the Indian's half-Mexican accomplice behind the livery.

Unfortunately, the Indian spied them first and hauled the livery owner's youngest boy against him as a shield. When Joe didn't shoot, some cowboy with more liquor

than sense in his skull did, and in the ensuing chaos a
child died and a killer got away. Though the money was
returned and the Mexican was tried and convicted, Joe
refused to let the death of that boy go unanswered. The
cowboy did three days in jail for public drunkenness, a
poor answer for his even poorer choice to play hero; but
Pale Indian had yet to be prosecuted. Though he'd likely
only be sent up on robbery charges, the Indian killed that
boy plain and simple.

With a calm he had to force back into place, Joe lifted
his pistol and stared down the barrel at the three targets
placed at random on the limestone boulder. His finger on
the trigger, left eye closed—one shot and the tin can flew
off the fence, proving his aim was true. Another shot and
the second can flew, and then a third.

Joe lowered his arm. Three for three. Just like always.

And yet he hadn't the good sense to use his sharpshooter's aim when it counted—when he could have
saved the life of a child by taking the life of that worthless
murderer.

"I still don't understand why You let that happen,
Lord," Joe said under his breath as he slid his weapon
back into the holster then slipped his boot into the stirrup. "Or rather, why I wasn't up to killing a man who
deserved it."

Following a tip on the Indian's whereabouts halfway
across ten counties had seemed like a good idea until
last night when the weather turned cold and the ground

turned hard. Now he had aches in places he didn't remember existed.

Not that any of this mattered when his pride had taken the worst bruising of all. Pale Indian had been in his sights just as surely as those three tin cans, and he'd somehow let him slip away. Joe thought of the killer now, dressed as if he'd come off the reservation, his white-blond hair stuffed under a wide-brimmed hat that all but hid his face. They'd stood at no more than a hundred paces in that alley, and yet he couldn't say he saw him clear enough to know him in the light of day.

The moment replayed in Joe's mind. Eerie calm on the other man's demeanor even as the child struggled and cried out. Then a volley of shots that went everywhere but their intended target. Chaos—and an escape. What the Indian would soon know is there was no escape, not when the Texas Rangers were in pursuit.

Joe rolled his shoulders to ease the kinks. To make things worse, the telegram that found him by way of Sheriff Arrington's office in Hemphill County indicated Pale Indian had been spotted getting off a train at the Horsefly depot. Of all the backwater towns in Texas, why choose the one town Joe had worked so hard to escape?

No matter. Joe had a job to do, and he'd use the familiar territory to his advantage rather than concern himself with going back to a place with nothing but unhappy memories. Two hours later, he began to recognize the landmarks of his birthplace. Joe shook his head. He saw nothing to prove him wrong in thinking the best thing about Horsefly was the trail leading out of town.

He'd said that so many times that it figured he'd now be plagued with an assignment right here in the place he'd happily left some years ago. But a ranger went where he must, and today he found himself in Horsefly.

If Pale Indian was here, he'd soon be caught. In a town the size of this one, no one could remain hidden for long.

This he depended on as he skirted downtown and followed the curve of the Guadalupe River over rolling farmland. Here and there he remembered a spot, thought on the memory, then discarded it. It wouldn't do to get attached to any place, much less this one. His allegiance was to the rangers now. And a homesick ranger was a dead ranger.

Come morning he'd check in with the sheriff, but for now his belly complained. Likely, Mrs. Vonheim had a pot of something warm and delicious simmering and a spare bed made up in the guest room. She always did, though he rarely took her up on her open invitation to visit. Partly, he decided, because his work had hauled him too far from Horsefly to easily return, and partly because it was easier to chase memories away when they didn't live down the road.

The widow's charitable nature went way back, tying the Vonheim and Mueller family trees together with equal strands of good deeds and companionship. Mama cared for Ida Vonheim and Tommy Jr. when Tom Vonheim was shot in cold blood while riding fences back in '79. Not long after, Ida Vonheim tended both Ma and Pa until the influenza took them, then insisted he let her see to him, too. Too sick to climb out of bed for his parents' funeral, Joe fought the fever while the older woman kept cool compresses on his brow and clear broth in his belly.

By the time the fever was gone, so was any desire Joe felt to stay in Horsefly, though he remained long enough to finish his schooling. Thus far, his mind had not changed, though his conscience prickled a bit when he thought about how easy it would have been to post the occasional letter or detour to visit on those times the trail had led him near enough.

No, it was easy enough to remember school days spent with his best friend, Tommy, the widow's only son, rather than dwell on the unpleasantness that caused him to high-tail it south and slap on a badge. At least Ida Vonheim had Tommy to keep her occupied, and unless he missed his guess, there'd be a whole slew of grandbabies to fuss over by now.

Tommy always was one to attract the ladies. One of Joe's regrets was that he couldn't manage to convince Tommy to ride out of town with him. "Someday," his friend would say. "Just not today." And off he'd go extolling the virtues of the latest female who'd fallen prey to his charm.

Joe swiped at his brow and glanced up at a sky that promised rain before nightfall. Reining in his mount as he came across the rise, Joe spied the Ames spread off to the north. Pretty girls, those Ames ladies. *Bessie Mae, plain as day.* He cringed at the memory of the rhyme he'd pronounced at the church picnic after Tommy's ribbing got the best of him. The one that stuck far longer than it should have.

Likely Bess Ames—or whatever her married name was—had long forgotten the stupidity he'd invoked, but Joe knew it to bother him on occasion. If he saw her, maybe he'd let her know what a heel he felt for being the cause of it. Or maybe he'd just keep that to himself.

Women were funny about things like that. Saying anything might be akin to opening a can of worms.

Joe shrugged off the thought. Why was it that he could put himself into the mind of a cold-blooded killer quicker than into the mind of a woman?

What was Pa thinking when he hired a man to patch the roof? She could have easily helped with the repairs before the rain set in. With her sisters married off and gone, it wouldn't have been the first time Bess Ames had been called on in a pinch.

And his excuse? She huffed as she recalled Pa saying it was unladylike to be climbing on roofs. Since when was he worried about what was ladylike? Hadn't she been the one to fuss over her sisters in that department while he allowed them to work alongside him or flaunt tradition in so many ways?

Why question me now?

"That's the widow's influence," she muttered as she threw a cup of sugar into the pitcher then stirred with a bit more vigor than usual.

Lately Pa had been spending an inordinate amount of time over at the neighboring farm. Helping out, he claimed, though Ida Vonheim had an able-bodied son, Thomas Jr., who could have easily done the work her father now cheerily performed had he not been overly occupied with his job at the railroad.

And to top it off, Pa had taken to whistling. Bess heard it now even as she dropped the spoon into the sink and reached for two glasses, adding them to the pitcher of tea now on the tray. Surely the menfolk would be ready for something cool to drink, what with the temperature rising to almost warm after last night's surprise frost.

Not that a frost in November should be a surprise, but with the weather staying on the decent side so far, the chill slipped through open windows like a thief in the night. Now the sun's warmth did the same, but Pa swore rain would come before nightfall. At least that was what he claimed his bones told him.

"Maybe your bones ought to tell you to stay off the house and away from the widow next door," she muttered as she lifted the tray. Even as she said them, the words pierced her heart. That Pa was still able to work alongside the heartiest of the hired hands was God's great blessing given his age.

And the fact that Frank Ames might find a moment's happiness with a woman after two decades spent mourning Mama was a blessing as well. This, Bess could admit in theory. Watching it unfold was altogether different, however, especially given the reminder that even Pa could find a spouse before her.

Bessie Mae, plain as day. The taunt gave ample reason why she'd been left to see to the care of an aging man. Bess sighed. "Unfortunately, I suspect he's an aging man in love."

Balancing the tray, she negotiated the porch steps to set the tray down on the old stump near the eastern side of the house. Shading her eyes against the sun, she peered up to see Pa's hired hand watching her.

"Thought you might be thirsty," she said to the fellow.

" 'Preciate that, miss," he said without breaking his gaze.

"Pa," she called. "I'm going to take the eggs to town." She waited a minute. No response. Only the steady stare of the stranger. "You hear me, Pa?"

Her father's gray head appeared at the roofline. "I hear you," he said. "Didn't think it required a response." He paused. "You plan to make lunch 'fore you go?"

Lunch? For some reason, the question tipped the scales on her brimming anger. "No, Pa," she said. "I figured your hired man could make lunch for you." A pause for good measure and she stepped back into the clearing. "Or better yet, have Mrs. Vonheim fix your lunch for you."

"Now that's a right good idea," Pa said, "except I figured to take supper with her. Meant to tell you not to worry over setting a place for me at the table tonight."

So she'd be eating alone? Again?

Consider it a blessing he's happy, Bess reminded herself. And yet all she could consider was what would happen should Pa do the unthinkable and put someone besides her in charge of caring for him. What would become of her then?

Frowning, she stormed to the barn and retrieved the basket of eggs she'd gathered on her rounds, then made for the road toward town. She'd almost reached the turn at Vonheims' farm when someone called her name.

The stranger, Bess realized when he loped up beside her. Until now she'd not been any closer than a few yards to the lanky man. Figuring him to be someone's relative from the old country, she first greeted him in German. At his confused look, she shook her head.

"What can I do for you?" she amended.

He stopped short then lifted his hat to offer a courtly bow. "Beggin' your pardon, miss, but Mr. Ames wanted to know if you're taking the buggy or walking to town."

Suppressing a groan, Bess squared her shoulders and picked up her pace. In her haste to show her father just how irritated she was, she'd forgotten all about the horse and buggy waiting for her. Now she'd be walking five miles each way, all for pride's sake.

"It's a nice day," she said as she stormed ahead,

praying the Lord would see fit to send someone with a buggy to fetch her home before the rain soured her plan. "Is that all?"

"No, ma'am," the fellow said, his voice cracking slightly. "He sent me with a message."

Bess continued walking, though she reluctantly gestured for him to join her. So Pa was too busy to come speak to her himself. *Figures.*

"What might that be? Perhaps to fetch more sweet treats for our neighbor?" she asked when he'd caught up to her. "I understand Mrs. Vonheim was quite taken with the *kolaches* he delivered last time."

A stain of red spread over his freckled cheeks. "I don't know about all that," he said, "but he did mention that you might want to fetch back some of those. . ." He seemed to struggle with the word.

"Kolaches?" she offered as she shifted the egg basket to her other arm.

"Reckon so," he managed before shrugging. "Though he didn't say what he planned to do with 'em."

Of course. "Fine," Bess snapped. "Tell him I'd be glad to."

A look of relief all but erased the fellow's worried expression. "I'll let him know."

"You do that," she said, picking up her pace. "And let him know he can make his own lunch, too."

"Oh, I don't think that's a concern," the hired man called.

Bess sidestepped a puddle then glanced over her shoulder. "No?"

"No, ma'am. I'm on my way over to Mrs. Vonheim's place next to tell her we'll accept her offer of fetching us a noon meal after all."

Well, that does it. Bess might have responded, but in the words of the pastor, "the comment wouldn't have been edifying." So instead she marched toward town, being careful not to jostle the eggs, a difficult undretaking considering the length of the march and how very much she wanted to throw the basket and watch its contents break and splatter.

Only a fool would've given in to the urge, however, and Bess Ames was no fool. The paltry amount she made on these twice-weekly trips had grown into a tidy sum over the years. Enough, in fact, to buy her a train ticket to a place where she might be appreciated.

The only trouble was, Bess couldn't for the life of her figure out where that place was. Even as her sisters each married up and left home, she'd given no thought to leaving Horsefly. Why would she when Pa needed her so?

But now? As far as she could tell, she was about as needed as a screen door in the wintertime.

Bess let out a long breath then put on a smile as she stepped into Kofka's Mercantile to make the first of her deliveries, her feet aching. By the time she reached the sheriff's office on Post Oak Road, her basket was nearly empty.

"A half dozen's all I've got left," she told Miriam, the sheriff's stout Irish housekeeper who tended both the sheriff's quarters and the jailhouse. "But if you'd like to lay claim to a larger share than usual, I can fetch them to you day after tomorrow."

" 'Tis a pity," she said as she removed the eggs and set them gently into the pockets of her apron. "While the jail's blessedly empty this week, the sheriff's expecting someone important. A ranger out of San Antone," she said as if announcing some sort of royal visit.

"Is that right?" Bess counted the coins and dropped them into the drawstring bag she used as a money pouch. Her next trip would be to the bank.

"It's right indeed." She leaned close. "I know you can keep a secret, Bess Ames. You've always been the reliable Ames girl."

The reliable Ames girl. Sadly, that was her in a nutshell. Not talented or even interesting. Not a crack shot or handy with a horse. Not even pretty.

Reliable. *Bessie Mae, plain as day.*

Bess tucked the pouch back into her pocket then noticed that Miriam seemed to be waiting for some sort of answer. "Yes, of course."

Miriam cast a glance over her shoulder where the sheriff sat hunched over what appeared to be a pile of paperwork, his chin resting on his palms. Upon closer inspection, Bess could see that his eyes were closed.

The housekeeper grasped the handle of the empty

basket. "It's Josef Mueller who's coming to catch that Pale Indian fellow. Sheriff Arrington sent a telegram saying he was on the way." She glanced over her shoulder at the still-napping lawman, then back at Bess. "You remember Josef Mueller, don't you? Fine-looking fellow, that one, best I recall, and now he's one of those Texas Rangers. Likely he'll catch this Pale Indian fellow. Wonder who he is."

Miriam prattled on, but Bess's mind had stuck on two words: Josef Mueller. Indeed, she remembered him. Fine looking or not, he was the one responsible for the awful school-yard rhyme that upon occasion still intruded on her thoughts.

Bessie Mae, plain as day.

Of all the days to be reminded of that. And of him. Oh yes, she knew Josef Mueller. Pale Indian, however, she'd never heard of. Bess was about to ask when the sheriff roused to sit up straight.

"Miriam," he called. "Either we've got company needing to be invited in or a door that begs to be shut. Which is it?"

"It's just Bess," Miriam called. "Come to bring the eggs."

"Yes," Bess added with a sigh. "*Just* Bess."

"Well, inside or out with you," he called with a chuckle. "The breeze is going to blow away my paperwork."

"More likely you'll lose it to sleeping on it, Sheriff Kleberg," Miriam called as she gave Bess a wink then closed the door.

As she stepped away, Bess could hear the good-natured banter between the pair even as she cast about for the familiar face of someone who might offer her a ride back home to the ranch. Then the door flew open and the sheriff appeared.

"A word with you, Miss Ames," Kleberg said. "I'd appreciate it if you'd not say anything about what Miriam's gone and jabbered about."

"What might that be?" Bess shrugged. "Oh, about Josef. Of course."

His strained expression relaxed. "Wouldn't want to let this Injun fellow know we're onto him."

She spied the pastor coming out of Eberhardt Emporium and waved in the hopes she'd caught him beginning his round of visits to parishioners instead of completing them. Perhaps she'd not have to walk home after all.

"Miss Ames?" the sheriff said.

"Oh yes. He'll never hear it from me," Bess said with the appropriate amount of sarcasm. It took a moment to realize the lawman was serious. "I was teasing, of course," she added. "I don't even know who this Pink Indian is."

"That's Pale Indian."

"Right." Bess shrugged as she watched the pastor turn toward the church. So much for begging a ride from him. With a sigh, she returned her attention to the lawman. "As I said, I've no idea who this fellow is."

" 'Course you don't." The sheriff's eyes narrowed as

he studied her from below the brim of his hat. "See that you're careful till we catch him."

"Careful. Certainly." Bess turned away with a grin. The biggest trouble she'd likely find today was sore feet.

After all, nothing ever happened in Horsefly, Texas.

Chapter 2

Joe stepped out into the late-morning sunshine, his belly full of Ida Vonheim's pancakes, eggs, and bacon. Likely she'd clean up the breakfast dishes then start on lunch, after which would come supper. He'd noticed a lack of repairs on the old place but hadn't found a way to ask why Tommy hadn't been doing his duties to care for his mama. Maybe the railroad job that kept him too busy to find a wife also blinded him to the obvious. Familiarity tended to do that. Though figuring out the why of it didn't get anything done.

Thus, his trip to town had been delayed while he allowed Mrs. Vonheim to show him to the hammer and nails so he could take on the more pressing of the repairs. He'd finished the items on her list in short order and gone on to a few more he'd found before the clock over the now-mended mantel sent him scurrying for his gun belt.

Of course, before he could head to town, Joe was

called back into the kitchen to taste fresh *springerle* just out of the oven. As the cookies were his favorite, the job wasn't an unpleasant one, but it did cost him another half hour of valuable daylight. When he finally got out the door, Joe was carrying two more springerle and a towel-wrapped mason jar of coffee in his hands.

"A week here and I'd be unfit to ride," he said as he settled onto the saddle. "If Tommy eats like this, he's likely round as a barrel." Hopefully, Tommy would pay his mama a visit before Joe caught up to Pale Indian and dispatched him back to San Antonio.

The mare picked its way across the rocky pasture then broke into a trot once she reached the road to town. Mrs. Vonheim's substantial fare kept him from having to stop for the biscuit and bacon she insisted he bring, though he did pause long enough to water the mare at the edge of the Guadalupe.

Soon enough, Joe caught his first glance at the growing town of Horsefly. Where once just a few sad buildings leaned against one another, now stood freshly white-washed dwellings and the smart spire of the church. Up ahead where the surprisingly busy road ran into Main Street, Joe spied the saloon—his second planned stop of the day.

First, however, he had to check in with the sheriff. Giving a passing glance to Kofka's Mercantile, which had been considerably smaller last time he saw it, Joe turned the corner onto Post Oak Road. At least the sheriff's office still looked the same. There had obviously been no need to expand this place or the jail when it likely sat empty except for the occasional overcelebrated cowpoke.

And Joe intended to keep it that way. If Pale Indian was hiding out in these parts, it wouldn't be for long.

Nudging past a pair of matrons comparing notes on the price of calico, Joe reached for the door of the sheriff's office only to find it fly open of its own accord. "Come on in here," a cheerful woman demanded. "The sheriff's been waiting for you, and I've got lunch on the stove. *Rinderrouladen* it is, and the best you'll find in Horsefly, that's for sure."

At the mention of the familiar German beef dish, Joe opened his mouth to protest, but the woman's hasty exit prevented it. Instead, he found himself shaking hands with a much-older-than-he-remembered Sheriff Kleberg.

"I'm not one for wasting time," Kleberg said. "That's why I had you hauled down here."

Joe shrugged. "But the sheriff over in—"

"It was me who told Arrington to get you heading this way," the sheriff said.

Joe's eyes narrowed. "I'm going to have to ask you to explain yourself, sir."

Kleberg chuckled. "Spoken like a true ranger. You don't sound anything like that kid who hung around the alley behind the jail and shot cans off the fence with his slingshot."

"I suppose not," he said. "But I'd still be obliged if you'd—"

"Explain myself. Right, well, what with the size of this town, do you think I'd be able to keep the fact that I know who this Injun feller is quiet if I marched down to the telegraph office and sent for you?"

"Why me?" he asked.

Kleberg shrugged. "You were the only man for the job, what with you being his best friend and all."

"Best friend?" Joe shook his head even as the blood froze in his veins. "Not. . ."

"Tommy Vonheim?" The sheriff nodded. "It appears so, Josef."

"You're wrong," Joe blurted out. "If it were him, I'd have suspected. I saw Pale Indian not two weeks ago. It couldn't be. . ."

But as he said the words, he realized he *hadn't* seen Pale Indian clearly enough to identify his face. Not with his hat hiding what the crying child didn't. Joe stormed around the desk and yanked the topmost poster off the jumble of pages tacked to the wall. "You can see for yourself. That man isn't Tommy Vonheim any more than you and I are."

Yet as he tried not to stare, he had to admit there was something familiar around the eyes. And there was the scar just south of the man's left eye that looked a bit like the one Tommy got when Joe dared him to try to catch his mama's banty rooster bare-handed.

Still, it couldn't be Tommy. Joe let the poster drop onto the desk and turned his gaze to the sheriff. "How can a man whose father was shot in cold blood turn around and go the way of a killer?"

Sheriff Kleberg remained silent. As wearers of the badge, they both knew tragedy could just as likely turn a man to evil as to good, especially when the tragedy came as a result of a crime that had never been solved.

Finally, the older man shrugged. "Maybe it ain't. Maybe Tom's just working a lot of hours at the railroad and not able to care for his mama like he used to."

It didn't take a Texas Ranger to see the sheriff didn't mean a word of it. "Or maybe he's on the run and not keen on showing his face much."

Kleberg's expression softened. "Now you see why you're the only man for this job. Any other fella would kill 'im and think nothing of it; but seein' as we've both known that family just about long as we've been alive, I'd like to do the Widow Vonheim the favor of not having to see her son strung up from a tree or carried through town with a bullet in him."

"That is, if he's guilty."

A nod to acknowledge Joe's statement, and then the sheriff pressed on. "I'd like to ask you to haul him out of town quick-like before anyone here's the wiser. 'Cept me, of course."

"Yes, of course," Joe said. "But whoever's under that hat I saw in San Antonio, he'll get a fair trial."

" 'Course he will. You're a good man, Josef." Kleberg paused, watching Joe almost without blinking. "Always were. Like your daddy was. And his before him. You'll do right by Tom in finding out if he's not our man. And if he done it, you'll do right by that, too."

Thoughts jumbled then reformed. Tommy's long absences. The Vonheim home's slow slide into disrepair. Ida Vonheim's inability to look Joe in the eye when the discussion turned to her son. . . .

Two questions rose above the rest: Where was Tommy Vonheim? And was his mother hiding him, possibly right under Joe's nose?

Bess took her time paying for the kolaches then slipped the paper-wrapped pastries into her coat pocket and headed for the door. Were she the defiant type, she might have conveniently ignored her father's request. Instead, she did as asked.

Good old reliable Bess.

Sighing, she stepped out into the heavy air and braved a glance at the clouds gathering overhead. Gauging the distance to the farm from here was tricky because she rarely walked the five miles.

"Pride goeth before a fall, you fool," she whispered as she adjusted the ribbons of her bonnet to hold it tight against the breeze. "In your case, it will goeth before a soaking."

And yet there was nothing to do but start walking. If Bess picked up her pace, she just might get home before the bottom fell out of those rain clouds.

Scanning the crowd, Bess saw plenty of familiar faces, but none she could admit her prideful mistake to. No, she'd stormed off without using good sense. It was only right that she'd likely end up walking home through that very thing: a storm.

Bess turned onto Post Oak then headed for the road leading to the ranch, only to remember that she hadn't put her egg money into her savings account at the bank. Tempting as it was to turn around and make the deposit, she kept walking even as the coins jingled in her pocket alongside the kolaches. Soon the town of Horsefly was behind her and nothing but rolling hills ahead.

In the spring and summer, the road passed through some of the prettiest land God ever created; and to take her mind off her already-aching feet, Bess forced attention on that fact. Still, where green pastures had stood just a few weeks ago, all was nearly barren now, what with the couple of chills they'd had. Oh, it would green up soon enough, but for now the mesquites sat short and squat on what looked to be miles of nothing much but brown.

Not that the horses seemed to mind. Or the cattle. And from the top of the hill, she could see plenty of both. Ignoring the thunderheads didn't keep them from sliding over the sun and stealing what was left of the afternoon warmth.

Suppressing a shiver, Bess crossed her arms over her chest and tried to walk faster. Unfortunately, the steep uphill grade prevented much progress—but it did help ward off the chill.

When the wind kicked up, she tightened her bonnet strings and began to sing. Only out here, with no one to witness it, would Bess dare sing "Nearer, My God, to Thee" at such a volume. All three of her sisters had been gifted with voices worthy of the church choir, while Bess's was more suitable to the back row. But the cows didn't seem to mind and only a few horses skittered away, so she sang all the verses she could remember then went right into singing "Just as I Am, without One Plea."

Up ahead she could see the twisted oak that marked the edge of the Schmidts' ranch. Bess smiled. Somehow she'd managed to walk two miles in what seemed like no time. *Must be the singing.*

"Only three to go," she sang before launching into the first verse of "Rock of Ages." When the sound of thunder interrupted, Bess sang louder. She was halfway through the fourth stanza when she realized someone was singing harmony.

In a very beautiful, very male tenor.

Chapter 3

Joe grinned as the mare cleared the top of the hill. There he found the other half of his impromptu duet: a stunning brunette with a lanky frame and a dress of butter yellow to match her bonnet. She looked as skittish as a colt and just as long-legged, and she sang loudly enough to wake the dead. Dangling from the crook of her arm was a basket that appeared to be empty.

Just who was this pretty stranger? Must be new to Horsefly. She certainly didn't look like anyone he knew. Another glance confirmed it. If he'd met this filly, he'd have remembered.

Tipping his hat, Joe put on his friendliest smile as he reined in his mare and stopped short a few paces away. "Well, howdy, miss. I don't believe we've been introduced. I'm—"

"It wasn't funny then, and it's not funny now, so just keep on riding to wherever you're going and leave me be, Josef Mueller."

How did she know his name?

The woman continued to offer him her back as she marched down the dusty road. His mama had taught him not to stare, and yet stare Joe did as the basket at her elbow swung against her left hip bone.

He had to look at the basket. Anything else wouldn't be right, what with the fact he hadn't seen a woman this pretty since...well, ever, if he were to be honest. When she stopped, the swaying stopped, and so did Joe.

"Just pass me by, Joe," she said, her backbone stiff and her shoulders a notch past proud.

There was something in her voice that his ranger training caused him to notice. Not anger, but maybe something close to it.

The mare wanted to trot, but he held the horse to a slow walk so he could keep a proper distance behind the gal whose face he couldn't quite place. "Do I know you?" he finally called out once he'd gone through every school-yard sweetheart's name twice. "Because you'll have to forgive me for not remembering you."

That seemed to do something that his sweet-talking couldn't accomplish. She stopped short and turned to face him. "Look, Joe. I know you're here to catch that Pink Indian fellow, but—"

"Pale Indian," he corrected as his senses prickled. Kleberg had told him no one knew about the Indian. Could this be an accomplice? Tommy always did attract the pretty ones. "How do you know about Pale Indian?"

"I sold eggs to the sheriff's. . ." Brown eyes narrowed. "Why does it matter?"

Thunder rumbled in the distance, cutting short any idea of lengthy response. At this rate Joe would likely be drenched before he reached Mrs. Vonheim's place. And yet he could hardly leave her when he knew nothing but the fact that she knew too much.

Joe climbed down from the saddle and held tight to the reins. Maybe she'd open up to him if he met her at eye level. And given her height, he'd just about do that.

Yellow Bonnet commenced walking faster, and it didn't take a ranger to figure out why when the first fat drops of rain pelted him. The mare didn't like bad weather; this much he'd learned on the trail from San Antonio. And so getting her—and himself—and this woman out of the rain became a priority. Even if she were some kin to the Schmidt family, the ranch house was a good half mile back.

He slid back into the saddle and nudged the horse into a trot. As he came alongside the woman, he pulled back on the reins. "I reckon neither of us want the soaking we're about to get." Joe swiped at the rain on his saddle horn. "I'd be obliged if you'd let me take you where you're going."

She looked for a moment as if she might consider it then shook her head. "As I said," she tossed over her shoulder, "go ahead and pass me by. I can get home just fine."

Off in the distance lightning zagged across the sky, and Joe counted the seconds until thunder rolled toward him. "Best I can tell, the worst of this storm's a good three miles east," he called. "So unless you're just about home, I figure you're not going to get a better offer than mine." He wanted to add, "Whoever you are," but instead held his tongue.

Another crack of lightning, this one close enough to feel, lit the worsening gloom. Thunder followed almost immediately, and with it came a strong east wind. Quick as that, the shadows had faded to near-darkness until the afternoon looked the same as night.

Joe knew immediately this was no normal autumn storm. "Looks like neither of us is going to get home dry," he said as he made an executive decision and spurred the horse on, "but at least we're both going to get home safe. When I reach you, jump."

"And if I don't?" From what he could see of the woman, her face held a little bit of arrogance and a whole lot of anxiety.

The rain plopped down in drops the size of half-dollars on the road between them, and the wind began to gust. He shouldn't tarry, nor could he leave her here.

"You'll still end up on my horse, miss," he said as he jammed his hat low on his head, "but I guarantee it won't be near as soft a landing."

She looked doubtful until a bolt of lightning cracked behind her.

With that, the horse tossed her head back and tried to shake the bit. "Settle down there," Joe muttered as he held tight to the reins. "Another minute and you can run for the barn."

He guided the stomping mare as close as he could to Yellow Bonnet; then, holding tight to the saddle with his left hand, he reached down to wrap his right arm around her waist. In a move he'd as yet practiced only with ornery goats back in San Antonio, Joe hauled the woman up and over the saddle then situated her across his lap sidesaddle.

With the added weight, the mare pranced and threatened to bolt. Or maybe it was the lightning, which was now so close Joe could almost feel the electrical charge as it hit a mesquite in the pasture up ahead. The woman squealed but never loosened her grip, even when the wind whipped the ribbons of her bonnet across her face.

"Hold on tight," he said. "I've got a good horse, but she's not keen on this kind of weather."

"Nor am I."

She wrapped her arms around him and grabbed two handfuls of his shirt as the mare took off like a shot, nearly sending them both tumbling backward. Only Joe's instincts kept him in the saddle, though they were seriously tested by the presence of the now-damp female.

"Where's home?" Joe asked when he regained his balance.

"Since nobody's moved the Rocking A, it's just down the road, Joe."

"The Rocking A?" He took his eyes off the road just long enough to glance at his companion. "You one of those Ames girls?"

"Yes," she said against his ear, though her voice was nearly hidden by the sound of the storm.

A gust of wind brought a torrent of rain, preventing any further conversation. So did the fact that Joe was acutely aware of the shoulder leaning against his and the scent of something flowery that seemed to come from beneath her bonnet. Then there were the arms wrapped around his back and belly.

A man who might consider any one of those things was a man who'd not get where he was supposed to be heading. Joe shook his head to clear the details and nearly lost his hat in the process. Thankfully the Ames girl caught it and placed it back where it belonged.

If only she'd taken a minute to set it on straight, he might have been able to see a little better. By the time the Ames ranch loomed ahead, however, the storm had grown to such proportions that Joe could barely guide the mare even if the brim of his Stetson hadn't shaded one eye.

Dense trees bordered both sides of the road, leading them over another hill and then down into a valley before the Ames home came into view. Set atop a hill with outbuildings behind it and the well off to the south, the ranch house was lit up downstairs and dark upstairs. Someone stood in the open door, likely Frank Ames.

Joe urged the mare up the hill while the Ames girl,

whichever one she was, kept her grip on his shirt until her pa raced out to pluck her from his saddle. Oddly, Joe felt the absence of the thin beauty immediately, though he could still smell the flowers even as the rain pelted his face.

Looking past the elder Ames to the younger one, Joe couldn't help but notice that whichever girl he'd returned to her pa, she was definitely the pretty one. Even in her sodden frock and flattened bonnet. Even as liquid ice poured down his neck and soaked him to the skin.

The woman paused on the porch to right her bonnet then gave up and tossed it aside. Hairpins went flying, revealing a length of glossy wet hair the color of mahogany.

Concentrate, Mueller. He still had another mile to go before the Vonheim house would welcome him, but at least he'd done his duty and delivered the lady to her doorstep.

" 'Preciate you bringing my girl home," Frank called as he ducked back onto the porch. "Come on in out of the weather."

Movement behind Frank Ames drew Joe's attention. There in the hallway was a blond-haired man. A man who could have easily been the man on Pale Indian's wanted poster.

Even though she knew she must be leaving a trail of water puddles behind her, Bess held her head high until she reached the safety of her bedroom. Only then, with the door solidly closed, did she sling the wet bonnet on the floor and remove her shoes and stockings.

Next, Bess stepped out of her skirt and dropped it beside her bonnet then fumbled with her petticoat. She'd only just washed her favorite yellow dress, and now she'd have to do it again. "And look at the mud caked on the hem. I'll be scrubbing for days to get that out."

Then she spied her reflection in the mirror atop her dressing table. "Of all the people to see me drenched like a wet hen, it would be Josef Mueller," she muttered as she pushed away the reminder of how it felt to lean against his muscled shoulder, to feel his arm around her, even if it was merely to keep her from falling and tripping his horse.

Oh, but hadn't the years been kind to Joe? And a Texas Ranger? "Mercy," she whispered. Then came the reminder in the form of the rhyme; her handsome hero had once been a school-yard bully with a wicked ability to rhyme and wound.

"Bessie Mae, plain as day. Well, isn't that the truth?"

Turning her back on the mirror, Bess made short work of changing into dry clothes then went back for her brush and wrangled her hair into submission. That feat accomplished, Bess walked to the window. Outside the fat pellets of rain peppered the pane and obscured the familiar landscape. She pressed her finger to the glass and traced the path of a raindrop, but her mind was back at the little schoolhouse on First Street. She was seven, not twenty-seven, and her papa told her almost every day that she was the prettiest girl in the second grade. Bess knew now that her father had learned to braid hair from the ranch foreman's wife, but back then she just thought he was good at braiding because he was good at everything.

Then came Josef Mueller, and she knew Pa hadn't been truthful with her. It was the second-worst day of her life.

"At least he's just visiting," Bess said as she rested her forehead on the cool glass pane. "Soon as Joe leaves, things'll get back to normal around here."

Then she thought of Ida Vonheim and the fact that her father would likely marry the woman sooner rather than later. Another drop traced a path down the glass, quickly followed by more, this time on the inside of the pane.

And this time they were teardrops.

Chapter 4

Ten minutes after he'd deposited Bess Ames at the front door of her Pa's house, Joe had the mare in a spare stall in the barn and was sitting at the kitchen table waiting for Frank Ames to pour coffee. Despite the offer of a towel, his damp clothes were sticking to him in places that made lingering uncomfortable, and there was a chill in the room. Still, he had a job to do, and finding out about the blond stranger came before creature comforts.

"You worked here long?" he asked the man who stood nervously in the doorway.

"Today's my first day," he said without meeting Joe's gaze.

"Cal's quite the roofer." Frank set a steaming mug in front of Joe then took the seat across from him. "Thanks to him we got the hole patched before the bottom fell out of those clouds."

"Where'd you live before you came to Horsefly, Cal?" Joe asked as casually as possible.

His ears turned red, and then, by degrees, the color spread to his face. Still he would not look at Joe.

"He's cousin to the Schmidts," Frank offered.

"Is that right?" Joe toyed with the edge of the towel. "Where'd you live before?"

This time Cal braved a glance in his direction. "San Antone," he said.

Joe's eyes narrowed. Had he found the man who might be Pale Indian so easily? It seemed so. "Why'd you leave?" he asked evenly then punctuated the question with a lift of his brow.

When Cal didn't answer immediately, Frank pushed back his chair and shook his head as he rose. "Ida tells me you're a ranger now, Joe."

He tore his attention from Cal to find Frank studying him. "Ida?"

"Ida Vonheim."

Joe couldn't help but notice it was Frank's turn to look embarrassed. *Interesting.*

"I am," he said. "Ranger company out of San Antone." Joe stared past Frank at Cal. "Sounds like you and I come from the same place. Small world, isn't it, Cal?"

"Sure is."

"I'll say." Frank shrugged. "Look at how you just happened to be coming down the road at the right time to save my Bess."

Joe nearly fell out of his chair. That gorgeous woman was... "Bess?" Bessie Mae, plain as day, had certainly blossomed in his absence.

Frank chuckled. "She lit out of here this morning with more spunk than good sense. I reckon she took exception to the fact I had Cal up on the roof helping instead of her." Another chuckle. "Ain't that right, Cal?"

Silence.

Cal was gone.

Frank shook his head then took a healthy gulp of coffee. "Don't mind him," he said as he set the cup back on the table. "He's not much for conversation."

Most bank robbers-turned-murderers aren't. "What do you know about him, Frank?"

The older man shrugged. "Gus Schmidt come by with him last week. Said his nephew was new in town and needed work. Said he'd vouch for him. Why?" He paused to narrow his eyes. "You're here on ranger business, aren't you?"

Joe only hesitated a moment before making the decision to draw Frank Ames into his circle of confidants. "I'm going to need your cooperation and your word that what I tell you won't leave this room before I answer that."

"You've got both," he said.

"No questions asked?"

"Don't need to," the rancher said. "Your daddy raised you to be a good God-fearin' man, and the state of Texas put a badge on your chest. That's good enough for me."

A sip of the strong brew, and Joe was ready to tell the tale. Choosing his words carefully, he caught Frank up on his reason for returning to Horsefly. "I'm not sure if Ben Kleberg wants me to take Tommy in or prove him innocent," he said. "I know what I'd prefer, but I've got to stay neutral."

Even as he said the words, Joe knew they weren't completely the truth. There was nothing he'd like better than to prove Pale Indian was someone—anyone—other than Tommy Vonheim.

Frank rose and walked to the stove then returned with the coffeepot to pour himself another cup. Joe waved away his offer of more then watched while the rancher studied him. Finally, he returned the pot to the stove.

"So either I've got a criminal for a neighbor or a criminal for an employee?"

Joe rose and carried his cup to set it in the sink. "Or neither."

The older man's expression was unreadable as he seemed to be considering both options. Finally, he straightened and stepped away from the stove. "All right, Ranger. How can I help you?"

"I'm already staying with Mrs. Vonheim, so I'll know if Tommy comes around." He paused to think a moment. "But I'll need access to your place, sir. If I'm going to keep an eye on Schmidt, it can't appear as though that's what I'm doing. I'll also need a cover story for anyone who wants to know why a ranger who's been long gone from Horsefly would return." A thought occurred. "And there's one more thing. Your daughter knows about Pale Indian."

He gave Joe a sideways look. "Oh?"

"Does Bess sell eggs in town? Maybe to the sheriff? She mentioned she did."

"She does. That's how she came to be walking back alone." He shook his head. "Actually, she generally takes the buggy, but she left here in a huff this morning. Guess I should've known she'd not take kindly to me dividing my time betwixt her and, well, I just should've talked to her first. Then maybe she wouldn't have left like she did." Frank must have realized he was rambling, for he smiled. "Guess it's too late for the short answer, but that would be yes, Sheriff Kleberg's usually the second stop on her morning route. I believe the emporium's first. Or maybe the mercantile. I rarely go with her, so forgive an old man for not remembering."

Frank Ames was hardly old, so he let the comment slide by without response. "Then it would be reasonable to assume she likely overheard something about Pale Indian while delivering eggs to the sheriff's office." He chose his words carefully. "You understand I will have to be certain of that before I can completely clear her."

"Clear her?" Gray brows rose. "Of what?"

Joe gave the man an even stare. "Until I told you about him, had you heard of Pale Indian?" When Frank shook his head, Joe continued. "Seems like the only folks who have besides the lawmen who want to catch him are his victims and his friends." Another pause. "I'd like to be sure she's neither of those."

"As would I, young man, but before we go any further, there's something else you need to know. I've got a connection to the Vonheim family that ought to be out in the open if I'm going to be involved in catching Tommy or setting him free."

"All right," Joe said, already guessing what that connection might be.

"That Ida Vonheim, she's quite a woman, and her husband was a good man, rest his soul. And, well. . ." Frank cleared his throat and looked away. "I believe the Lord's trying to put us together, Ida and me, though I'm just as certain Bess isn't so keen on it."

Not a complete surprise, as his hostess had mentioned Frank Ames more than once during their brief time together. Joe settled on a nod as the appropriate response.

Frank's attention returned to Joe. "She's never said it, but I wonder if being the last Ames girl still under my roof hasn't caused her some measure of discontent."

"Could be." Hard to believe that one hadn't been the first to wed, at least if beauty were a measure of marriageability. "Which one are you going to listen to, Frank?"

A slow smile began. "Wise words, young fellow. And as for this situation with the Indian fellow, I believe I've got an idea that just might work."

Joe glanced out the window and noted that the rain had let up considerably. Maybe he'd take a look around the Ames place before heading back to Ida's dinner table. Likely he could find the elusive Cal Schmidt and extract an answer or two.

"Joe, you want to hear my plan?"

He turned his attention to the rancher. "Sorry, sir. Yes, please."

"All right, so you've got a man to catch and I've got a daughter to protect."

"Protect? I'm not looking to arrest her. Just need to be sure she's—"

"I know all that." Frank waved away his protest. "What I mean is, if either Cal or Tommy is the man you're looking for, then my daughter's living in close proximity to a criminal and she doesn't know it. Bess is a friendly gal, and she's known Tommy since he was a kid in knee pants. Cal she's not so fond of yet, but he's right here sleeping in the bunkhouse. Then there's the issue of why you're in Horsefly. Can't exactly say you're hunting a local, now, can you?"

Joe waited while the man warmed to his topic.

"Yes, well, here's my idea, and understand I'm going to have to run it by the Lord before I decide it's something I'll be party to. But what say you tell folks you've come back to Horsefly on a mission of another sort?"

"A mission?" Joe shook his head. "What kind of mission would bring me back here? Most everyone knows

I'm a ranger and have been for years. What could possibly bring me back to Horsefly? And what does that mission have to do with finding Pale Indian and keeping your daughter safe?"

Frank Ames chuckled. "Oh, that's the best part, young man." He reached over to clasp his hand onto Joe's shoulder. "You're a ranger, all right, but word is you've been promoted to a desk job up there in San Antone. Is that right?"

"Well, I do spend less time on the trail than I used to. Why?"

The hand on his shoulder gripped tighter. "How old are you, Joe?"

"I'll be thirty-two come spring. Why?"

"A ranger in possession of a good salary and a desk job is surely going to start thinking about a wife, don't you think? And what better place than Horsefly, Texas, to find one?"

Shock rendered him speechless. Then came the sound of footsteps. Had Cal Schmidt returned? Automatically, Joe's hand went to the revolver at his side.

"Pa?" came a familiar female voice from somewhere on the other side of the wall.

"Come on in here, Bessie Mae," Frank Ames said with a wicked grin. "Ranger Mueller and I were just talking about you."

Chapter 5

anger Mueller?

Bess pasted on what she hoped would be a pleasant expression then allowed her father to give her a hug before facing Joe Mueller. "I didn't realize you were still here," she said to him. "If you'll excuse me, I'll leave you men to your conversation."

Before Pa or the ranger could respond, Bess scurried out the door and headed for the staircase. Her foot rested on the second riser from the top when Pa's voice stopped her cold.

"Elizabeth Ames, I've never tolerated rudeness in my home and I'm not about to start now."

Rude? Elizabeth?

She turned slowly while she adjusted her smile. There at the bottom of the stairs stood her father and Joe Mueller. While Pa wore a familiar irritated look, Joe just seemed to be staring, his soggy Stetson dangling from his left hand. Likely he rarely heard a grown woman being treated like a child.

And yet she knew she deserved the reproach. "I'm sorry, Pa. It was not my intention to offend."

Pa gestured to Joe. "Then you ought to come on down here and thank Ranger Mueller here for seeing you got home safe."

Back straight. Smile in place. Hand tight on the rail.

Bess made her way carefully down the stairs until she reached the bottom riser. This put her just above eye level with her school-yard tormentor. Though she planned to make amends with Joe as her father asked, she ignored the ranger to address Pa first. "Forgive my impertinence, Pa." True conviction hit her swift and hard. "Starting with this morning. My behavior was inexcusable."

Pa seemed surprised. "It was, but I do." The look on her father's face told her there would be more discussion on the topic later. "Well, all right then. I'll leave you two to finish this conversation." He turned to Joe and offered his outstretched hand. "I'll look forward to seeing you around the ranch, Joe."

Seeing you around the ranch? While Pa disappeared back into the kitchen, Bess worked her surprised expression back into something more neutral before turning her attention to the rain-soaked ranger.

Their gazes collided, and Bess tightened her grip on the rail. In the parlor, the clock struck the half hour.

"My father's right," she finally said. "I'm grateful to you for my safe return home." *Though I'll likely have bruises by nightfall.*

Joe ran his free hand through still-wet hair. "Though you'd likely have preferred not to have been tossed across my saddle like a sack of potatoes."

Actually. . . "You've got a point," she said. "A buggy might have been a bit more suited to the weather."

"A buggy." He paused. "I understand you went off without yours this morning."

Heat flooded her face. What else had Pa told the ranger? "It was a lovely morning for a walk."

Inwardly she groaned. *I sound like a silly schoolgirl.*

He didn't appear to know what to say next, so Bess decided to end the agony. "Well, I do thank you for all you did, Joe."

"What?" His shoulders straightened. "Oh yes, well, I should go. I'm sure Mrs. Vonheim will be wondering if I've drowned."

Mrs. Vonheim. She tried not to react to the mention of Pa's sweetheart.

"Something wrong?" Joe asked.

So it didn't work. "Wrong?" She shook her head. "No, nothing." *Nothing I'd be willing to tell you, anyway.*

Joe looked doubtful but, after a moment, set the hat on his head. "All right then. I suppose I ought to be going."

A scrape that could only be a kitchen chair against the wood floor echoed across the hall. "Joe, hold on there," Pa called.

So her father had been listening. Bess sighed and leaned heavily against the rail. She watched carefully. *What is Frank Ames up to?*

Joe turned and met Pa halfway. The pair shook hands and seemed to exchange glances before the ranger turned to leave. Or maybe she imagined it.

"Joe," Pa called as the ranger opened the door. "Bess makes a fine roast. What say you join us after church on Sunday? That would be nice, wouldn't it, Bess?"

"Nice," she echoed, unable to believe her ears.

Thankfully, Joe appeared ready to turn Pa down. At least that was what the undecided look seemed to say. "I'd have to be sure Mrs. Vonheim doesn't have plans to make her own Sunday dinner, though." He glanced over at Bess. "I'm staying at the Vonheim place while I'm here."

She gave a half nod, sufficient to let him know she heard.

"Then you'll definitely be here, because Ida told me just this afternoon that she'd be pleased to eat with us on Sunday."

Ida? Bess jerked her attention toward Pa as the words sunk in. "She did?"

"She did," her father said evenly.

"Well then, I'll see you both on Sunday." Joe tipped his hat to Bess then made good his escape.

When the door shut, Pa gestured for her to follow him into the kitchen. She did, reluctantly.

"I know what you're going to say, Pa," she said from

the doorway. "And before you do, you should know that I'm very happy you've found some measure of happiness with Mrs. Vonheim."

"You are?" Pa settled in a chair and rested his elbows on the table. "You sure?"

Bess sighed. "I'm sure I will be."

He smiled. "That's my girl. Now what's for supper?"

"Supper?" Bess asked. "I thought you were taking supper with Mrs. Vonheim."

"I changed my mind." Her father shrugged. "Figured I'd rather spend time with my daughter tonight."

"That's not the truth at all, is it, Pa?"

"Bess," came his warning tone. "I changed my mind, and that's that. Now if you don't mind, I'm going to go check on things in the barn while the rain's let up a bit." He rose. "Go on and get started. I'd like to get to bed early tonight. It's been a long day."

"All right, Pa, but don't expect kolaches."

He stopped at the door and glanced over his shoulder. "Why?"

"Let's just say there's not much left of the ones I bought in town this morning."

Pa started to laugh. "Oh no."

"Oh yes," Bess said. "And it's going to take more than one washing to get the remains out of my pocket."

"Next time I'll fetch them myself," he said with a chuckle.

"Next time I'll take the buggy." Bess attempted to keep

a straight face but soon joined her father in smiling even as she reached for the dish towel.

"Well, thank the Lord for Joe Mueller." When she didn't respond, Pa continued. "He's a good man, that Joe." A pause. "And he's spoken favorably of you."

Bess froze. "He's what?" She let the towel drop onto the counter. "How can he speak of me at all? Joe Mueller doesn't even know me anymore." *And when he did, he treated me awful.*

"Now don't you take that tone with me, Bess Ames. I believe the Lord led Joe here, and I'll not hear anything about it from you."

"Why would the Lord lead him here? According to Marian up at the sheriff's office, the ranger's based out of San Antonio, so technically if he's here at all, it's not to stay."

Pa crossed his arms over his chest. "So you've been discussing him as well?"

"I've done no such thing. But try and stop Miriam when she's busy telling a story." Bess turned back to her dishwashing.

"Yes, well, just promise me you'll give the ranger a chance, Bess."

"A chance?" She glanced at Pa over her shoulder. "What an odd thing to ask of me. What sort of chance would Joe Mueller be asking for anyway?"

"I suppose we'll find out soon enough," he said,

though Bess had the distinct impression her father already knew the answer to her question.

And that troubled her more than anything.

Chapter 6

The dining room smelled of roast beef and apple pie, and the table had been set in what was surely the Ames family's best china. Sunlight streamed through windows framed by curtains that matched the napkin stretched across his lap.

Joe looked across the table at Bess Ames, a vision in blue gingham, and wondered whether the pretty girl had forgotten how to smile. She'd certainly seemed unhappy when he slid into the Ames family pew at church this morning. When he sang, she frowned. And on the ride back from town, she'd failed to appreciate the fact he'd arrived in a buggy rather than on horseback, something he'd done just to make her grin. And she'd only ridden beside him because her pa insisted.

Neither had his gift of her missing egg basket made her happy, though it had cost him several lost hours while he searched for it along the road from town. A muttered thank-you was all he'd received, and even that seemed reluctant.

It was enough to make a man think he'd lost his ability to woo a woman. Not that he was trying to do that, of course, though it did wound him a bit when she missed his attempt to help her from the carriage and stepped right past him.

"Didn't the reverend have a nice sermon, Joe?" Mrs. Vonheim asked as she dabbed at her chin with her napkin.

"Yes, ma'am," Joe said. "I've heard some preaching in my day, but today was exceptional." He slid Bess a glance and noticed she seemed to be studying him. When Joe met her gaze, the Ames girl looked away.

"Bess, wasn't Ida's pie delicious?"

This time Bess met her father's stare. "It was," she said. "Might I have the recipe, Mrs. Vonheim?"

"Of course, dear," Ida said, "but only under one condition."

The Ames woman set her fork down. "What's that?"

Frank relaxed visibly and then offered Bess a smile before reaching to place his hand atop Ida's. "Why don't I show you that new foal we've got out in the barn, Ida?"

"I would like that very much," Ida said. "But might I have a word with Bess first?" She hesitated. "Alone, if you gentlemen don't mind."

Joe rose first, unwilling to witness any family trouble. While he was willing to keep to his agreement with Frank to watch over Bess, he had his limits.

By the time he reached the porch, Frank was on his heels. "I think it's going pretty well, don't you?"

"Depends on what you're trying to accomplish, Frank." Joe stepped off the porch, avoiding the patch of mud still remaining from the deluge of the last two days. "I'd give that conversation that's about to happen even odds on whether it's going to be good or bad."

Frank clapped his hand on Joe's shoulder. "Have faith, boy," he said. "Ida and I have been praying about this."

"Well, good," he said. "Now about your employee Cal. I spoke to Sheriff Kleberg yesterday afternoon."

"And?"

"And it turns out Kleberg's known Cal since he was a kid. Something about Kleberg's wife and Cal's grandmother being kin." Joe shrugged. "It's enough to satisfy me for now, but I'm still not convinced. The sheriff's going to check out the suspect's whereabouts for the past month."

"The suspect?" Frank stopped short. "You sure you're still remaining neutral?"

"I'm trying," Joe said.

"Well, that's all we can ask, now, isn't it?" Joe pointed to the toolshed. "If you've got a few minutes, I'd like to show you the pistol I found behind the well yesterday."

"Pistol?" Joe shook his head. "Why didn't you mention this sooner?"

"Because it's an old flintlock, Joe, and not in any condition to be shot. Likely carried downhill with the flood. Have you ever seen one of them?"

"I have," Joe said, "but it's been awhile. Mind showing me?"

"Come with me. I've got it taken apart so I can clean it, but I think you'll still find it interesting." Frank turned toward the shed, and Joe followed. "About Bess, I couldn't help but notice things are a bit cool between the two of you."

Joe stepped over the rocky outcropping. "I don't know what I'm doing wrong, Frank. At this rate no one in Horsefly's going to believe I came here to make a wife out of Bess Ames. Why, she won't even give me the time of day." He paused. "I'd appreciate any advice you might give me. Otherwise, I'm going to forget about this plan and come up with another one."

"I wonder if maybe. . ." Frank paused to gesture toward the road. "There's somebody coming."

Joe followed his gaze to see the lone figure riding toward them. It only took him a minute to recognize the rider.

"Tommy."

"Bess, I'd like to speak to you woman to woman." Ida Vonheim settled back against her chair and rested her hands in her lap. "And not to talk pie recipes."

"All right." Bess fumbled with the napkin then set it aside to give her attention to the blue-eyed woman at the head of the table.

"I understand your father's spoken to you about me." Her gaze never wavered, even when Bess remained silent. "I love him, Bess, but I won't come between a father and daughter, and I'd never dream of taking the place of your mother in your heart."

Well, that wasn't what she'd expected.

The older woman sighed. "So I'm here to turn propriety on its ear and ask you for your blessing on our relationship."

"My blessing?" The words soured in her mouth. "But I don't have the right to—that is, my father's a grown man and he—"

"And he would never hurt you, Bess. Unless you approve of us, I'll leave him to you." She rose. "Much as it will pain me and, likely, Frank, I'll do it to keep from driving a wedge in this family."

Something softened inside Bess. "You do love him, don't you?"

"I do."

"As do I." Bess rose as tears threatened. Ida Vonheim held out her arms, and Bess fell into them.

"Well, aren't you two chummy?"

Bess stepped out of the older woman's arms to see Tommy Vonheim standing in the doorway. Behind him were Pa and Joe Mueller.

"Am I too late to get a plateful of whatever it is that smells so good in here?"

In between bites, Tommy entertained the group with tales of life on the railroad. By the time the last piece of pie had been consumed, Bess remembered why she'd always enjoyed her neighbor's company.

If only he hadn't been best friends with Joe Mueller.

"Much as I hate to eat and leave, I'd love to see my own bed tonight," Tommy finally said. "And my mother looks as if she might be tired as well."

Mrs. Vonheim didn't look that way at all to Bess, but she said nothing, and neither did Ida. While Pa walked mother and son out, Joe remained behind. "I'll help with the dishes, Bess," he said, rolling up his sleeves.

"No need." She turned her back and hauled an armload of dishes into the kitchen then reached for the pump to fill the sink.

A sound behind her told Bess that Joe had ignored her. One more trip to the kitchen and he'd cleared the table. *Maybe he'll leave now,* she thought.

But he didn't. Finally, Bess had enough of the lawman standing behind her. She whirled around to face him, prepared to do battle.

"Go home, Joe Mueller," she said. "There's nothing else for you here."

He appeared to consider her statement. A curt nod, and the ranger walked out, leaving her alone with her thoughts. She'd already returned to her work at the sink when she heard footsteps heading her way.

Good. It was time to talk to her father about making

peace with Ida Vonheim. "Pa," she called as she reached for the dish towel to dry her hands. "I've got something to tell you."

"It's me, Bess," Joe said. "Not your father."

Bess threw the towel onto the counter but remained in place. Words escaped her. A good thing considering the fact she'd likely need to apologize should her thoughts be heard.

"Turn around, please," he said then waited until she did. "There's something I'm long overdue in saying."

She complied and found that Joe Mueller had moved closer than she expected. He reached out to touch her sleeve. "Bess, I did you wrong back in school, and I never have made it right." Joe shrugged. "If I could go back and change things, I would, but all I can do now is ask you if you'll forgive me for that awful rhyme I made up about you." He paused to grasp her wrist. "Will you? Forgive me, that is?"

All those things Bess had planned to say to Joe some-day dissolved under his even stare. "Forgive you?" she whispered. "I—that is, there's nothing to forgive."

His expression told her he didn't believe a word of it. Bess looked away to study the pattern on the kitchen rug. "All right, it did hurt." She lifted her gaze to meet his. "A lot."

"Bess," he said softly as he released her wrist. "I was such an idiot. I would have said anything for a laugh."

She hid her trembling hands in the pockets of her

apron. "The fact it was true didn't mean you should say it."

"Oh, Bess." This time when he reached for her, it was to touch her shoulder. "When I look at you now, I can't believe I ever thought you were. . ."

Her eyes found his. "Bessie Mae, plain as day?"

"Not anymore." Joe leaned toward her and brushed his knuckles against her cheek as he moved a strand of hair from her face. "You've grown into such a—"

The front door slammed shut, and Joe took a step backward. "Joe, you still here?" Pa called.

"I am, sir," Joe responded as he scrubbed at his face with his palms. "In the kitchen with Bess."

"Good, because I decided to go fetch that flintlock. It's in pieces, but I think—" Pa rounded the corner with something in his hands then stopped short. "Oh, I'm interrupting."

"No," they said in unison.

"What is that, Pa?" Bess asked as she swiped at her eyes with the dish towel.

"You're crying, Bess Ames." He turned to Joe. "What did you say to upset her?"

"It's fine," she said, "and Joe didn't say anything to upset me." She glanced up at Joe. "Everything's fine, isn't it?"

"Yes," he said with the beginning of a smile. "It's fine."

"All right then," Pa said. "If you don't mind, Bess, I'm

going to show the ranger this flintlock I found out by the well."

"No, go right ahead," she said. "We were done." Bess turned back to tackle the dinner dishes, all the while listening to the conversation between the men.

"And you found it in the mud?"

"Saw the barrel sticking out of the mud after the big rain the other day," Pa said.

"It looks as if it was buried only a short time." Joe paused. "See, the only damage seems to be to the wooden stock and mother-of-pearl decoration. If it had been in the mud very long, you wouldn't have any of that."

"What do you make of it, Ranger?"

"It's a mystery," Joe said, "but lucky for you, Mr. Ames, I specialize in solving mysteries." The men shared a laugh; then Joe continued. "The gun seems familiar," he said. "So I'll ride into town tomorrow and send a telegram to headquarters to find out if someone's reported it missing or stolen." A pause. "After Tommy and I have a chat, that is."

"Yes," Pa said. "Been awhile since you two spoke, ain't it?"

"Too long. I'll have to find out why that railroad of his doesn't take him through San Antonio." A pause. "Or maybe it does. I bet there are records to answer that one. I'll make a note to check."

"Yes, Joe, you'd need to know that so next time he's in town, you two can get together and catch up."

Odd, but Pa's tone sounded anything but natural. In fact, their conversation had veered from casual to downright odd.

Bess turned to peek at the item they were inspecting and recognized it immediately. "That's Tommy's gun. Remember, Pa? He used to come over and shoot cans off the well with Lucy because his mother didn't like him shooting at their place."

Pa gave her a strange look. "Why didn't I know about this?"

She shrugged. "Probably because you wouldn't have liked it had you known Lucy was shooting that old thing. I told her it looked dangerous, but she'd laugh every time."

Joe tapped his temple with his forefinger. "Maybe that's why it seems familiar to me," he said, though Bess could tell he wasn't completely convinced. "I'll let you know when I hear back from headquarters."

"Speaking of headquarters," Bess said, "shouldn't you be going back soon?"

Soon as the question was out, Bess knew it was the wrong thing to ask. Pa's frown told her as easily as Joe's surprised look.

"I'm not trying to hurry you," she quickly amended. "Just wondered."

The ranger seemed to study her a moment. In truth, she'd only blurted out the question because the thought of his leaving was suddenly something that didn't appeal.

Hadn't he almost told her she was anything but plain as day?

"I'm in contact with headquarters, but I don't have a timetable for heading back just yet." Joe gave her a sideways look. "Well, long as we're wondering about things, I've got something I'm wondering, too."

"What's that?" Pa asked.

The ranger turned to Bess. "I'm wondering if you'd take a buggy ride with me tomorrow, Bess."

" 'Course she will," Pa offered as he looked past Joe to dare Bess to argue.

Chapter 7

When Joe stepped out into the chill night air, Tommy and his mother were long gone. He took a deep breath and held it until his lungs burned then let it out slowly. The ritual helped him focus, a habit he'd learned on the trail.

The ranger in him had waited all evening for some sign that his friend had gone wrong. Anything—a word, a gesture, a mark on him—that might confirm what the sheriff claimed. Thus far, he'd only seen Tommy Vonheim, long-lost friend and railroad man.

Only once had he felt ire rise against the German, and that was when he'd paid a bit too close attention to Bess Ames. The joke they'd shared was something he now could not recall, but the way she looked at him, the smile she offered. . . . That had nearly sent him across the table—stupidity normally reserved for pimple-faced youths.

This fact alone made Joe want to avoid Bess Ames altogether. For somewhere between saving her from a rainstorm and promising her pa to keep a watch on her, he'd started thinking too much about her.

He barely knew the woman, and yet tonight in the kitchen he'd have kissed her if Frank hadn't walked in. *Kissed her.* Joe shook his head. A ranger never loses his focus. It could mean the difference between life and death. And with Tommy back, so could it mean the difference in catching Pale Indian or letting more innocent lives be lost.

This thought carried him back to the Vonheim place, where he paused on the porch to listen to mother and son carrying on what sounded like a spirited conversation. "I am careful," Tommy said.

The cry of a barn owl broke through the night's silence, obscuring the sounds inside. When the bird's call ended, so had the discussion in the parlor. Joe reached for the doorknob only to find the door fly open.

"I wondered when you'd come inside," Tommy said. Eyes as blue as spring flowers stared at him. He'd caught many a woman's attention with those eyes. Somehow the weaker sex seemed to be taken in by this fluke of nature, though Joe had never understood it. Now Joe stared back, wondering if he was looking into the face of a friend or a cold-blooded killer.

"It's cold out here."

"I like it," Joe said. "Long as I've got a bed to sleep in,

I don't mind the weather."

"That's right—you're a ranger." Tommy stepped onto the porch and let the door close behind him. "Funny how that turned out. I always said I'd be the one who turned lawman."

"You wanted to track down your pa's killer." Soon as the words were out, Joe realized his mistake. The genial expression on Tommy's face had gone south, and in its place was a steely look that masked any emotion.

"How long's it been since you were in Horsefly?" Tommy finally asked. "I was just trying to figure that out."

"More'n ten years, I'd say." Joe leaned against the porch rail and stared past the small yard to the pasture and the sparse mesquites beyond. Here and there a patch of limestone rock seemed to glow brilliant white under the winter moon. "Nothing much has changed. I'll admit that. Town's a little bigger. That's about it."

Tommy chuckled, or at least it sounded that way. "Never well, far as I can tell." He came to stand beside Joe. "So why now?"

Joe shot him a look. "What do you mean?"

"I mean, why come back here now?" The owl hooted again, and Tommy turned in that direction, offering Joe a profile that had changed little since grade school. He was taller—fully over six feet—and broader across the shoulders, but other than that, Tommy Vonheim was the same kid who chased squirrels and knocked tin cans off walls with slingshots alongside Joe all those years.

The same kid who'd shared his mama when Joe no longer had one of his own. In the spirit of that friendship, Joe reached over to clasp Tommy on the shoulder. "A man needs a place to come back to now and then, don't you think?"

Tommy seemed to consider the statement a moment. "I suppose he does." He paused. "But doesn't he also need a reason to return?"

The casual tone was gone. Joe's ranger training kicked in as he straightened his backbone and turned to face his friend. "I'm afraid you've caught me."

His eyes went wide then narrowed. "Oh?"

Joe stuffed his fists into his pockets and shrugged. "I'm after someone."

Tommy froze. Then, by degrees, a smile began. "Anyone I know?" his friend finally asked.

"Could be." Joe let his arm fall to gently rest on his sidearm. "I'm still trying to figure it out."

It was Tommy's turn to face him. "Oh, that's priceless, Joe. Let me figure it out for you."

Fingers tightened on the gun, though Joe kept his face neutral. As far as he could tell, Tommy wasn't carrying a weapon; but he'd never been a man to depend on supposition.

"You always did have a crush on Bess Ames. Everyone but you could see it." Tommy snorted with glee. "Makes sense you'd finally come back for her," he said as he gave Joe a playful nudge. "Though I'll tell you you'd best marry up with her before I decide to. She's a real stunner, and smart to boot. Wait. That intelligence of hers might work against you."

Joe released his grip on the gun and let relief wash over him as he joined in the laughter. Shooting a friend on his mother's porch wasn't in the plans for tonight, especially when he hadn't proven his guilt or innocence yet.

Abruptly Tommy stepped toward the door. "It's cold out here. Come on in and have a beer with me like old times."

Joe shook his head. "Don't touch the stuff anymore."

Tommy gave him a look of disbelief before reaching for the doorknob. "You are getting old," he said as he disappeared inside.

"With age comes wisdom," he replied, praying it was the truth.

"Bundle up, Bess," Pa called from the dining room. "There's a chill in the air. And be sure to take him past that little plot where you're going to be putting in a garden. There's a pretty view from the bluff up there."

"Say, Pa, I've got a great idea. Why don't you go on this silly buggy ride with him?" Bess said as she gathered her wrap around her shoulders. "Since you're taking such an interest in all this."

"Don't be impudent."

"Then don't play matchmaker." Bess stuck her head in the kitchen doorway and spied her father immersed in today's edition of the *Horsefly Herald Gazette*. "You're not very good at it."

Pa snorted and went back to reading his paper. A knock at the door sent Bess back into the hallway. There she found Cal. "There's a horse and buggy coming up the road, ma'am," he said as he studied the ceiling.

"Thank you, Cal." She moved toward the door, leaving her father's ranch hand in the hall. When he followed her outside, Bess found herself in the uncomfortable position of having to make conversation with a man who seemed unable to speak.

"So you're cousin to the Schmidts," she finally said.

Cal nodded but offered nothing further. Bess glanced down the hill and willed Joe to hurry.

When Cal moved to stand beside her, Bess searched her mind to find another topic to discuss. "So," she finally said, "how did you come to be in Horsefly?"

The Schmidt cousin's face flushed bright red. "You ask a lot of questions."

"I do?" Joe's carriage came over the rise. Now he was close enough for her to hear the horse's hoofbeats. "I'm sorry."

Cal looked away. "Family," he said softly. "A man reaches a point and he needs family. Especially at Christmastime."

"Yes," she said slowly. *Family at Christmastime.*

Much as she rarely admitted it, Bess missed her sisters. With Charlsey, Lucy, and Sarah all happily married and spread to the four corners of creation, it was hard to remember a time when they'd all been under the same roof.

A plan hatched, and Bess tucked it away for consideration after she returned from her excursion with Joe. "I think you're right. Family's important."

She waved to Joe then excused herself to Cal, who glanced at his watch then back at her. "Would you tell the ranger I'll be right back?"

"Yes'm," he said softly. "I'll tell him."

Bess slipped inside and tiptoed toward the kitchen, pausing in the doorway to watch her father for a moment. With his spectacles affixed to the end of his nose and the graying temples he'd sported recently, it was obvious Frank Ames was no spring chicken. And yet he certainly wasn't too old for the plan she hoped she could carry out.

"Pa," she called. "Got a minute?"

"'Course I do, Bessie." He set the newspaper back down and slid the glasses off his nose to place them atop the *Herald Gazette*. "But didn't I hear the ranger coming up the road?"

"You did, but I've got Cal entertaining him." She settled on the chair beside her father. "Pa, I never got to tell you what happened when Mrs. Vonheim and I had our chat."

He shook his head. "Didn't figure I needed to know. A man's shy of asking about what goes on among womenfolk."

She smiled and reached to touch his hand. "I like her."

Her father lifted his gaze to meet hers. "I like her, too, Bessie Mae."

"I know you do." Bess contemplated her words before continuing. "Maybe it's time, Pa."

"Time?" He shook his head. "Want to explain that?"

"Not really," she said as she rose. "Besides, I don't think I need to."

"Bess," her father called when she'd reached the hallway.

She backtracked to peer around the door frame. "What is it?"

"Stick close to the ranger, honey," he said as he reached for his spectacles and set them in place on his nose. "You never know what's out there, and he's a man trained to protect a lady."

Bess shook her head. "What sort of silliness is that? This is Horsefly, Texas. Nothing ever happens here."

Chapter 8

Joe slapped the reins and set the horses to a fine trot once they left the winding ranch road for the wider avenue to town. "A fine day for a drive," he said to the beautiful brunette at his side.

Only then did he notice that Bess had worn the same yellow dress as the day he met her at this very spot on the road. In the rain. With her shoulder pressed against his and the smell of flowers in her hair.

He swallowed hard and turned his attention to the road ahead. To the right was the Schmidt place. Joe made a note to call on Mr. Schmidt. Though everything about Cal Schmidt had checked out, he still found it hard to let the ranch hand leave his suspect list so easily.

What he couldn't decide was whether it was because he didn't believe the fellow was truly innocent or because to admit Cal wasn't Pale Indian was to start believing Tommy was.

Sliding Bess a sideways look, he found her staring at him. "Where are we going?'"

"I thought we'd take a drive through town first."

What Joe didn't say was he'd been asked one too many times at church last Sunday why he was still in Horsefly. A ranger didn't stay in one place longer than it took to capture the bad guy unless he was either retired or. . .well, there wasn't any other reason.

So he'd decided it was time to take Frank Ames's plan to heart. Though Bess didn't know it, today was the day she'd be introduced to the people of Horsefly as Joe Mueller's potential sweetheart.

He sighed. Something about the ruse didn't sit right with him, but he was unwilling to try to figure out which part.

So if Bess wondered why a glorious day that could be spent in the country would involve the busy streets of Horsefly, she didn't let on. Rather, she smiled, toyed with her bonnet strings, and then leaned back to lift her face to the sun.

Maybe Tommy was right. Maybe he had been carrying a torch for Bess Ames since grade school. His heart sure did a flip-flop when he looked at her. And she was a fine woman from a fine family.

What was it her pa had said? A ranger in possession of a good salary and a desk job was surely going to start thinking about a wife. Was he?

No. Not when Pale Indian had yet to be caught.

Joe was awfully quiet. He'd hardly spoken on the drive to town. Now with the buildings of Horsefly in view, he seemed no more talkative. She was about to say something when he pulled up on the reins and guided the horses to a stop in a sunny outcropping well off the road. From there she could see the town in the valley below and the shimmering water of the Guadalupe River.

"I owe you an apology, Bess."

"Another one?" she asked lightly. "This has become quite the habit of yours."

It was flirting, plain and simple, and Bess felt the fool as soon as the ridiculous statement was out. What business did a twenty-seven-year-old spinster have playing the coquette to a broad-shouldered Texas Ranger?

He gestured toward town, seemingly oblivious to her silliness. "I have a selfish reason for taking this route."

"Oh?"

A nod. "I'd like it very much if everyone in Horsefly could see you riding by my side." With that, he slapped the reins and set the horses back on the road toward town. As the buggy picked up speed going downhill, Bess felt her bonnet ribbons give way.

"Stop, Joe. I did it again," she called as the bonnet flew from her head and landed somewhere behind them.

He hauled back on the reins and brought the horses to a stop. "What's wrong?"

Bess pointed to her head then shrugged, again feeling

like the fool. "I've lost my bonnet. You see, I have this habit of worrying with the ribbons, and what with the wind and all, it just...oh, I'm rambling." She leaned forward to escape the buggy, only to feel Joe's hand on her arm.

"Wait here and I'll go after it."

When Joe didn't immediately return, Bess rose to turn around and see if she could spy him. Failing that, she slid over and took the reins to turn the buggy around. That was when she saw him facedown on a limestone ledge, his arms outstretched.

Pa's warning came back to her now. *Stick close to the ranger. You never know what's out there.*

"Joe," she called. No response, so she tried again.

Now she had to choose: Leave Joe and go for help, or leave the buggy to help Joe. She chose the latter, bounding from the buggy with her skirts flying. Rather than announce her presence to whomever had sent the ranger down the canyon, Bess elected to move as silently as possible as she picked her way from rock to rock until she was almost close enough to touch the still-prone ranger.

From her vantage point, Bess could see that while his body remained still, his right arm seemed to be grasping at something. "Joe?" she whispered. "Are you hurt?"

This time he turned his head in her direction, his face flushed. "No. Go back to the buggy."

Bess surveyed the situation then returned her attention to him. "But I—"

"The buggy, Bess. Go. Back."

Reluctantly she nodded. Rather than retrace her steps, Bess circled around the ranger. When she reached the other side of the outcropping, she realized the problem.

"You're stuck."

He lifted his head to stare in her direction. If this expression was what criminals saw, no wonder the ranger had such good luck catching them.

Swallowing hard, Bess moved forward a half step. There she could see his fist wedged between two limestone boulders, the strings of her bonnet dangling in his fingers.

"Your hand. You can't . . ." Giggles threatened, but she managed to tame them by looking away. "Let go of the bonnet," she said, "and then you can pull your hand out."

Joe shook his head.

"Stubborn man."

His glare wasn't as effective given his position, but he seemed not to notice.

"All right then," she said. "I'll have to come and fetch the bonnet."

Bess made her way with ease over the rocky terrain, her skill honed after a lifetime of skittering up and down the hills on the ranch. In no time, she reached the ranger and thrust her hand toward the bonnet.

"Here," she said as she snagged the yellow fabric. "I've got it. Now let go and—"

That was when the rocks slid from beneath her, carrying Bess and the bonnet down the canyon.

The slide wounded Bess's pride more than anything else. This she realized when she came to a stop against a boulder firmly embedded in the side of the hill.

She set her bonnet atop her head but hadn't time to tie the ribbons before Joe Mueller came bounding down the rocky incline. He caught her in his arms and held her to his chest, nearly knocking the breath out of her.

"I thought I'd lost you," he said. "You were there and then you were just gone."

Bess could hear his heart racing even as hers began to match it. "I was careless," she said as she braved a look up into his eyes. "Took a step without looking."

"Yes." His face was close. Too close. "You did."

"I forgot," she said, her voice reduced to a whisper, "to look where I was going."

He blinked, and impossibly long lashes swept high, tanned cheekbones. "Yes," he said softly, "sometimes that's how it happens."

"Yes, sometimes. . ." Words blew away with any remaining lucid thoughts as she leaned against a broad and familiar shoulder.

"Sometimes," he echoed, "it's better to go ahead and let go."

Her last sane act was to look into his eyes. The hands that held tight to his arms should have pushed him away. Instead, she held on tight and closed her eyes.

Besides, she was a twenty-seven-year-old spinster, and nothing ever happened in Horsefly, Texas.

Chapter 9

I t was only a kiss. That's what Joe told himself when he repeated it. Twice.

From her lack of understanding of the technique, he easily deduced it was her first. And second. And third.

"Bess," he said against silky hair that indeed smelled as flowery as he remembered. "You've dropped the bonnet again."

Dark eyes opened and then widened even as she tried to move backward. Pinned as she was between a rock and a ranger, there was no place to go.

Acting the gentleman was never so difficult, and yet Joe knew he must. He rose and dusted off his trousers then stepped past her to retrieve the troublesome bonnet. By the time he returned, he found Bess sitting on the rock fretting over a smudge of dirt on her dress.

Gently he set the bonnet atop her head then, with trembling fingers, tied the ribbons into some version of a bow. Doubling the strings over, the bow became a knot.

"There," he said. "Now it won't come off."

Bess peered up at him, seemingly unable to move. He was about to ask if she'd somehow been injured in the fall or, heaven forbid, during the kiss, when she blinked hard and cleared her throat.

"Joe," she said softly. "Why did you kiss me?"

Why indeed? Any number of reasons occurred, but Joe couldn't find his voice. Finally, he managed a smile. "Because," he said as he offered her his hand, "I fell."

Dark brows gathered. "What does that mean?"

"Bess," he said as easily as he could, "don't ask me to explain."

Her stare confounded him with its innocence. How long had it been since he'd met a woman like Bess Ames, let alone kissed one?

"Why not?" she asked as she let him help her to her feet.

Joe looked beyond Bess to the canyon and the Guadalupe below. From where they stood, a good part of Texas was visible. No, he amended, *the* good part of Texas.

"Turn around and look at that," he said to Bess as he steadied her with his arm around her waist. "What do you see?"

"Is that a trick question?"

She glanced over her shoulder at him, and he saw the bee-stung look of lips he'd only just kissed, causing him to almost forget his point. Clearing his throat, Joe forced his gaze back on the expansive landscape. "That's home, Bess." He pointed to the horizon. "*Your* home."

Bess stiffened in his arms. "Oh, I see what you're saying. Well, don't worry about me, Joe Mueller." She whirled around, her back straight, and began making her way toward the road. "Don't expect me to be one of those women who kisses a man then expects him to marry her. Because I'm not. I'm just not, and even a kiss like yours—"

"Three kisses," he corrected as he followed in her wake.

"Three kisses like yours," she amended as she crossed the rocky ground as nimbly as a deer despite her womanly attire. "Nevertheless, I'm a woman of the world, Joe, and I understand that while these things happen, there's no need to lay claim to someone just because he—"

That was where he stopped her—with a fourth kiss. This time right there in full view of the horses, the buggy, and Cal Schmidt, who happened to be riding by with his uncle, his aunt, and their eight children.

While Joe went over to shake hands with the men, Bess did her best to endure the reproachful stare of Mrs. Schmidt. A curt nod was all she could manage before slinking back to the buggy, knowing every grass stain and smudge of dirt would be highly visible on the yellow frock. And from what she knew of Mrs. Schmidt's ability to spy a misbehaving child from long distances during Sunday school, it was very likely the woman was taking inventory at this very moment.

Before she came to town for tomorrow's egg delivery, Bess would likely already be the topic of conversation, for the other thing she knew about Mrs. Schmidt was that she adored offering up juicy tidbits clothed as prayer requests.

She sank back against the cushions of the buggy seat and waited until she heard Joe's boots approach. "I'm horrified," she said as he slid onto the seat beside her. "I'm sorry, Joe. I don't know what came over me. I've caused you quite the problem and I know it. It's just that I—"

Kiss five silenced her.

"Bess," he said, work-roughened hands still caressing her cheeks, "if you don't stop talking, I'm not going to be able to stop shutting you up with kisses, and then we really will have a problem."

His expression told her he meant it.

Bess lifted her forefinger to her lips and pressed it there. A nod told him she agreed, and he responded with one of his own. Too soon, the buggy was in motion.

"What are you doing?" she asked when she felt the contraption turning back toward town. "You can't parade me through town with a stained dress and Mrs. Schmidt's tales leading the way."

The ranger leaned her way and brushed her cheek with his lips. She decided that one was kiss five and a half.

"Only the guilty slink away, Bess Ames. Now sit up straight, and for goodness' sake, leave those bonnet strings alone."

Moments later the buggy rolled into Horsefly with Bess doing her best impression of an innocent woman. *It was just a kiss*, she told herself. *And likely the only ones you'll get.*

"Ranger, Ranger," someone called.

Joe pulled up on the reins and swiveled to greet the telegraph operator. "Got something here for you," he said before tipping his hat to Bess. "Ma'am," he said.

She returned the greeting while she watched Joe's eyes scan the page. A moment later, he folded the telegram and stuffed it into his pocket.

"Something wrong?" she asked.

His nod was curt, his manner giving away nothing of the man who'd just kissed her in the canyon. "If you don't mind, I need to make a stop at the sheriff's office."

"No, of course," she said. "I'll find something to do, so don't worry yourself."

In his haste to leave the buggy, Joe barely acknowledged she'd spoken. Before she could blink twice, the ranger had disappeared into the sheriff's office, leaving her sitting in the middle of Horsefly with stains on her dress.

All she could do was hide behind her bonnet and wave to anyone who might recognize her until Joe finally bounded back out onto the sidewalk with Sheriff Kleberg right behind him.

"Think about my offer," the old sheriff called.

Joe seemed to be waving him away. "Not until this is handled," he said.

"Understood." The sheriff looked past Joe to make eye contact with Bess. "Howdy, Miss Ames," he called. "Nice day for a drive."

"Yes, isn't it, Sheriff Kleberg?"

"Give my best to your pa," he said before giving Joe one last look and disappearing inside.

"Joe," Bess said carefully, "is everything all right? You look troubled."

The ranger shrugged off her question. "It's fine, Bess. Just fine."

And with that they were off, heading back to the ranch the same way they came: in silence. It took all Bess could do not to fiddle with her bonnet strings as they neared the canyon. From the looks of Joe's expression, he could use another detour and several more kisses.

Bess sighed. And so could she.

No, she decided. Any further kissing she did with Ranger Josef Mueller would be done in such a manner that she was neither hiding nor ashamed. She'd learned her lesson during the seemingly endless time she'd sat waiting for Joe.

A woman worth kissing was a woman worth wedding. And if Joe only wanted to toy with her affections, he'd have to find someone else to kiss.

As Joe pulled the buggy to a stop in front of her house,

Bess opened her mouth to tell Joe exactly that. Editing the marriage part, of course, for a lady would never bring up the subject of marriage to a man, even if she were a twenty-seven-year-old spinster and he an eligible single ranger with an uncanny ability to silence her with a kiss.

Unfortunately, Pa and a half dozen ranch hands were gathered near the barn, and Joe headed their way as soon as he lifted Bess out of the buggy and set her feet on the ground.

Not even a good-bye did he spare her, the cad.

"Well," she said loudly enough for him to hear, "of all the nerve." And with that she stormed inside even as her curiosity begged her to stay and listen to the men as they threw about words like "pistol" and "arrest warrant."

"No," she said as she bounded up the stairs. She couldn't care less what anyone said about anything right now. Joe Mueller had just kissed and fled, and that was an unpardonable sin.

Throwing open her bedroom door, she aimed for her bed then found it occupied.

By Tommy Vonheim.

Chapter 10

"S o the gun was Tommy's after all?" Frank asked as his ranch hands gathered around.

"It was, and that's what's going to get him caught." Joe offered the telegram to Frank.

"Says here the fellow who was caught with him in San Antone identified a flintlock pistol as Pale Indian's weapon of choice."

"Guess the fact he was facing the gallows loosened his tongue." Joe heard a scream and ran. "Bess," he called as he threw open the front door. "Bess, where are you?"

All he heard was the ticking of the parlor clock. Then came the muffled noises at the top of the stairs. Joe glanced behind him and saw the ranch hands bounding up the porch steps. "Wait," he said then met them on the porch. "You three go that way and cover the back. You," he said as he gestured to a pair of tall fellows, "one on each side of the house. The rest will cover Frank and me." He paused. "You all armed?"

Satisfied they were, Joe gave them one more warning. "Keep your weapons at the ready, and if anyone except me, Bess, or Frank here comes your way and you don't like the looks of 'em, shoot to kill."

Frank nodded his approval and the men scattered. "You thinkin' there's trouble with Bess?"

Joe gave the rancher a sideways look. "I've got a feeling there's always going to be some kind of trouble with Bess." He chuckled. "And likely I'm overreacting. But knowing what we know now, I'm going to have to be cautious until Vonheim's in custody."

"So he's Vonheim now?" Frank asked. "What happened to Tommy?"

"Tommy was my friend, Frank. Vonheim's a killer and he needs to be brought to justice." Another muffled sound stole his attention.

"Likely she's dropped her hairpins again," Frank said. "She's prone to doing that. Well, that and her bonnet. She worries with those ribbons until I'm surprised they don't fall off. Always did, even as a little girl. Why, her mama used to—"

A scream split the silence. Joe bounded up the stairs, grasping for his revolver. "Which room's hers?"

Frank showed him. It was locked.

"Bess," he called. "Open the door."

Silence.

"Bess?" Joe threw his shoulder into the door twice

357

before it flew open. There he found Bess crumpled on the floor. Beside her knelt Pale Indian.

The hat. The clothing. The Indian moccasins. All of these things he remembered from the alley behind the livery in San Antonio.

The face he knew from childhood as his friend Tommy Vonheim.

Joe leveled the revolver at the Indian. "Back away from her."

"I didn't mean to hurt her," he said. "I was trying to get her to hear me out and she wouldn't do it. She just kept telling me I had to leave and she wouldn't listen." He was almost in tears now, this man Joe barely recognized. "Frank," he continued, "you're why I'm here."

Joe tore his eyes from Vonheim for just a moment as Bess roused. "Stay put," he ordered her, and she either listened and complied or was unable to defy him. Joe preferred to believe the first option.

"What've I got to do with anything, Tommy?" Frank asked.

"I want you to take care of Mama." He shook his head. "I don't know that I'm worth getting a blessing from, but I sure would like to see you marry up with my mother. She'll need you when I'm gone."

"You're not going anywhere," Joe said, "except to face a judge and jury."

Vonheim shook his head. "You know that would kill my mother. I can't let her know what I've done. You can't do that to her, Joe."

Anger throbbed at Joe's temples. "I didn't do this, Joe. Your bad choices landed you where you are."

The Indian rose and offered up empty palms. "I'm not armed, Joe." When there was no response, Vonheim continued. "There's no good end to this, and I know even though you're my friend, you won't let me go."

"I can't," Joe said through clenched jaw.

"I know." He shrugged. "You were always the good guy. Me, I liked playing bank robbers and horse thieves."

"This isn't play, Pale Indian," Joe said. "This is real life, and you've got to pay for what you've done. That boy in San Antonio didn't get a chance, and neither do you."

Vonheim dropped his hands to his sides and turned his back to Joe. "What're you doin', Tommy?" Frank said gently. "Can't we just let a judge and jury settle this? Your mama'll love you no matter what happens."

He turned around and looked past Joe to Frank. "Yes, I know she will," he said. "And she'll miss me something terrible when I'm gone. Promise me you'll take care of her, Frank."

"Well, of course I will. I love your mama, son, which is why I can't let anything—"

Vonheim bolted toward the window and threw himself against it. Glass shattered as the windowpanes splintered and the Indian fell through. A volley of shots rang out, and then only silence.

Joe scooped up Bess and held her against his chest

until she opened her eyes. "Tommy," she whispered. "He frightened me and I fell. He was talking about his mother. Something about you taking care of her." She spied her father. "Pa? Where's Tommy?"

Frank walked past her to look out what remained of the window. "Appears he fell, Bessie Mae," he said.

"Fell?" She made a weak attempt to stand then gave up and sagged against Joe's shirt. "What happened?"

Frank knelt beside them. "His mama mentioned he wasn't well," Frank said gently. "It appears he might have lost his balance over there by the window." The rancher gave Joe a direct look. "Ain't that what happened, Joe?"

Slowly he nodded, knowing Tommy's mother would hear the same story.

A week after Tommy Vonheim's funeral, Joe packed his saddlebags and showed up on Bess's doorstep to say good-bye. Bess tried not to cry even as he pulled her into his arms for a kiss. She'd lost track of the number somewhere between Tuesday and Friday, but she did count two more farewells before he disappeared down the trail.

"I'll come home for Christmas," he called from somewhere beyond the mesquites.

"You'd better," she replied as she returned to her room to read the letters that would make good on her plans.

That evening at supper, Pa was grinning. "What's got into you?" she asked as she set out the plates.

"I asked her, Bessie Mae." His grin turned into a

chuckle. "I asked Ida Vonheim to marry up with me soon as it was proper. Didn't want to intrude on her grief."

"And what did she say?"

"She said she'd marry me tomorrow, Bessie." Another laugh. "Looks like I'm going to be a married man. Not sure I remember how."

Bess went to hug her father. "Pa, what about a Christmas Eve wedding? The church'll already be decorated."

"A Christmas wedding! Why, that's a great idea." He rose and hurried from the room.

"Where are you going?" she called.

"To tell Ida the good news."

Christmas Eve dawned bright and beautiful with a chill in the air that competed with the anticipation Bess felt. She was keeping a secret that Ida, her soon-to-be new mama, was in on. While Pa went to cut the tree for the parlor, Bess made short work of completing the arrangements for the wedding. By the time the tree was up and adorned with the Ames family decorations, Bess's nerves were stretched thin.

The only piece of her plan that hadn't fallen into place involved Joe Mueller. Thus far she'd had neither letter nor telegram from the absent ranger. By the time she climbed into the buggy beside the groom-to-be, Bess had decided Joe wasn't coming.

A thousand reasons pelted her mind, but she refused to consider any of them. Rather, she reached across the bench and grasped Pa's free hand then slid him a smile.

"We're still gonna need you at home, Bessie Mae. Don't you ever think you're not welcome."

Bess sighed. "Thank you, Pa. We'll see how things turn out." The last thing she wanted to be was the third person in a newlywed's home.

The buggy arrived at the church, and Bess slid out to hurry to the church's side door. There she found Ida waiting for her. The older woman looked beautiful in the new dress Bess had helped her pick out. "Where are they?"

Ida opened the door to the pastor's study, revealing the best Christmas gift of all: her sisters and their families.

Time for hugs and greetings was short, as the groom now stood at the altar beside the pastor. As the music rose, Bess gestured to the door. "Shall we go out oldest to youngest?" Charlsey asked.

"No, dear," Ida interjected. "Let's do the opposite." She shrugged. "For fun."

"Of course." Bess hugged each sister as she left the study on the arm of her husband. Finally, it was Bess's turn. "I guess I've got to go it alone." *Bessie Mae, plain as day.* The statement haunted her for the first time since Joe left.

Ida reached for her overlarge bouquet then divided it in half. "Here, dear," she said. "It'll give you something to hold on to."

Bess took it reluctantly, feeling a bit silly as she stepped into the church. None of her sisters held flowers, so what would possess Ida to insist?

If only Joe were here.

Then she spied him. Standing at the altar. Beside Pa.

Her sisters were grinning. A glance behind her told Bess that Ida was, too.

"Go on, dear," Ida said. "You and Joe can have your turn at the preacher first. Frank and I have waited this long. We can surely spare a few more minutes."

"But I..." She shook her head as she turned her attention to Joe. "He hasn't even asked me to marry him yet."

"About that." Joe moved toward her. "You see, a fellow takes his time getting to know the young lady, but I'm due back in San Antonio by New Year's Day. I'd have to say this makes our situation a bit of an emergency."

Bess glanced around at the citizens of Horsefly gathered in the old familiar pews. Even Mrs. Schmidt smiled at her. "But you...we haven't courted properly."

His gaze scorched her. "Considering the timetable we're working with, I'd say our courting schedule might be hurried up a bit."

"I see." She smiled. "So how long have we been standing here?"

"Two minutes," Cal Schmidt called, pointing to his watch.

Joe moved closer. "Two minutes already?"

"At least," she whispered. "Almost three."

"Guess that makes it time." Their noses were nearly touching as he wrapped his arm around her shoulder. "Definitely time."

"Time for what?" she whispered against his cheek.

"Time for me to make up a new rhyme about you." Joe paused to lean back a notch and look into her coffee-colored eyes. "Bessie Mae," he said softly, "you're going to kiss me today."

And she did.

"Excuse me, you two," the pastor called. "There's a little formality called a wedding vow you'll need to speak before you can do that."

"Shall we, Bess?" Joe asked. Then he shook his head. "Wait—all teasing aside, let me do this properly."

Right there in the middle aisle of the church, Joe got down on one knee. "Bessie Mae, will you marry me today?"

And the bride-to-be said yes.

MRS. VONHEIM'S SPRINGERLE COOKIES
(makes approximately 5 dozen)

4 eggs
2 tablespoons butter
2 cups sugar
4 cups all-purpose flour
2 teaspoons baking powder
¼ teaspoon salt
¼ cup anise seed

Beat eggs; then add butter and sugar. Cream together. Sift flour, baking powder, and salt. Add dry ingredients to butter mixture and combine. Knead dough until smooth, adding more flour if necessary to form smooth dough. Cover and chill in refrigerator for at least 2 hours. Roll onto slightly floured board to ½ inch thick. Roll springerle roller over dough to make designs. Cut at border. Sprinkle anise seed on clean tea towel and place cookies on top. Allow to stand uncovered overnight to dry. Bake 12 to 15 minutes at 325 degrees; then remove from oven and cool completely. Store in airtight container.

MIRIAM'S RINDERROULADEN
(serves 4)

1½ cups beef broth
4 flank steaks, approximately 6 oz each
2 teaspoons Dijon mustard
½ teaspoon salt
¼ teaspoon pepper
2 slices bacon
2 pickles, sliced in strips
1 large onion, chopped
¼ cup vegetable oil
4 peppercorns
½ bay leaf
1 tablespoon cornstarch

Heat beef broth and set aside. Spread mustard equally on each steak; sprinkle with salt and pepper. Cover each with bacon, pickles, and chopped onion; roll like a burrito. Secure with toothpicks. Heat oil in heavy saucepan; add steak rolls and brown well on all sides. Pour in hot beef broth, peppercorns, and bay leaf. Cover and simmer 1 hour and 20 minutes. Remove steak rolls and set aside to drain. In bowl, blend cornstarch with small amount of cold water and mix well. Stir into saucepan and bring to a boil until sauce is thick and bubbling. Pour over steaks and serve immediately.

Kathleen Y'Barbo is a bestselling author of more than 35 award-winning novels and novellas with over 850,000 books in print. In addition, she is the publicist at Books & Such Literary Agency and writes a weekly blog post on book promotion called Marketing Matters at www. booksandsuch.biz/blog. Kathleen is a tenth-generation Texan, a graduate of Texas A&M University, and the mother of three grown sons and a teenage daughter. Find out more about Kathleen at www.kathleeny-barbo.com.

A Letter to Our Readers

Dear Readers:

In order that we might better contribute to your reading enjoyment, we would appreciate your taking a few minutes to respond to the following questions. When completed, please return to the following: Fiction Editor, Barbour Publishing, Inc., P.O. Box 719, Uhrichsville, OH 44683.

1. Did you enjoy reading *Wild West Christmas*?
   ❑ Very much—I would like to see more books like this.
   ❑ Moderately—I would have enjoyed it more if _____
   _____
   _____

2. What influenced your decision to purchase this book?
   (Check those that apply.)
   ❑ Cover   ❑ Back cover copy   ❑ Title   ❑ Price
   ❑ Friends   ❑ Publicity   ❑ Other

3. Which story was your favorite?
   ❑ *Charlsey's Accountant*   ❑ *A Breed Apart*
   ❑ *Lucy Ames, Sharpshooter*   ❑ *Plain Trouble*

4. Please check your age range:
   ❑ Under 18   ❑ 18–24   ❑ 25–34
   ❑ 35–45   ❑ 46–55   ❑ Over 55

5. How many hours per week do you read? _____

Name _____

Occupation _____

Address _____

City_____ State_____ Zip_____

E-mail_____